FLASHPOINT

BRIAN SHEA

STACY LYNN MILLER

SEVERN RIVER
PUBLISHING

1

After twenty-four hours on the road, paying cash for food and gas and avoiding toll roads, Thomas was sure he and the muscle his boss had paired with him hadn't left a discernable trail. Anton Boyko's orders were specific. Thomas and Viktor, Anton's most trusted lieutenant, were to drive from Brooklyn to some little town near Dallas no one outside of northern Texas had heard of before opening the envelope in Viktor's pocket. On their way, they were supposed to meet with a guy known as the Raven to pick up the right tools for the job.

The mapping application on his phone told Thomas to take the next turn on the highway ten miles from the Arkansas-Texas state line. The geo-coordinates directed him to a barbeque stand on a frontage road. He brought their sedan into the lot and glanced at the other cars' license plates. Their plate was the only one not from Texas or Arkansas and would stick out to anyone noting them. He parked near the road for an unimpeded getaway if something went wrong.

When Thomas opened the driver's door, the mouthwatering scent of smoked hickory meats filled the air. In the fifteen months since hooking up with the Boyko organization, he'd had meetups in all sorts of shitholes in New York's five boroughs, so this assignment was a breath of fresh air. Or, more precisely, freshly cooked pulled pork air.

Viktor joined him at the rear bumper, wiping the moisture from his brow with a forearm in the Arkansas spring heat. The temperature was a perfect seventy-four degrees, but his partner would sweat buckets in a snowstorm.

"I'm going to take a leak," Thomas said, stepping toward the side of the building.

Viktor grabbed Thomas by the arm and spun him around. Evil filled his eyes, which had kept Thomas awake for most of their road trip. "Anton may trust you, but I don't. Our orders are to get food and sit at a bench."

"Unless you want me pissing in line, I'm hitting the head. I'll take the pulled pork." Thomas followed the sign tacked to the building, showing the bathrooms were around the back. His bladder was fine, but he wanted to get a feel for the meeting location without Viktor watching his every move. His training had taught him to identify the high ground, avenues of escape, and possible unfriendlies.

The families and tourists in line and at the red picnic benches didn't fit the profile of a criminal who might have special "tools" for whatever job Anton had sent him and Viktor to complete. He wished Anton had a description of the Raven, but he'd said he'd hired the man based on reputation. A reputation for *what* remained a mystery.

After scouting the fenced-off lot in the back and circling the building, Thomas determined the only high ground was in the trees across the frontage road. It was also the point of rapid egress. If anything went down, they'd be sitting ducks against a sniper hidden in the pines, so before turning the final corner, he took the safety off the Beretta in the waist holster hidden under his bulky golf shirt.

He caught up to Viktor at the pick-up window, grabbed his basket of food and drink, and sat at the only empty picnic table facing the street and parking lot to minimize his exposure to a sneak attack. *Old habits*, he thought. The most important lesson he carried forward from his previous life was never to sit with his back to an entrance. While eating, he kept one eye on the other patrons and the other on the parking lot.

Soon, a small, timid man wearing casual clothes and dark-rimmed glasses with a backpack slung over his shoulder approached the empty end of the table. Tourist was written all over his face. Holding a basket of food, he asked, "Excuse me. Do you mind if I sit? I'll only be a few minutes."

"Knock yourself out." Viktor returned to stuffing his face with brisket and Coke.

Thomas shifted his focus, dividing it between the crowd and their new tablemate sitting on the same bench as him. The man fumbled with his backpack between bites and placed a large white jeweler's ring box on the tabletop. It appeared he was there to propose at a barbeque stand of all places. Thomas smirked, recalling one proposal he'd seen. Though the young man didn't get the answer he'd hoped for, he did it right by proposing where he and his intended had first met. Maybe this guy had met his bride- or groom-to-be over pulled pork.

Thomas returned to his vigil of watching.

"Interesting bird," the man said, pointing toward the power line near the street. "What kind of bird do you think it is?"

Viktor looked over his shoulder to peer across the street, but Thomas snapped his head toward the man, suspecting a setup. He drifted his right hand to the butt of his pistol under his shirt, thinking he'd have to be accurate if he had to take a shot. From his angle, three families with children were directly behind the man.

Viktor shrugged and said, "I have no idea."

Idiot, Thomas thought. He wouldn't recognize first contact unless it kissed him on the lips. "It's a raven," he replied.

"Yes, it is." The man slid the box down the table, halfway toward Thomas. "The operating instructions are inside. They should be easy enough even for Einstein to follow." He gestured his chin across the table toward Victor.

Thomas chuckled. "I can figure it out." Whatever *it* was.

"I need your employer to transfer the final payment."

"Of course." Viktor dialed his cell phone. "We have it. Make the transfer."

Moments later, the man's phone dinged. He glanced at the screen and pushed the box closer to Thomas. "It's been a pleasure, gentlemen." He slurped the rest of his drink, picked up his backpack and trash, and left.

Thomas cupped the box in his palm. "Let's go." He gathered his trash, tossed it into a nearby receptacle, and walked to the car. Finally, he would find out what job he was supposed to perform.

Once in the car, Viktor opened Anton's instructions. "Boyko says the Feds have flipped someone close to him and are close to issuing an arrest warrant. We must buy enough time to flush out the informant from witness protection. We have until Monday morning to get this done."

"Which only gives us two days. What's the job?" Thomas asked.

"We're to take out the U.S. Attorney in charge of the case, using the device the Raven has created, and report when it's done."

Thomas opened the box from the Raven, revealing a folded piece of paper in the lid and a liquid-filled packet resembling a detergent pod attached to a small electronic device next to a remote-control button on the bottom. He read the instructions. *Handle with caution. This is a dissolvable, vibration-triggered chloroform deployment system. (1) Install the device inside the driver's vent. It can remain in place for a month before deployment. (2) To turn on the device, press the remote control once within a hundred yards of the vehicle. When the yellow light turns green, the device is armed. (3) When the car is in motion, movement vibration will trigger the system. The chloroform will incapaci-tate the occupants within five minutes. (4) Traceable components will dissolve within 40 seconds of contact with water.* How it worked was straightforward and frightening.

Hours later, two convenient flat tires brought their target to an auto shop near her home. And five hundred dollars slipped to the repair tech-nician was enough to have him install the device. The tricky part remained—deciding when to activate it within the next thirty-six hours—but the path became apparent after scouting the AUSA's movements for one day.

Before the sun rose on Monday morning, Thomas and Victor camped out in their sedan four houses down from the prosecutor's home, waiting for her to begin her commute into Dallas at the start of the workday. Since parking, Viktor had voiced his suspicion about who might have turned informant on Boyko and what they deserved, narrowing the pool down to two people. Thomas couldn't disagree with his reasoning, but reading between the lines, he took the diatribe as a warning against betraying the Boyko organization.

Thomas sipped his coffee calmly, showing Viktor his veiled threats didn't scare him.

When the first orange slivers of daylight appeared in the eastern sky, the garage door opened at the target house, and the BMW they'd followed for the previous day and a half pulled out. Thomas pressed the remote once, showing his partner a solid green light. There was no stopping the plan now.

"Do you think this will work?" Viktor asked.

"It had better. Otherwise, Anton will have our heads."

When the BMW cleared the curb, Thomas started a timer on his phone, surmising the device should have started its slow release of chloroform fifteen seconds earlier. He knew from the movies it was a colorless gas but had to look it up last night to learn the driver would smell something like acetone but sweeter and likely think nothing of it.

The prosecutor turned down the street toward the exit from the Rowlett subdivision. It should take her two minutes and thirty seconds to make it to the four-way stop sign at the main road bisecting the two primary communities on the western peninsula of Lake Ray Hubbard. She lined up at the intersection with the other waiting cars. Fifteen seconds later, she finally completed the turn.

Three minutes and forty-five seconds had elapsed. The gas should have filled the cabin with a prominent sweet scent.

After turning the corner behind the woman, Thomas gritted his teeth when she accelerated and settled at five over the limit. Their plan would only work if she hit the land bridge connecting the cities of Rowlett and Rose Hill at the four-minute fifteen-second mark or later. Luck was with him. He breathed easier when she reduced speed for a slower driver ahead of her.

Thomas glanced at his phone when she crossed onto the bridge. Four minutes and twenty-three seconds. "Perfect," he said. The gas should have her on the precipice of passing out.

Viktor sat taller in his seat when the car in front of them swerved left and right. The woman was clearly fighting to stay awake. If she went left next, Thomas would help her to the other side by wedging his car between her and the median divider. He kept his traveling distance close, ready to intervene, but he was betting on the instinct for drivers to veer right toward the shoulder after encountering trouble with their car. He bet correctly.

The car accelerated, swerved right, and launched over the earthen berm. After careening through the brush, it landed in the water and abruptly stopped with only scant sunlight outlining its frame. The front end angled down, hastening the speed at which the car took on water.

Thomas pulled over to assess whether the job was successful and to show his concern to other passersby. Three other cars behind him pulled over too. He and Viktor emerged from the sedan and approached the slope leading to the water. The prosecutor's car continued to sink and float away from the shoreline, ensuring the evidence from the chloroform device was destroyed.

Two men from another car jumped into the water and swam toward the vehicle. By the time they reached it, only the roofline had remained above the waterline. One dove under and returned to the surface a second later. He yelled, "A woman is in there!" He dove a second time and came up, shaking his head. "I can't get to her. She's dead."

Another person shouted, "I called 911. Rescue is coming."

Thomas and Viktor returned to their sedan quietly. While Thomas pulled away from the scene, Viktor dialed his cell phone.

Anton Boyko's breakfast had long gone cold. He'd been at the back patio table for a half-hour, picking at his food, thinking about when he'd taken over the most powerful and feared crime syndicate in Brooklyn twenty-two years ago. He'd quashed power struggles from loyalists of his predecessor and expected the FBI to leverage the other stragglers against him. However, Anton had kept the police and federal agents at bay by living by one axiom —never place blind trust in anyone who wasn't family.

On Thursday, he learned his truism had failed him. And today, the most profound betrayal of his life had made his favorite omelet unappetizing. He and Sasha hadn't seen eye to eye in eight years. Anton thought they had mutually agreed to despise one another from their respective corners of the country while limiting contact to Christmas and his mother's birthday. He was wrong and now faced the weightiest dilemma of his life—kill his only child if he couldn't talk sense into him.

The truth was hard to swallow. The man Anton had groomed to take over the business was a federal informant in witness protection—a closely held secret he would share with only two men. The first was his cousin. Viktor had been with him since his days of strong-arming kids on the playground for nickels. He'd trusted him with his life countless times and counted on him to handle this matter with secrecy and sensitivity.

Thomas Falco was the second man Anton had brought into this unpleasant business. Compared to his other lieutenants, he was new and undeserving of a task of such importance, but Anton had little choice. Falco had a connection to his son no one else in his organization had, which made him the only one capable of flushing Sasha out of witness protection. His unique position, however, didn't equate to blind trust. Viktor would keep him in check. Now, the fate of the business he'd built for two decades, along with his own, rested in the efficiency of those two men.

Since eating wasn't possible, he flipped through the morning newspaper for the tenth time, willing his phone to ring with news about the assistant U.S. Attorney who had convinced his son to bear witness against him. Her single act might have fractured his family and business beyond repair, and she had to die.

His phone finally rang. The number on the screen told him this was the call he'd waited for. He answered it. "Viktor."

"It is done, Anton."

"Good." He released a long, steady breath. The prosecutor was dead, but he wasn't out of danger yet. "Now I need you to find Sasha before the feds regroup and he testifies against me."

"He's the rat?"

"You know the troubles we've had. I want you to find my son and bring him back alive."

"Now I understand why you sent Falco with me," Viktor said. "Sasha trusts him."

"Yes. He'll know how to flush out my son. Don't come back until you have him."

"How do you suggest we proceed?" Viktor asked.

"Kostas." Saying his name filled Anton's mouth with a sour taste. He blamed that man for everything wrong between him and his son and would take care of him once and for all. "He will trust Falco, but when he's no longer useful, I want you to punch his ticket."

"Kostas or Falco?"

"You decide."

2

You got this. Lexi read Nita's "right message at the right time" text before returning the phone to her cargo pants pocket. She needed the pick-me-up after taking a week off, a week the ATF owed her since Lange had called her to duty during her honeymoon. A week at the Ponder home wasn't her idea of a romantic vacation, but following the harrowing events in Napa, the time alone under the same roof with Nita and her father was precisely what they needed to connect as a family. Leaving them today was more emotionally challenging than she'd expected.

Lexi took a deep breath, slung her backpack over her shoulder, and walked into the federal building, unsure of the reception she would receive. When she'd left for her ill-fated honeymoon last month, before everything went haywire with Benjamin Foreman and the United States President, she'd had the respect of every agent on the floor, built on consistent solid work. She'd even made inroads into the frosty relationship with her new boss, Willie Lange. However, the media coverage since leaving California had placed a giant question mark on her ability as an ATF agent, erasing months of progress.

Pundits had pounced on the incident at the golf tournament where she'd mistaken a fly for a weaponized drone on live television. She'd launched the crowd into a wild panic and had the president ushered off the stage in a mad rush. The media had dubbed the incident "Flygate" and questioned whether her success in Spicewood and Las Vegas had gone to her head. She wasn't a social media hater, but after the first nasty meme depicting her floating with fly wings on her back showed up in her feed, she deleted the apps from her phone. She also avoided the television at home unless a race or rerun was on.

With twelve minutes left before she was officially on the clock again, Lexi headed to the one person who could read the room with her eyes closed and would give her the unvarnished truth. She knocked on the door labeled "Intelligence" before easing it open.

Kaplan Shaw was seated at her desk with her nose buried in a computer screen. She waved her over while typing something on the keyboard. "Come in, Lexi. Ready for your first day back?"

"I'm looking for some intel before diving in headfirst. What should I expect?" Lexi asked. "A handshake or a roasting?"

"I'd call it eighty-twenty. Most are still with you, but some are convinced you went off your rocker," Kaplan said. The latter group had to come from agents who had grumbled when the FBI deputy director handpicked Lexi to lead a national task force. She thought she'd won them over, but the wall sitters didn't require much to choose a side.

"No one would believe what really happened, including you." Lexi still had nightmares about the micro-drones lending chase and zapping her unconscious.

"Don't sell yourself short. Considering two senators are dead, I'd believe nearly anything involving Benjamin Foreman and the Raven. I may have to get you drunk as a skunk and pry it out of you one night."

"I believe you would," Lexi laughed. "I also came to get an update on the Raven and his engineer, Robert Segura. Anything more on the money trail?"

"Nothing that points to either of them. Every trail circled back to Senator Gotkin and Benjamin Foreman, but they're both dead. It's like Segura fell off the earth. I wouldn't be surprised if he's assumed a new identity."

"You're probably right. How about lunch later today?"

"I'd like that."

Lexi climbed the stairs to her floor, expecting a mild reception but bracing for the worst. The smell of freshly brewed coffee hit her after opening the stairwell door and mixed with the dull drone of Monday morning chatter from agents catching up after a weekend.

Lange's office door was open. Lexi considered popping her head in but had learned her lesson soon after their first meeting to be prepared to answer detailed questions whenever they talked. Lange was demanding, but her approach forced the agents under her command to keep up with their assigned cases. It was an effective management style worthy of emulation.

Lexi slung her backpack higher on her shoulder, turned down the aisle between rows of cubicles, and stopped dead in her tracks. A flyswatter had been tacked outside each workstation in a gauntlet of mockery. She would have been embarrassed if she wasn't right about the nano drones, just not about them being at the golf tournament.

The deeper she traveled through the division's version of a college prank, the louder the chatter became. Six agents came into view when she stepped past the end of the aisle and entered the gathering area by the coffee station. One raised his coffee mug and announced in a playful tone, "Superfly is here."

The others turned, raised their cups, and cheered. "Welcome back, Superfly."

Heat flushed Lexi's cheeks. She placed all but one of those agents in the camp supporting her, so she took the ribbing as good-natured. "Nothing like a warm welcome." One handed her coffee in a paper cup with a fly drawn on the side. "Very nice, Franks." She raised the drink toward the group. "Gotta fly to my desk."

Lexi continued past the printers, finding Ronald, her favorite logistics clerk and former office mate, at his desk. She expected his typical toothy smile greeting but was met with set eyes and pursed lips—his angry look.

"Good morning, Ronald."

"Those guys are idiots."

Lexi circled his desk and placed an arm over his shoulder. "They were having a little fun."

"At your expense. I don't like it one bit."

"Pay them no mind."

"How can you ignore them?" Ronald shook his head.

Lexi clearly wasn't getting through to him. Appealing to his affinity for Marvel quotes might help. "Because truth is my shield. Knowledge my armor."

He smiled with the right corner of his lips cocked up higher than the left. "Doctor Strange. You must know something they don't."

"Let's keep this between us." Lexi winked and entered the cubicle she shared with her partner. Nathan Croft was at his desk, pouring over their file on the Raven. The whiteboards tacked to the wall between their work areas contained lists of investigative data sources, most of which were crossed off. "Good morning, Nathan."

He looked up, chuckling. "Like the new office decorations?"

"It took imagination and team effort," Lexi said, focusing on the good nature of her office mates, not the underlying commentary on the public nature of her perceived screwup. "I gotta give them that much."

"But I agree with Ronald. They're idiots." Nathan put his hands on his hips, punctuating his disappointment. "If they knew the truth, they'd give you a ticker-tape parade."

"But the truth can never be told. It's enough knowing what we did."

"Intellectually, I get it, but you're the biggest hero this country has seen since 9/11. All these yahoos think you made a fool of yourself on national television and pissed off the president."

"Let them think what they want. We need to find the Raven." Lexi put her backpack at her workstation, wiggled her computer mouse, and laughed when the screensaver appeared. Nathan had replaced the generic selection with a still picture from the old sci-fi movie, *The Fly*, with the main character dressed in a cheesy fly head costume. "Somehow, this is much funnier coming from you."

"I thought you would appreciate it." Nathan's grin faded. "Ready for an update?"

Lexi dragged her chair next to his and focused on the whiteboard on the wall between their workstations. The items listed were an investigator's checklist for tracking down a suspect after coming up empty from searching the traditional law enforcement systems. It included social media, trailer park records, tax rolls, social security records, motor vehicle and driver's license records, voter rolls, property records, SEC filings, engineering college records, public school rolls, and state and federal prison rolls. By the number of items crossed off, it appeared he had a busy week searching for Robert Segura, the Raven's engineer.

"What did you find out?" Lexi asked.

"The trailer park he listed as his permanent residence in Houston was a bust. It's a rental. He prepaid for the year from the account Kaplan is tracking. The manager said no one had been in the trailer for three years. He has no social media, driver's license, criminal record, property, business, or voting record in Texas. This guy was a ghost until I checked student registrations at engineering colleges." A grin grew on Nathan's lips.

"You're like Kaplan when she gets on the trail of someone," Lexi said. "You get this glint in your eyes."

"I take that as the highest compliment."

"You should," Lexi said. "Kaplan is the best at what she does. What did you find?"

"He went to MIT. His student application said he's from Brooklyn, New York. He listed an orphanage as his home address."

"Was he on a scholarship?"

"No. Each year, his tuition, room, and board were paid in cash."

"Interesting. What did the orphanage say?"

"He was brought in when he was seven years old after his parents died in an apartment fire in 1985. He lived there for six years until he went missing in 1991. The orphanage reported him as a runaway, so no one investigated. He showed up five years later at MIT and stayed there until 2001."

"That's the year I quit my father's NASCAR team and went to college. We could barely afford the local school. My gut tells me the Raven footed Segura's bill."

"Mine does, too," Nathan said.

"Anything more?"

Another sly grin formed on his lips. "Once I knew he was from Brooklyn, I narrowed my search to New York. I ran into a brick wall until I checked the state prison records. Upstate is housing a prisoner named

Alexander Segura, also from Brooklyn. He's forty-two, two years older than Robert, so he could be a brother or cousin."

"You're brilliant, Nathan. We need to request an interview."

"The prison replied to my request first thing this morning. We're on for tomorrow, but we still have to clear it through Lange and schedule a flight."

"Then we better talk to her." Lexi pushed back her chair.

"Maybe you should go alone."

Lexi squinted. While their relationship as partners changed for the better after saving the president, Nathan never passed up an opportunity to brief the boss on this case. Something else had to be at play. "Should I be concerned?"

"She hasn't told me anything, but keep in mind she thinks you screwed up."

Lexi sighed. "I know. My future rests on the support of Director Hanlon. Let's brief her and hear my fate together."

Before exiting the cubicle, Nathan gripped Lexi's upper arm. "No matter what happens, this is your case. You've earned it."

Lexi showed her gratitude with a firm nod before re-entering the gauntlet of flyswatters. Once through, she knocked on Willie Lange's door and waited for a verbal invitation before entering. Agent Lange was at her desk. She'd added several personal items to the office since Lexi was last there before going on vacation. One prominent item on the desk was a hollow blasting cap mounted on a small piece of varnished wood. Lexi guessed it was a remnant of the first explosive she'd disarmed.

Most explosive experts kept a souvenir of the first time they faced death, like a business owner framing the first dollar made after opening a shop. Lexi had also held back a piece but had stuffed it inside a shoebox at the bottom of her bedroom closet. After losing her leg, her prosthetic was enough of a daily reminder of the job's dangers.

"Good morning, Agent Lange. Do you have a minute? We'd like to update you on the Raven case."

"Sure. Come in." Lange's flat expression didn't have the "glad to have you back" sparkle, suggesting she had news to break. Regardless, Lexi jumped into her briefing.

"While I was gone, Nathan searched for the Raven's engineer we unearthed in California." She explained how MIT student registration records led them to an orphanage in Brooklyn and a potential relative in prison. "We arranged an interview tomorrow and would like to fly to New York." Lange gathered her eyebrows together as if fighting back a grimace. Maybe asking to go on a trip on her first day back wasn't a good idea. "We could return the same day to keep the spending down."

"It's not a matter of money, Agent Mills." Lange ran a hand along the back of her neck. "Director Hanlon called me personally last week. He wants you off the case."

"Off the case?" Lexi yanked her head back as a coldness gripped her chest. "I expected you to toss me off as the lead, but to take me off the case is a knee-jerk reaction."

"I can't disagree." Lange lowered her shoulders in defeat. "But the director was clear. He considers you a liability, so he doesn't want you in a position where you might make the news cycle again."

"This isn't fair, Willie." Nathan stepped forward, crossing his arms at his chest. "Lexi has gotten us closer to finding the Raven than I ever did. She's earned this. If there's one thing I've learned from working with her, it's that I can't do this alone."

"Then pick a partner," Lange said.

"I pick Lexi. She knows all the players and how to get things done. Anyone else would be a giant step back. If you knew what I know about Lexi, you would—" Nathan paused when Lexi tugged on his sleeve. His jaw muscles visibly rippled. He unclipped his service weapon and badge from his belt. "Then I quit. I'm retirement eligible. I'll put in my papers today."

Lange's eyes widened with surprise. The color drained from her face. "Retire? Is this the hill you want to die on?"

Without a moment of hesitation, he replied, "Yes."

Lange took a deep breath and leaned back in her chair as if weighing her choices. "You're boxing me into a corner, Nathan. I'm not prepared to lose you." The way Lange phrased her response and her shocked expression hinted something more was between her and Nathan than a professional relationship.

"The decision is yours, Willie. Either keep Lexi on the case, or I'm walking."

"Fine. Lexi stays, but you're the lead. You need to keep her on a short leash. Otherwise, both of us will start collecting our pensions before summer hits, and Mills will have to dust off her resume."

"Deal," Nathan said. "What about New York?"

"Book the flight."

Lexi and Nathan exited Lange's office. She stopped him at the mouth of the gauntlet. "Would you really have retired?"

"Yes. You're a freaking hero, Lexi. I wouldn't be alive if you hadn't MacGyvered your way out of Foreman's cabin. Office pranks were one thing, but you having to take one this big for the team pisses me off."

"There's more at stake than my job or reputation. I'll do whatever is necessary to keep the status quo." Lexi patted his lower arm, expressing her gratitude. "Let's get Ronald to book our flights."

Lexi continued down the aisle. All but one agent had taken down their celebratory flyswatter, the one Lexi figured would prefer to see her fired. At the end of the cubicles, nearly the entire floor of agents had gathered at the television mounted above the coffee station. It was tuned to a local news station. The sound was down but closed captioning was on. "Breaking News" was blazoned across the screen. It was hard to make out, but Lexi thought she saw the words *U.S. Attorney Dead*.

"Can someone turn up the TV?" she asked.

The sound came on. The anchor talked about an early morning accident in an eastern suburb of Dallas involving a car that had plunged into Lake Ray Hubbard. Good Samaritans had tried to rescue the woman driver, but she was pronounced dead at the scene. The suspected cause of death was drowning.

Lexi wracked her brain, recalling how many U.S. attorneys she'd worked with since coming to the Dallas division. She counted three. Each was professional and dedicated to their job. A picture flashed on the screen, causing Lexi to gasp. A painful sadness stabbed her when she realized the victim was a friend. Nathan steadied her by the elbow when her knees wobbled.

"Delanie," she said.

"Wasn't she the AUSA who helped us take down Milo Tilton in

Harrington last year?" Nathan asked. Lexi couldn't speak and replied with a slow, heartbreaking nod. "It's a shame. She was a good person. I liked her."

Lexi was no stranger to losing people she'd worked with side by side. Trent Darby had died from a Tony Belcher landmine and Kris Faust from a Raven weaponized drone, and she'd witnessed both deaths. However, hearing about Delanie's death through a news report didn't sit well. Speaking of her in the past tense felt wrong. Accepting she was gone would take some time.

Lexi finally said, "We worked together on Task Force Zero Impact for six months and became good friends. We butted heads a few times but wanted the same thing."

"What was that?" Nathan asked, using a soft voice.

"To make Tony Belcher pay." Lexi recalled the months of hauling in one Red Spades and Gatekeepers member after another. Delanie was available all day and night and could make a deal within minutes to get the task force on the trail of the next link in the chain until Lexi reached the top—Tony. "I'll miss her."

She returned her attention to the television and listened to the anchor's commentary. The Justice Department's Northern District of Texas official statement said Delanie Scott had the highest conviction rate of all U.S. Attorneys in Texas and was recently tapped to head a major case crossing multiple jurisdictions. The screen changed to a reporter interviewing a police officer at the scene. The officer said the accident was under investigation, but witness statements confirmed only one car was involved, and bystanders could not free her from the submerged cabin.

Lexi was familiar with the bridge in Rowlett and speculated about what might have caused the crash. Was it due to mechanical failure, a tire blowout, or had she fallen asleep at the wheel? Delanie worked relentlessly, often to the point of exhaustion, something Lexi had also done with regularity. She'd driven home half asleep many times and could have ended up like Delanie on any occasion.

Lexi's phone buzzed with an incoming phone call. She recognized the unique ringtone and answered without looking at the screen. "Noah, you heard."

3

Thomas followed the GPS instructions on his phone. Unsure why he and Viktor were driving to a bistro in Fort Worth, he suspected the job might have something to do with Anton's son. He last saw Sasha at the family home a year ago. The argument between father and son that night was the only time Thomas had seen Anton lose his temper, let alone his composure. It ended with Sasha's nose broken and Anton banishing him from the Brooklyn compound forever. Sasha's mother, Anton's wife, had mentioned him only once before Christmas, worried his flight might be delayed due to a rare ice storm blanketing Texas.

Viktor directed Thomas to park in the alley behind the restaurant. "Once the joint closes in ten minutes, Kostas will come out to empty the trash," Viktor said. "We need to talk to him. He doesn't go home until he tells us where to find Sasha."

Thomas' suspicions were correct. This was about Sasha. It wasn't common knowledge in the Boyko organization, but Kostas was why Anton fought with Sasha and would never consider him a son again. If Anton wanted to talk to Kostas, he must be desperate. Common sense told him Sasha was the informant or knew the person's identity, and Kostas would help them get the information from him. Thomas wanted to know two things. How did Viktor know where Kostas worked? And how far did Anton expect them to go to get what he needed from Kostas? Thomas guessed Anton had been keeping tabs on Kostas since Sasha left Brooklyn and expected them to do whatever was necessary to find his son. Thomas also knew not to ask questions. If Viktor wanted him to know something, he would tell him.

For the last three months, closing on Monday night had become Kostas' least favorite shift at the bistro. He'd considered looking for other work, but since the Covid lockdown, jobs with LGBTQ-owned businesses had dwindled. Even the Beebo Club, the only surviving nightclub in the Dallas-Fort Worth metroplex, had closed its doors permanently following the savage shooting massacre months before Kostas and Sasha moved to town last year. Tending bar there would have been his ideal job, but serving tables for his friend was the next best thing. Working in the community made him feel safe, except on nights like tonight.

The West Fork Bistro had an underground reputation as a gathering place for queer men and women without the owner marketing the establishment as a gay business in a state traditionally unfriendly to the community. Business professionals and the local hipsters visited for lunch, and the singles came for dinner and potential hookups at night.

Mondays, however, had been taken over by a group of construction workers who were gutting and remodeling the building next door. The crew, as Kostas called them, had started coming after work for football and continued when the season ended. From the first night, they were loud, demanding, and rude. One had targeted two gay male patrons for ridicule, so word had spread quickly. Mondays at the bistro were no longer safe for the community. If business wasn't otherwise down so much on Mondays and the crew wasn't tame compared to the stories he'd heard from other restaurants in the area, the owner would have asked them to leave and never return months ago.

Kostas hated the dilemma, but those men kept the bistro in business, and he had to be pleasant to them. Closing time was minutes away, and their group was getting ready to leave, but neither was coming soon enough. Their verbal barbs were particularly acrid tonight but came short of pushing Kostas to consider turning in his apron like he had last week.

Jake caught up to Kostas once he'd cleared some of the empty dishes and was out of earshot of the table. "How are you holding up? Need help running off the crew?"

"Would you? My patience for them is running thin."

"Happy to help. Have you closed them out?" Jake asked.

"Not yet. They usually order drinks right up to the wire." Another reason to loathe the crew. Randy was a decent boss, but he could only afford to pay the staff for an hour past closing to clean the kitchen, dishes, and dining room and prep for the morning service. These guys often stayed ten to twenty minutes past closing until someone asked them to leave.

"At least they're trained for last call in the kitchen."

"That's like ordering a diet Coke with your Big Mac meal. It helps but not much."

Jake laughed. "I'll get them out in the next five minutes, but you gotta help with the trash run tonight."

"Deal." Kostas could always count on Jake to act as a buffer. The crew didn't intimidate him, and he wasn't afraid to express himself outwardly, even during the Monday closing shift. If anything, he dialed it up, adding dark eyeliner and pink streaks in his short curly hair. He presented as gay, daring the crew to take their best shot.

Kostas gathered the condiment containers from the other tables for refilling while keeping an eye on Jake. After closing out the tab, Jake handed out the four individual bills at the table, earning a laugh with each delivery. "Sorry to break the news, fellas, but it's closing time. Let me guess. The burger and four bottles of Guinness goes to the pretty boy. The turkey sandwich and Corona Lights goes to the stud with the six-pack." Jake gave him a wink. "The beef sliders from the appetizer menu and bottomless Coke goes to the guy on a budget." Jake flamboyantly slapped the fourth check down. "Which means the crispy chicken on a waffle, four shots of scotch, and milkshake goes to the man without a care in the world." He added a hip wiggle. "I wish I had your daring."

The first customer gave the last one a playful shove. "It looks like someone has a crush on you."

"Look who's talking, pretty boy." He returned the shove, pulling out his wallet. Each threw down cash, grabbed their jackets, and left.

Jake locked the door behind them and took a deep bow under the five-minute mark. He gathered the cash and receipts and joined Kostas at the table where he was filling condiments.

"Impressive," Kostas smirked. "I wish Sasha had your humor."

Jake's smile faded. "Have you heard from him?"

"Not since his text two weeks ago." Kostas slumped in a chair. Sadness and confusion overwhelmed him again. He'd thought he was past the hurt, but Sasha was his first love. Getting over him would take much more time. "I still don't understand why he left. Everything was fine. Our jobs. Our apartment." He pulled from his pocket a titanium ring. "I was going to propose last weekend on his birthday."

"Maybe he found the ring, and it spooked him."

Kostas shook his head. "No. This was supposed to be my second proposal. When I asked him the first time, he said he still had to come out to his family. It didn't go well, so we moved here. After we settled, he said to wait a year and ask again. It's been a year." He inspected the ring, willing himself not to cry again. It had taken him weeks to find the right ring, but when he saw this one, he knew it had been made for his boyfriend.

"It's beautiful."

"Sasha is a science buff with a fixation on meteorites." Kostas pointed to the decorative elements in the center. "This is a Gibeon Meteorite inlay with a dark ceramic blue accent. Dark blue is his favorite color."

"I'm sure he'll be back. Like he said in his text, he needs a little space."

"I don't know. It's not like Sasha to leave without talking things through. We've been through rough patches but always worked through them."

"Have you checked with his family?" Jake asked.

"No. They wouldn't talk to me if I called." Kostas couldn't tell Jake that he and his boyfriend fled New York after the big blowout to escape Brooklyn's most feared mob leader, Sasha's father. The great Anton Boyko had plans for his son, but his being gay wasn't one of them.

"Have you thought about going there to talk to his family?"

"That would be the worst idea in the world." Kostas took Anton's threat seriously—he'd kill him if he ever stepped foot in Brooklyn again.

"How about we make sandwiches from tonight's extras and head to your place? I can call Ashton. We'll eat and listen to horrible music the rest of the night." Jake threw an arm over Kostas' shoulder, clearly out of compassion, not attraction. He was devoted to his husband and never once during the year of working together demonstrated a wandering eye.

"I appreciate the offer, but I want to get to bed early. I want to stop by more places Sasha and I used to frequent and ask if anyone has seen him." It was a long shot, but Kostas wasn't ready to give up on the love of his life without a fight.

"Well, the offer stands. We're only a phone call away." Jake patted his back. "Let's finish closing up and take the trash on our way out."

Within a half hour, the cook had the stove and grill cleaned and the items stored in the pantry and walk-in cooler. Ten minutes later, Jake and Kostas had the last dish and glass drying on the racks and the requisite number of flatware settings wrapped in a cloth napkin for the morning service. They each grabbed a full trash bag and slung it over their shoulders. Kostas killed the lights, and Jake locked the back door behind them with his key.

After tossing the bags in the dumpster, they headed down the dark alley where dim security lights over the service doors of four other businesses lit their path toward the side street and to their parked cars. Spoiled trash and stale urine created a robust musty smell in the cool night air.

Halfway to the corner, a parked sedan blocked most of their path. Kostas hadn't seen it before, so it likely didn't belong to an employee of the surrounding businesses. Stray cars in alleys in this part of town at this time of night usually meant a drug deal or a prostitute performing a service.

The driver's and front passenger doors opened when they got closer to the vehicle. Two men stepped out and moved to the front bumper. The shadowy light made it impossible to determine who they were, making the hairs on the back of Kostas' neck stand on end. Thinking they might be members of the crew back to get in a few good licks on Jake for his cheekiness while ushering them from the bistro, Kostas adjusted his keys in his hand, gripping the apartment key as a weapon.

He and Jake slowed.

One man stepped forward. Kostas couldn't be sure, but he looked familiar. He looked like the bouncer from the Brooklyn nightclub who had saved Sasha from a beating by four gang members.

Kostas squinted. "Thomas?" He'd seen the other man with Anton's men once but didn't know his name, nor did he want to.

"Kostas," Thomas said, "we need to talk."

The serious tone stopped Kostas in his tracks. When he first met Thomas Falco, he was a bruiser, making a buck at one of the Brooklyn hotspots. And when he ushered a bloodied Sasha to the Boyko compound instead of the hospital following a beating, Anton rewarded his quick thinking with a job. Thomas had to be there on behalf of Sasha's father, not as a friend.

"What do you want?" Kostas asked with an unsteady voice.

"We need to find Sasha," Thomas replied.

Jake leaned closer and whispered into Kostas' ear. "Who are these guys? Should I call the cops?"

He whispered back, "They work for Sasha's father. Stay cool." Kostas redirected his attention to Thomas. "I haven't seen him in two weeks, and he won't return my messages."

"But you know how to reach him," the other one said, stepping forward. "You need to come with us."

"He's not going anywhere with you," Jake said, positioning himself between Kostas and the men. He was fearless to the point of foolhardiness.

Kostas pulled him back. "You need to get out of here."

"I won't leave without you." Jake was eye candy for most gay men. He was thin but in top shape with well-defined muscles and would probably take one of these guys, but not two.

The other man pulled a pistol from underneath his jacket. Thomas did the same, but a heavy sigh made him appear reluctant. Kostas' stomach tightened. He likely wouldn't make it out of this unscathed. "I'll go with you but leave my friend out of this."

Jake grabbed Kostas by the coat sleeve. "What are you doing?"

"Saving your ass."

"It doesn't need saving." Jake swung at the other man with the gun. He caught him off guard, hitting him in the jaw. The pistol dropped to the ground.

"Shoot him," the man yelled.

Thomas lunged forward. Kostas feared he was about to pull the trigger, but Thomas slammed the butt of his gun against the back of Jake's skull. Jake wobbled. Kostas reached out to catch him, but he slipped through his arms, falling to the asphalt.

While the other man caught his bearings, Kostas knelt on the ground, concerned for his friend. He shook Jake and called his name, but he didn't respond. He snapped his head toward Thomas. "You may have killed him."

"Just get in the damn car, Kostas," Thomas said.

Kostas pressed a hand against Jake's chest and felt it gently rise and fall to shallow breathing. He was alive, but blood seeped from a gash in his head. If he let on that Jake wasn't dead, he feared Thomas or the other man would finish the job. "You killed him, Thomas. You killed him."

Thomas knelt, clutching Jake with both hands by the collar, and issued another punch. Jake didn't react. "He's gone."

"We need to dump the body," Viktor said.

"Leave him." Thomas sifted through the man's pockets, located his wallet, and removed his cash before wiping his prints off using Jake's T-shirt. "It will look like a robbery." He ushered Kostas toward the sedan and tossed him into the backseat. The other man slid beside him while Thomas got into the driver's seat, started the engine, and drove away.

Kostas suddenly feared for his and Sasha's lives, thinking if Anton had sent two armed thugs to find Sasha, something was desperately wrong. Wherever Sasha was, he hoped it was far, far away.

4

Since Tony Belcher had attacked Lexi's family, she was rarely far from her service weapon. She'd stopped storing it in a locked case at home, deciding the precious seconds required to open it might mean the difference between life and death. She kept it loaded in her nightstand drawer when she slept and took it into the bathroom when she showered, leaving it within reach on the countertop. Stowing it at the prison check-in point with her cell phone made her feel vulnerable, like a piece of her armor was missing and her ability to protect what was left of her family was on hold. Lexi needed to interview the prisoner and fly home before the Raven or any other thug with a gripe against her caught on.

Nathan pushed through when the electronic buzzer sounded at New York's Upstate Correctional Facility greeting center. Lexi followed. They trailed a correctional officer down a brightly lit hallway. A sign on the wall read, "Welcome to the Island."

"What's the island?" Lexi asked their escort.

"Only staff and visitors on official business are allowed in this part of the facility. Everywhere else inside the walls is the sea of inmates. It's our island of civilization where we don't have to worry about every pen or paperclip becoming a weapon."

Lexi offered a respectful nod for the daily danger the correctional officers faced.

They passed a breakroom with couches, tables, and a television. A soda vending machine was a few feet inside. Lexi pulled their escort to a stop. "What's the rule on offering an innate a soda?"

"It's fine, but he has to finish it before returning to the block."

"Thanks. Give me a second." Lexi dipped inside the breakroom, inserted three dollars into the machine, and selected a bottle of Coke. *Highway robbery*, she thought.

After she returned, they continued their walk and reached the entrapment area, a narrow corridor between two secure doors. A sign on the wall read, "Leaving the Island." The second door buzzed open once the first one closed. The next wall message was a painted quote from the novelist Hammond Innes. It read, "He who lets the sea lull him into a sense of security is in grave danger." It was a solemn reminder for every correctional officer. No one was safe once they passed through this door.

Their escort led them inside an interview room. The space was clean. The fresh paint on the cinder block walls, an acoustic ceiling with ample fluorescent lights, and a steel desk with three metal chairs were newer than Lexi expected. Everything in there couldn't have been more than two or three years old, likely the product of free-flowing Covid money.

"Officers should have the inmate here in a minute," the escort said. "Would you like any water?"

"No, thanks," Lexi said before the escort left.

Nathan sat at the table and opened the file he'd assembled. It contained Alexander Segura's rich criminal record, including the prison file documenting his behavior during his stay at Upstate. Two items caught Lexi's attention when she reviewed the file on the plane. Beyond asking for a lawyer after his arrest, he refused to speak during the interrogation and trial, which meant he was tough. Secondly, his mother visited only twice yearly since his incarceration eight years ago, which suggested he was lonely.

When Lexi sat next to Nathan, he pointed to the soda bottle. "What's with the drink? We have his DNA, and guys like him aren't swayed by small gestures."

"It's a conversation starter." Lexi shook it a few times before placing it at the corner of the table. "I've interrogated my share of Gatekeepers and Red Spades who were uncooperative. You introduce us and tell him why we're here. If he doesn't talk, don't say anything more. Follow my lead."

Nathan shrugged. "Okay." His questioning tone suggested he didn't think her tactic would work.

Moments later, the door opened. Two officers and an inmate dressed in green overalls and restrained by shackles and a full belly chain stepped inside. A guard directed the prisoner to sit in a chair before releasing the waist chain and securing his hands to the crossbar on the table.

"Can you give him enough slack to drink if he wants to?" Lexi asked. The guard gave her a curious look. "We'll be fine." She sized up Alexander Segura. His short stature, slim build, and dark hair strongly resembled Robert Segura. He carried himself more confidently than Robert, which could have been a product of prison life.

"We'll be right outside." The guard adjusted the restraints and exited with his partner.

"Mr. Segura, I'm Agent Croft. This is Agent Mills. We're from the ATF and are here to ask you about a family member."

Lexi expected Segura's long, silent look. He wouldn't respond to questions, so she had to get him to ask them. While Nathan remained silent, she loosened the cap on the soda bottle, slowly releasing the carbonation. Segura's gaze drifted to her. She'd successfully gotten his attention. Now, she had to set the trap.

Lexi took the top off the bottle and laid both on the table, one foot in front of her. She crossed her arms at her chest and stared at the bottle. A minute passed, but Segura remained quiet, telling her he would be tough to crack. Most suspects she tried this on broke their silence in the first thirty seconds. She had to bump it up a level.

Lexi chuckled for a few seconds, keeping her stare on the bottle.

Segura cocked his head. She had him.

"What's so funny?" Segura asked.

"The guards are getting screwed by the soda vendor." Lexi leaned closer and carefully inspected the bottle, pointing her finger up and down its length. "See how the carbonation is already gone?"

"Yeah. What about it?"

"It should take an hour for it to stop bubbling. I bet this stuff is at least a year old." She picked it up and inspected the expiration date. "Yep. Expired. I bet the vendor has a thing against cops."

Segura laughed. "I know how he feels."

"Want it?" Lexi gestured toward him with an upturned palm.

"Is it safe to drink?"

"Yes, but it won't taste like it should."

"Sure, why not?"

Lexi slid the bottle closer, and he took it. "Look, we need to track down a relative from Brooklyn, Robert Segura." She kept details vague to not tip her hand. As far as she knew, Alex could have worked with Robert and the Raven before his arrest. Any offer of enticement would have to start small.

"What's it to you?" Segura asked.

"The better question would have been what's in it for me," Lexi said. "You have another twelve years on your aggravated murder conviction. A gift, if you ask me."

"I'm not asking."

"Then tell me something. What is the one thing you want to make your time in prison more palatable? My guess is your mother," Lexi said. Segura's eyebrows rose a fraction. Lexi had his interest. "Brooklyn is four hundred miles away. She's getting old and can only make it up here twice a year."

"They couldn't have sent me farther away. I'm practically in Canada." Segura tugged on his chains, rattling them.

"What if I can get you transferred to Green Haven? Would you talk to us about Robert?"

"I'll need a guarantee."

"That's a start. Before I make a call, I need to know if he's a relative."

Segura nodded slowly. "Cousin."

As she prepared to make the call, a wave of sadness swept over Lexi. Her first instinct was to call Delanie Scott. She had as much juice as Maxwell Keene, her friend and Deputy Director of the FBI. Delanie was one of the few prosecutors who could get the ink on a deal before the ice melted in her drink. Never working with her again was hard to accept, but

Lexi had someone else in mind with an equally vested interest in tracking down Robert.

Lexi pushed her chair back. "We'll be right back." She opened the door and got the attention of the guards. "I'll need my cell to make a call. Can you keep the inmate here until I get a reading on how long this will take?"

One looked at his watch. "You were allotted an hour and still have forty-five minutes. Knock yourself out."

While Lexi and Nathan retraced their steps to the island through the entrapment area, her partner asked, "What do you have in mind, Lexi?"

"Calling in the big guns to make the transfer happen today, so we don't have to come back another day and chance losing him." Lexi returned to the island side of the check-in desk, asked for her cell phone, and retreated steps away for privacy. She scrolled through her contacts list and dialed. She was given the private number to provide President Brindle critical updates on her investigation into the Raven and locust technology, and this interview was crucial.

Chief of Staff Martin Torres answered on the second ring. "Agent Mills, it's good to hear from you. Do you have an update?"

"We have a solid lead on the Raven's engineer, but I'll need your help to extract the information." Lexi explained the situation and her proposal for a transfer. "Normally, I'd reach out to my contact in the Justice Department, but she was killed in a car accident yesterday."

"Ah, Delanie Scott. We're all saddened in the White House."

"She was a good friend. I'll miss her." Lexi cleared the emotion from her throat to focus on the task. "This man, Segura, isn't the cooperative type. We need to strike while he's in an agreeable mood."

"The president gave me a standing order to avail every resource at our disposal to help you in your investigation. Send me the particulars. I'll personally contact the New York governor and explain the urgency. Expect an email of the approved transfer within the hour."

"Thank you, Mr. Torres." Lexi slipped the phone into her pocket after emailing Torres the information he requested. She turned her attention to Nathan. "Torres is on it. Let me buy you a Coke. We should get what we need before it loses its fizzle."

Nathan smirked, shaking his head. "You know how to get things done, Mills, which is why you should be the lead on this case."

"What's done is done." Lexi could live with losing face in front of her peers, but Lange trying to pull her from the case stung more than she cared to admit. She'd expected more support from her boss and was disappointed it took Nathan's threat to retire for her to go out on a limb. But that limb was for Nathan, not Lexi.

Half an hour later, Lexi and Nathan returned to the interview room with a printed letter from the governor approving the transfer to Green Haven Correctional Facility, seventy-five miles from Brooklyn. She presented it to Alexander Segura. "This is only valid if you talk to us. Now, what can you tell us about your cousin?"

"A month or two after his parents died in a fire, Social Services tracked down my mom. She went to where he was living to see about taking him in but came home empty-handed."

"Did she say why?"

"Some older boy gave her the creeps. She said he told her to stay away from him. That it was his job to protect him. She thought he might make trouble and wanted nothing to do with him. Besides, she barely had enough money to care for me. I couldn't blame her."

"Do you recall where he was staying?"

"Some place for orphaned boys in Brooklyn."

"Did any other family take him in?" Lexi asked.

Segura shook his head. "My grandmother was handicapped and couldn't take him in. We lost track of him for fifteen years. Then he suddenly appeared with the same creepy guy when our grandmother was on her deathbed. A bunch of shit went down. He told her about how rough it was in the orphanage and how he wouldn't have survived without Starshiy."

"Starshiy?"

"That's what he called the creepy guy. I swear the prick showed up to make her feel guilty, and it worked. Before she died, she changed her will, giving him the deed to her apartment. That was the last time I saw him. It's good he never showed his face again because I would have killed him. My mom was supposed to get the apartment. The worst thing about the whole deal is that he's hardly there. It sits empty most of the time while my mom lives in government-assisted housing. What a guy."

Lexi jotted down the apartment address, thanked him for his cooperation, and left the interview room feeling had. Alex hated his cousin and would have given up the information without the deal if she'd told him Robert was a primary suspect in a case in which he could face the death penalty. At least she didn't give more away than a transfer closer to home.

When Lexi was at the check-in desk and returned her service weapon to its home on her waist, it was like putting on her armor. She was prepared to defend her family against the Raven again. Walking to the parking lot, she checked her phone for messages and discovered a missed call and text from Maxwell. She listened to his voicemail once inside their rental car. *"Hope you're holding up, Lexi. I wanted to make sure you knew about the funeral service for Delanie set for Thursday afternoon. I'll text you the details. See you then."*

Lexi closed her eyes, realizing Delanie's death still seemed surreal. Maybe seeing her body in a casket would finally make it concrete like it did at her mother's funeral. It had to. She copied Maxwell's text and sent it to the task force group chat, adding *Delanie's funeral is set. Hope to see you all there.*

5

Twenty-four hours to Texas for a job he was in the dark about. Two days casing Delanie Scott and Kostas Fisher. Another twenty-four hours on the road back to Brooklyn, babysitting Kostas in the back seat behind tinted windows with the help of street tranq to keep him from escaping or alerting a passerby on the road. By the time they pulled into the Boyko compound, it was four o'clock in the morning, and Thomas was exhausted from catnapping with one eye open. He trusted Viktor to not put a bullet in his head about as much as he trusted Congress to balance the budget. It was possible, but not in his lifetime.

Thomas dragged Kostas from the back seat, still limp and groggy from the drug cocktail. He and Viktor grabbed Kosta's arms and took him to a storage room with a cot in the wine cellar. The basement had only one exit, no windows big enough to escape through, and was insulated sufficiently to muffle screams from the main residence and Boyko's wife. It was the perfect location from which to extract information.

After padlocking the door, Viktor led Thomas to Anton's office, excused the man guarding it, and turned on a corner lamp from the wall switch. The amber light brought out the rich tones of the wood desk, chairs, and built-in bookshelves. "Wait here. I'll wake him."

After Viktor left and closed the door, Thomas considered retrieving the burner phone hidden in his tighty-whities, where most guys refused to frisk when looking for a weapon or wire. Someone should know he was back if Anton disapproved of how he handled the job, but Thomas suspected Anton had bugged the room with video and audio surveillance. He'd have to talk his way out if things went south.

Moments later, the door swung open. Anton and Viktor entered. Their somber expressions were unreadable. Anton sat at his desk and turned on the banker's lamp near the front edge. "I understand you brought Kostas. Well done, but I'm concerned about what made you think you didn't have to follow Viktor's order regarding the witness."

"I did everything Viktor ordered me to do. I killed the lady, disabled the security cameras behind the café, and took Kostas, but he didn't think things through in the alley. Several businesses in the area were still open; someone may have heard the shot and called the police. If they had come searching out of curiosity, we would have had another body on our hands. He looked dead to me. I thought it was better to make it look like a robbery gone bad, so the police would think someone local did it."

"I see. That's a much different story than I've been led to believe. You did well, but I won't stand for disobedience. When one of my lieutenants gives you an order, you follow it. Do you understand?"

"Yes, Mr. Boyko." Despite knowing he'd done the right thing, Thomas didn't qualify his response. He'd seen firsthand how Anton dealt with those who failed to follow orders. He beat his wife at the drop of a hat and wouldn't hesitate to put a bullet in Thomas' head.

"I'm glad you understand. Take me to Kostas."

Kostas woke with the worst headache and cotton mouth of his life. It felt like someone had plunged an axe down the middle of his head and left it there. He'd taken his share of party favors over the years, but whatever was in those pills Thomas and the other man gave him packed a big wallop. He had no idea what time it was, let alone the day. However, he was sure he'd been in the back seat of a car for hours.

He opened his eyes to assess his surroundings, but his vision was slightly blurry from the drugs. The room was cold and musty. He blinked more to clear the fog, discovering stacked boxes and crates against a wall. More of the room became clear. He appeared to be in a storage room smaller than his bedroom. He was likely in a basement based on the unfinished cinder blocks on two walls. The army-style cot he was on was the only furniture, but a nearby upturned five-gallon bucket had two full water bottles and a bag of potato chips.

Kostas pushed himself to sit upright and chugged half a bottle to address the dry mouth and headache. It was a decent start, but he'd experienced enough hangovers to know he would need to hydrate for a day to feel better. Once he got his bearings, his memory started to clear. He remembered closing the restaurant with Jake and going out the back. "Jake," he whispered, recalling Thomas had pistol-whipped his friend. But Jake was alive when Kostas checked. Why, then, did Thomas say he was dead? Either he couldn't tell the difference, or Thomas wasn't the one to fear. Nevertheless, Kostas was in danger and had to escape.

His strength had returned, so he tried the door, but it was locked. He moved boxes, looking for another way out, but two walls were made of blocks. The other two were interior walls covered by unfinished sheetrock. Kostas had helped his dad one summer remodeling the upstairs of his childhood home and knew the frame studs would be sixteen inches apart, wide enough for him to slip through. He figured the wall with the door likely led to a hallway or opening, and the other framed wall might lead to another room. If he could break through the drywall, he could escape.

Kostas picked a section close to the cinder block wall and moved the boxes and crates to the center of the room. After stuffing the food and water into his jacket, he knocked on the wall, locating a void between two studs. He kicked the wall firmly with his right leg, breaking through the first layer three feet above the concrete floor. The fragments scraped against his jeans but caused no damage to his lower leg. The sound was loud enough to alert someone outside the door, so Kostas grabbed the bucket and prepared to use it to knock out anyone who rushed through. He counted to ten, but no one came, so he resumed his escape effort.

A peek through the wall confirmed a second layer of sheetrock on the other side of the wood frame. Kostas peeled back drywall edges to the screws on the studs, clearing a passageway six feet tall. His next kick through the wall would be blind, so he decided to use less force to avoid hitting an immovable object too hard and breaking his foot. He raised his leg waist high and pushed until the material cracked under pressure, and his foot passed through and instantly hit something solid. Whatever it was, it moved, giving Kostas hope he could break his way out.

No light spilled through, so he must have burrowed into another room. Kostas picked at the opening to clear a passageway tall enough for him to fit. A few more pieces and he would be through.

The door opened.

Shit, he thought. He shimmied through the opening and used a shoulder to push the box, or whatever was blocking his escape out of the way.

"Whoa." Thomas leaped forward and grabbed him by the arm when he was halfway through the opening. He said softly, so only Kostas could hear, "Don't make this worse for yourself. Tell Anton what he wants to know."

Was this a good cop, bad cop type of thing? No matter the case, Kostas had a sinking feeling if he didn't get out of there now, he never would. He threw off Thomas' arm, slithered the rest of the way through the opening into the dark room, and fell to his knees to wade through whatever was there. The only illumination came from the hole he'd made.

"It's another locked room, Kostas," a man yelled. "You're trapped. Come back now, and we won't hurt you."

Kostas wasn't buying his empty promise for a second. Sasha had told him stories of his father's shady business and brutality, but he'd thought they were exaggerations. That he'd conflated his homophobia and strict parenting style into wild accusations. He now knew every horrible word was true. Anton Boyko was a ruthless mobster and killer.

He clawed through cardboard storage boxes until he reached a cleared path. The door should be to his right if the room was configured like the one he'd escaped from. He crawled, feeling his way in the dark, and touched the wall. Coming to his feet, Kostas reached the door and twisted the knob. It was unlocked. He shoved the door open, prepared to run, but two men with guns met him, forcing him to a skidding halt.

"I warned you." The one who had kidnapped him with Thomas

stepped closer and threw a solid punch to Kostas' belly. A water bottle absorbed most of the hit, but the man wound his arm for a second round, targeting his face this time. The crushing blow sent stinging pain radiating through his left cheek, blurring his vision. Another punch hit his back flank, a direct shot to a kidney. A wave of pain and nausea forced him to his knees.

"That's enough for now," someone said.

Someone lifted Kostas to his feet by the arm. He looked up and recognized Anton from the pictures Sasha had shown him. "Where is my son, Kostas?"

"I don't know where he is, Mr. Boyko. Two weeks ago, he texted me when I was at work, saying he needed some space. I tried calling and texting for a week but haven't seen or heard from him since."

"I don't believe you. Unlock your phone." Anton snapped his fingers, and the other man handed him the phone he confiscated before leaving Fort Worth.

Kostas *was* telling the truth, so he unlocked the device using facial recognition and returned it to Anton. "See, not a word from him in the last two Mondays. I'm starting to worry."

Anton returned the phone to his man. "This only proves you two haven't communicated through this phone. I want a list of the people he knows and places he frequents."

"So you can rough up every friend until he surfaces? I don't think so."

The other man launched another punch into his kidney, doubling him over again. Kostas fought the urge to throw up. A second punch to the face. A third to the gut. The rotation continued for three more cycles until Kostas couldn't stand or see through the blinding pain and swelling eyelids.

"Give me the phone," Thomas said. "We can get a list of people from his contacts list. Unless he's paranoid, it should also have a location history."

Anton lifted Kostas' chin until their eyes met. "I know you're holding back. We will either break you or kill you. The decision is yours."

Kostas shivered, each movement aggravating a rib or organ the subject of an earlier beating. He believed every terrifying word Sasha had told him about Anton and envisioned a slow, agonizing death. *Damn you, Sasha.*

Where the hell are you? "He left me, Mr. Boyko. I wish I knew where he was, but I don't."

Viktor continued to pummel Kostas while Anton looked on with anticipation. Thomas doing nothing angered him the most. He was supposed to be Sasha's friend, yet he stood by while Kostas grew weaker with each consecutive blow.

Then a miracle happened. Thomas leaned closer to Anton.

"He might not know where Sasha is, but he might be able to flush him out." Anton didn't respond, but Thomas continued. "My guess is Sasha doesn't have his phone on because it can be traced, but he likely still has access to email. We can have Kostas send a message asking to meet with him. It would have to be serious to entice him into sneaking away from witness protection. I know Kostas had leukemia as a child. He can tell Sasha it has returned, and he wants to meet him in a safe place, perhaps at the club where they first met. If he refuses to send it, I can. I know enough details of their relationship to make it sound real. However, we shouldn't kill him now. Sasha might be watching the place, so we'll need Kostas to be there."

"All right, Mr. Falco. We will try your idea, but he dies if this doesn't work." Anton waved his hand, and the beating mercifully stopped.

6

Noah Black turned south onto the gravel access road leading to the Mills family home in Ponder. He came to a creeping stop to avoid triggering the sensor and alerting Lexi that he was there. After flipping up the visor that had shielded him from the setting sun during most of his drive from the airport, Noah let himself recall the bitter memory of the last time he was there. He'd endured many harrowing events with Lexi—the attack at the governor's mansion, trapped in a missile complex with a ticking bomb, and rescuing Nita from a kidnapping with a bomb sitting next to her—but the most gut-wrenching experience happened here six months ago.

He still had nightmares about the day Tony Belcher wreaked havoc on Lexi's family. Discovering the trail of blood on the tile was enough to turn his stomach. He'd feared everyone inside the house, including Nita, had been butchered after finding Lexi's parents unconscious on the kitchen floor. Lexi's pale look of fear when she first saw them was horrifying. He couldn't let her be the one to determine whether they were alive or dead. No son, daughter, parent, or spouse should ever have to do such a thing with a loved one.

Twisting his fingers tighter against the steering wheel, he regretted not being here for Lexi's wedding. If he had, he could have been her rock when her mother died the next day. But he was still reeling from stepping over a line he'd sworn to never cross. Tony Belcher was unarmed and no longer a threat in the Vegas hotel, but he took the shot before Lexi could. His reasoning was sound. If anyone could live with the guilt of crossing the line, it was him, not her. What kind of friend would he have been if he didn't spare her that pain? But coming to terms with what he'd done had meant he wasn't there in Lexi's hour of need. It was an omission for which he'd never forgive himself.

"I'm here now, Lexi," he whispered, swallowing past the growing lump in his throat.

Noah coasted his rental car farther down the road, noting several security improvements since the attack on Lexi's family. She'd installed motion sensor floodlights along the road, but enough sunlight still hung in the sky to keep them off. Wireless cameras were strategically positioned around the property, warning of someone coming from any direction.

He parked beneath the large shade tree behind the main house between Lexi's SUV and the four-car garage. The garage doors were down, so Lexi's father likely wasn't in there tinkering with a pet project. After he exited and stood between his car and Lexi's, the porch's screen door creaked as it slowly opened.

"Stop right there," someone called out.

The shadows beneath the cover made it difficult to discern who was at the door, but the voice sounded familiar. "Nita? It's Noah."

Nita stepped farther out, cradling a long gun in her arms. "What are you doing here? I thought you were flying in tomorrow."

"I wrapped up my case early, so I changed my flight." Noah walked forward, inspecting her weapon more closely. "What the hell are you doing with a shotgun?"

"I'm a lousy shot, so Lexi got this for me after the wedding."

"How romantic," Noah laughed. Leave it to Lexi Mills to buy her wife the best rated home defense shotgun on the market. Its small size made it easy for Nita to handle, and the magazine provided her ample firepower to take out a squad of invaders.

Nita leaned the weapon against the side of the house and gave Noah a loose hug. It had been a year since they shared an awkward moment when she slipped from sobriety, but she clearly still felt uneasy about it. Their drunken kiss in a public bathroom had almost cost her the love of her life.

"It's good to see you," she said. "FaceTime isn't the same as the real thing."

"No, it's not, but it's been nice seeing you two now and again."

Nita gestured toward the door. "Let's get your bags. Lexi's in the shower."

Once inside the kitchen, Noah heard the television and spotted Lexi's father entering from the hallway connecting to the living room. "Noah." Jerry opened his arms wide, welcoming him into his home. "I wasn't expecting you until after the funeral tomorrow." He pulled Noah in for a hardy hug.

"I hope you don't mind putting me up for an extra night?" Noah asked.

"Of course not. What's one more night among friends? We're all glad to have you here for the weekend." Jerry backed up a step, inspecting Noah from head to toe. "You're looking thin. Nita's taken up pie duties. Let's get a slice or two in you."

"I'd love some pie."

"It's Jessie's recipe, but I still don't have it down yet," Nita said. She retrieved four dessert plates from the cabinet and served two pieces to him and Jerry. "I'll tell Lexi you're here."

After hearing her phone beep with an alert, Lexi cranked the shower handle clockwise, bringing the flow of hot water to a stop. The unique chime told her a motion sensor on the property was triggered by something bigger than the critters that often used their land as a thoroughfare. She opened the shower door to reach for a towel, shivering when a rush of cool air kissed her damp skin.

Balancing on her natural foot, she dried off enough to not create a water trail to the counter before gripping the grab bar and hopping to the phone beside her service weapon. The notification screen confirmed an alert from the home security system. She pressed on it, but facial recognition was a bust with her wet, scraggly hair, so she entered the passcode, leaving water streaks on the screen.

The security app popped up, saying the access road sensor had detected motion. It provided a direct link to the cameras picking it up. After leaning on her elbows to relieve the strain on her right leg, she scrolled through the video recordings and discovered someone had arrived in a white sedan. They parked next to her SUV and got out. The camera caught his face and brought a broad smile to Lexi's lips.

"You sneaky little thing." Lexi hurried to dry herself off and sat on the toilet to get dressed. Before she slid her underwear on, the door opened, and Nita appeared in the opening. She leaned against the door jamb with her arms crossed against her chest and scanned Lexi up and down with a hungry look.

"I was going to tell you we have a special guest for pie, but dessert is right here."

"You are tempting, but I saw Noah was here." Lexi shimmied her underwear the rest of the way up.

"Just a small sample." Nita stepped between Lexi's legs, angled her head down, and gave Lexi a lingering, passionate kiss. She let a hand drift, caressing the top of a breast.

Noah could wait a few minutes, Lexi thought for a fleeting second, but after six months, she was anxious to see him. She pulled back. "As much as I'd love to continue this—"

"I know, but I'm collecting a raincheck in bed tonight." Nita winked.

"It goes without saying."

"I'll let him know you'll be right down." Nita added an extra sway to her hips while leaving the bathroom. The show was clearly for her benefit.

Lexi finished dressing and doffed her prosthesis over the liner and two layers of socks—the optimum fit for her new socket. Her prosthetist had done a fantastic job measuring her changing limb size, and this socket had the snuggest and most comfortable fit since Lexi had become an amputee.

After running a comb through her hair, she descended the stairs but stopped before making the final turn to the kitchen. The last time she saw Noah Black in the flesh, his body language had significantly changed from what it was before their final confrontation with Tony Belcher. He was always relaxed around her and alternated between playful banter and relentless devotion. She was the same with him. But since that day in Las Vegas, he was stiff around her. She hoped they could get back to the easiness they once shared.

Lexi released a deep breath and entered the kitchen. Noah and her father were across from each other at the table for four, chatting and chewing on bites of pie. Nita was sitting nearest the refrigerator in her mother's traditional seat. She leaned against the backrest with a slight grin and followed their conversation, turning her head back and forth between both men.

Noah looked up, locking gazes with Lexi. He smiled with his eyes, but his expression wasn't filled with joy. Moisture shimmered along his lower rims, reflecting the pain behind his prolonged absence. When he nodded his greeting, Lexi couldn't hold back the tears any longer and closed the distance between them. He stood and pulled her into a long embrace. Friendship. Trust. Love. Respect. It was all there. By the time Lexi broke the hug, she was unsure how much healing he still had to do, but he seemed well on his way.

"You couldn't have called and let a girl know you were coming early?" Lexi smiled.

"And ruin the surprise? But maybe I should have. Nita greeted me with a twelve-gauge."

"She did, huh? I'll feel better the next time I have to leave her and Dad alone."

"Things sure have changed around here. I saw the cameras and sensors." Noah knitted his brow. "Are you expecting trouble?"

"The Raven is gunning for me, so I'm not taking any chances. Though, the place isn't as secure as I'd like it to be."

"I am not turning this home into some castle by putting up an eight-foot metal fence," Lexi's father said, rolling his eyes.

"Sir Mills." Noah bowed dramatically but quickly dropped his smile. "Don't underestimate the Raven, Mr. Mills. From everything Lexi has told me, he's to be feared as much as Tony Belcher, if not more."

"I don't disagree, Noah," her dad said. "I've taken precautions but won't cower behind walls."

"Now I know where Lexi gets her stubborn streak."

"I'll take that as a compliment," Lexi said.

Her father raised a fist to his mouth to cover a deep yawn. "It's getting late. I don't know about you youngsters, but I'm heading to bed." He stood and reached for his plate, but Nita interrupted.

"I got it, Dad." She grabbed their plates but left one out and winked at Lexi. "In case you still want dessert."

Lexi returned her gesture. "Leave it."

"I'll head upstairs after I clean up," Nita said. "You two go catch up."

After her father said his goodbyes, Lexi turned to Noah. "Want to see what my dad and I have been working on?"

"Sure." Noah shrugged.

Lexi grabbed two Corona longnecks from the fridge, handed one to Noah, and led him to the garage. Floodlights came on, illuminating their path. Lexi entered the security code on the wall-mounted pad, raising the righthand door. Her restored Shelby was in one bay, and the project she'd worked on with her dad in earnest since returning from Napa was in another.

Noah's face brightened with excitement. "Nice rides. The Shelby turned out great." He walked around it, inspecting the body, the new paint job, and the fresh interior. "It's a great tribute to Gavin."

"It is." Lexi's heart still ached at Gavin's memory. He was her father's longest friend. They'd started the Jerry Mills Racing Team with him as his trusted crew chief. Gavin was also Lexi's first mentor, bringing her on as a certified mechanic. He'd taught her more about building and repairing cars than her father had, which was saying something. He'd also taught her how to think methodically, a trait that made her good at her job as an explosives expert. But most importantly, he'd remained her friend when her father pulled away after she came out as gay. Gavin was a sweet, kind man who didn't deserve to die in a Tony Belcher attack.

Noah switched his attention to the Camaro. It was still a work in progress, but he seemed equally impressed. "Is this the one from Harrington? The one you trashed?"

Lexi laughed. "I wouldn't say I trashed it, but I certainly put a few more dents on it."

"At least you caught that dirty deputy." Noah sipped his beer.

Lexi snickered at the memory of pushing Thomas Perez's classic Camaro to its limit, executing the perfect pit maneuver to spinout the bad guy and keep him from escaping. She'd scared Perez to the point he nearly pissed his pants in the passenger seat. "Thomas is a great guy. In return, we're restoring it for the cost of the material and parts."

"That's really nice of you." Noah took another swig. "If I know you as well as I think I do, taking this on was more about repairing your relationship with your dad than the car. Has it helped?"

Lexi smirked. Noah knew her well, and not much got past him. "Yes, it has. And it's helped him focus on something other than missing my mom." She sat on one of the two folding chairs she'd set out for her and her dad.

Noah joined her. "I'm sorry I didn't come to the funeral. I should have been there for you."

"It was too soon. You still needed time and distance to process things. I'm sorry I put you in that position."

"You didn't. Belcher did. He was a madman who needed to die. We saw firsthand the reach the Belcher brothers had beyond prison walls. Who knows the havoc he would have brought on your family if we had arrested him."

"Intellectually, I know it's true, but emotionally, I have a hard time reconciling why you shot him."

"I saw the fire in your eyes, Lexi. I couldn't let you go down that path. It was too far of a leap for you, but it was a short one for me." Noah took another big swig. "You have no idea how often I've flirted with that line since returning to Nogales. It's open season down there for the worst the cartels have to offer. The drug trafficking, human smuggling, and murder and rape of migrants seeking a better life. But what gets to me the most is child sex trafficking. It's never-ending, and it breaks my heart."

Lexi set her bottle down and shifted in her chair to look Noah in the eye. He appeared beaten down by a constant flow of unspeakable crime and depravity. "Stay. Come to work in Dallas. I'm sure Maxwell or I could get you on with the FBI or ATF. Or Governor Macalister can find you a position with the Texas Rangers. Sarah Briscoe would love to have you on board. You can move your aunt up and stay right here. We have the space."

"I don't know, Lexi." His tentative headshake gave her hope that Noah didn't consider her suggestion completely absurd.

"We're family, Noah. We need to stick together. At least tell me you'll think about it."

"I'll think about it."

Lexi checked her watch. It was getting late, so she pushed herself from the chair. "You better get settled in. We have a long drive ahead of us tomorrow. We meet up with Kaplan at seven in Fort Worth to carpool down. Do you want the guest room upstairs or downstairs?"

"You better make it downstairs." Noah also stood. "I don't want the newlyweds keeping me up all night." He gave her a playful shoulder shove.

Lexi's cheeks flushed with embarrassment. She shoved him back. "Come on, you."

After getting Noah set with fresh bedding and a bath towel, Lexi ascended the stairs quietly to not wake her dad. She cringed when the second to the last step creaked loud enough to scare a burglar. *I gotta fix that*, she thought.

Lexi opened their bedroom door. The lights were off, but the dim glow of a candle flickered inside. Nita was in bed, lying on her side with her head propped up by an upturned palm. "It's about time," Nita said. "I was beginning to think you might pass on dessert."

Lexi unbuttoned her shirt slowly. "You know my sweet tooth."

7

Following a four-hour drive, Lexi parked her SUV in the funeral home parking lot. She glanced at Nita asleep in the passenger seat and giggled at the drop of drool at the corner of her mouth. She shook her wife's arm gently after unbuckling, slowly waking her from a well-needed nap. "Nita, we're here," Lexi said softly. "We ran into construction, so we don't have much time before the service starts."

Nita opened her eyes extra wide, inhaling deeply. "Okay. I'm good. Do we have time to use the bathroom?"

"I think so. Other people are still arriving." Lexi gestured toward Nita's mouth. "But you might want to wipe that off first."

Nita straightened in her seat and flipped open the visor mirror. "For heaven's sake." She wiped the corner of her mouth.

"I'll go with you," Kaplan said from the back seat.

Everyone hopped out. Noah exited from the back seat, groaning and stretching his back. "I'd forgotten that hanging out with you means long road trips."

"I bet you wish you'd flown into San Antonio instead of Dallas," Lexi said.

"Common sense would say yes, but seeing you and Nita last night makes every ache and pain worth it."

The four gathered at the bumper. Nita placed a hand on Lexi's forearm and spoke firmly to her. "No shop talk today. You need time to grieve."

Lexi kissed her on the lips. "I won't." The group followed the signs toward the chapel. Noah elbowed Lexi in the side and gestured his chin toward the entrance. "It's Lathan and Coby." The men disappeared inside.

If Lathan Sinclair and Coby Vasquez were there, Lexi figured Maxwell Keene and his wife were nearby. When she spoke with Maxwell yesterday, he'd said they were carpooling from the FBI building in Dallas.

Once inside, Lexi scanned the chapel reception area and spotted Amanda Keene studying a memorial poster board with photographs resting on an easel. Lathan and Coby joined her, so Lexi guided her group toward them.

Amanda's eyes lit with recognition. "Lexi. Nita. I'm so glad you made it." She hugged them before turning to Noah and waving him closer with both hands. "Come here, Noah. I've missed you." She pulled him into a tight embrace.

"I missed you, too," he said.

"I was surprised to learn you were coming when I talked to Maxwell yesterday," Lexi said. "Did you know Delanie well?"

"We met twice in Maxwell's office, but I think it's important to show solidarity from the law enforcement family."

"I couldn't agree more," Nita said.

"Lathan. Coby." Lexi hugged them. While the rank and file of the task force didn't have direct dealings with Delanie, her work directly impacted how they did their job. It was good seeing them there, Kaplan included. Only Simon Winslow and Mel Thompson were missing, but Mel had her grandson to watch, and Simon was leading the governor's security detail for a trip to the border.

Following greetings all around, Nita and Kaplan went to the bathroom while the others filed into the chapel, staking out seats on the pews. The space had a seating capacity of about a hundred, and the room was already half full. Lexi glanced toward the front. More photo boards and ample white and lavender flower arrangements on stands flanked the casket. Another bouquet rested on top. She didn't expect the coffin to be closed but assumed injuries sustained during the accident were too significant for the mortician to make Delanie presentable.

Lexi continued to scan the room but didn't find the person she was looking for. She whispered to Amanda, "Where's Maxwell?"

"He's speaking with the family in the private area. He wanted them to know an army of law enforcement was there if they needed anything before things started."

That was so like him, Lexi thought. Maxwell was the deputy director of the FBI with loads of responsibility, but he always took time with his people. And when the situation called for it, like today, he ensured the families knew how important their loved one was to the job and him.

Nita and Kaplan returned. Noah had left space for Nita to sit between him and Lexi, but Nita asked Lexi to slide over and sat between her and Amanda. Whether she added a buffer between her and Noah for Lexi's sake or her own didn't matter. She thought it necessary, which was concerning. Nita had kissed him during the lowest point she'd hit in years, but they didn't share the kiss, which was a difference with a significant distinction. It was a slip Lexi had long forgiven, but it was now clear Nita hadn't forgiven herself. She had to do a better job of laying the groundwork for Nita to heal.

Lexi whispered into Nita's ear, squeezing her hand, "You're stronger than you realize."

Nita looked confused. "I love it when you say that to me, but why now?"

"It takes strength to forgive yourself. I know it's within you." Lexi knew she'd correctly guessed Nita's motivation when her lips trembled. She scooted closer, throwing an arm over Nita's shoulder. She kept it there for the entire service, reminding Nita of their trust and proving it was as solid as ever.

After the speeches of love, compassion, and tenacity, the mourners stood in line to view the casket. When it was Nita and Lexi's turn, they stepped up. Lexi placed a hand on the polished dark walnut. It was cold, impersonal, and failed to give her the closure she needed to accept Delanie's death. However, the anguish on the faces of Delanie's parents and brother made it painfully real.

The guests gathered at the Veteran's Hall five blocks from the funeral home and took turns offering condolences to the family. The food was catered and served from foil tins. Water and soda were available from large white ice chests, and pop hits from the early to mid-1990s played in the background. Lexi wasn't sure of Delanie's precise age but assumed this was the music she'd grown up with and enjoyed the most.

Lathan and Coby returned to the table with multiple plates of pasta and salad. Each handed one to Lexi and Nita to save them a trip through the line. Lexi picked at her food, but the service had left her with little appetite. She'd experienced the same reaction at Kris Faust's funeral until she spoke to Kris' mother and promised to catch the man responsible for her death.

Unfortunately, no one was to blame for Delanie's death but herself. Lexi had read the preliminary investigation report into the accident and the witness statements detailing that her car had swerved moments before plunging into the lake. Since toxicology reported no traces of alcohol or drugs in her system and an inspection of the vehicle found no mechanical defects, the sheriff concluded Delanie must have been distracted or fallen asleep at the wheel. Lexi couldn't promise to find justice for Delanie's death. Couldn't turn her guilt and sadness into a relentless search. She still had a quest to fulfill for Mrs. Faust but refused to give up on it.

"Please tell me this wasn't on Delanie's all-time playlist," Coby said. Lexi focused on the music in the background and recognized the song instantly.

"It's achy, breaky soul crushing," Lathan said, earning muffled laughs from the group.

"I kinda liked the last song," Maxwell said, sliding a plastic cup toward his wife. "Want some ice, ice, baby?"

"Be nice, Maxwell," Amanda said with a coy smile. "Your friends might cringe at the playlist our kids have in mind for your funeral." She turned to Lathan. "You'll be dancing the macarena in the aisle."

Everyone at the table tried but failed miserably to hide their snickers.

Maxwell puffed his chest. "I stand by my choice in music. Critics be damned."

This was precisely the type of reception Lexi wanted for her funeral. She wanted her friends and family to remember her with laughter.

Lexi turned her attention to the large round table in the room's center, where Delanie's immediate family was seated. No other guests were visiting at the moment, so this was the perfect time for Lexi and her former task force to pay their respects. She stood. "It's time, team."

Lathan, Coby, Kaplan, Noah, and Maxwell pushed back their chairs and followed Lexi to the center table. She stopped between Delanie's parents. "Mr. and Mrs. Scott, I'm Lexi Mills, and the people behind me were part of Task Force Zero Impact. We worked with your daughter for most of last year."

Delanie's mother reached for Lexi's hand and cupped it in hers. The grief in her eyes was heartbreaking. "Yes, she spoke of you and the task force often. Dellie considered it the highlight of her career."

Lexi forced back the tears threatening to fall. Delanie had a long, storied record with the Justice Department, yet she considered her time with Lexi's team the pinnacle of her career. She was honored. "I can honestly say no prosecutor was more professional and dedicated to the job than she was. Prosecutors and law enforcement sometimes butt heads." Lexi snickered, remembering one deal she didn't care for. "We were no exception."

"She mentioned your occasional disagreements but said she respected you more for them. Like Mr. Keene said earlier during the service, our Dellie went the extra mile to ensure evil people paid the price for their crimes, no matter the risk. She didn't care if it meant losing her job."

Lexi had thought Maxwell's choice of words during his speech was odd, but it made sense in the context of job security. "Delanie won us over with her love of the law and relentless pursuit of justice. I was proud to have her as a friend and will miss her dearly."

Mrs. Scott patted Lexi's hand. "Thank you, Miss Mills. Hearing of the wonderful things Dellie accomplished and her impact on others is comforting. It tells me our daughter was a good and well-loved person."

"She was," Lexi said. "If there's anything we can do for you and your family, please ask."

"I will," the woman said. She focused on Maxwell. "Thank you, Mr. Keene, for speaking at the service earlier. Telling everyone about our daughter's work and the type of person she was meant more than you realize."

"It was an honor, Mrs. Scott," Maxwell said.

The group returned to their table, shuffling seats so Lexi and Maxwell sat beside each other. Since Lexi had promised Nita not to talk business today, she leaned closer and spoke softly so only he could hear. "You should know my boss removed me as the lead on the Raven case. The director wasn't happy with the bad PR from the golf tournament in Napa."

"Do you want me to put in a word at Justice? I'm sure I can get you reinstated."

"No. It's probably for the best at this point."

Maxwell jerked his head back, the creases at the bridge of his nose becoming more prominent. "That's not like you. You never shy away from responsibility."

Lexi considered looping in Maxwell about what really happened in California, but she owed the president her trust. "This was always Croft's case. He's been investigating the Raven for two years. I trust him to work it as well as I would."

"If something changes, let me know."

"I will. We have a solid lead and plan to follow up on it on Monday," Lexi said.

"What kind of lead?"

"We have a possible address for his engineer in Brooklyn."

Maxwell harrumphed. "Before you head to New York, I'd like to meet with you and your partner tomorrow to discuss the case."

"Can it wait until Monday? Noah is in town for the weekend and heads back to Nogales Sunday."

"Bring him. He might like to hear some of this. Kaplan would too."

8

It had been a year since Thomas had come to Hailey's Comet. It wasn't trendy, but he'd made a decent living there for several months. As a part-time bartender/bouncer, he'd made incredible tips while letting the customers drone on about their shitty lives. From listening to Sasha Boyko, he'd learned the Comet was one of the few bars in the borough his father didn't have influence over, which was why it had become his favorite hangout without crossing the river.

The last time he was at the Brooklyn nightclub, he'd intervened after a pair of thugs decided to use Sasha's face as a punching bag in the restroom for no other reason than he was gay and had looked at one of them in a too-friendly way. Kostas had tried to help but was knocked out with a single punch. The decision to step in had earned him Sasha's and Kosta's gratitude and a job in the Boyko organization. However, his goodwill with Kostas ended when he showed up in Texas with a gun.

He pulled the panel van into the dark alley, parking it in the spot reserved for the club. *Thank you, Hailey*, he thought. *I could always count on you*. If his old boss hadn't agreed to let him park there, the plan to draw out Sasha might not work.

Viktor unbuckled from the passenger seat and crouched to slide into the back, where they'd tossed Kostas. They'd bound his hands and feet with plastic straps and gagged him with tape over his mouth to ensure he wouldn't give them trouble on the way to the club.

Viktor clicked open a switchblade knife and wagged it in front of Kostas' face. "No funny business, or we'll kill both of you. Understand?" Kostas nodded vigorously before Viktor sliced the bindings from his wrists and ankles. "If you do exactly what Falco says, no one will get hurt. Remember, we have you wired and tagged"—he shook Kostas' left foot with the locked anklet containing a GPS tracker—"so we'll hear everything you say and know where you are every second."

Kostas' eye roll suggested he didn't believe Viktor for one second about not getting hurt. Only last night, Viktor gave him the beatdown of his life.

Thomas checked his and Kostas' microphones and earpieces to keep in communication with Viktor. He opened the side door, grabbed Kostas by the arm, and yanked him into the alley. "Let's go."

After Thomas typed in the code on the security panel, they entered through the back entrance reserved for employees near the delivery door. The smell of stale beer hit him like a truck, and the muffled thumping of loud club music vibrated through his chest. During the day, this part of the club was teeming with stockers, cleaners, and dishwashers, preparing for the opening at four o'clock in the afternoon to catch the happy hour crowd. But the back was empty at night, except for the occasional busser running in for supplies.

The stockroom was unoccupied, so Thomas pressed through to the main room. The music became clearer and more ear-pounding once through the double swing doors. The smell of burning weed filled the room, as did dim white lights, some flashing to the beat of the music.

The place was more packed for a Thursday than Thomas remembered, likely because of the first stretch of warm spring weather hitting the city this week. The wall of booths and tables in the center were all taken, but the long counter with barstools against the far wall was sparsely occupied. Thomas guided Kostas to an end so he could keep a watchful eye on the room.

Moments later, a server dressed in a black mid-thigh skirt, white button-down shirt, and a bow tie approached with an order pad in her hand. The black and white outfit was required, but the skirt was optional.

This server was out for big tips. Always. "What will it—" She paused, focusing on Thomas. "Tommie, long time no see. What brings you back to the Comet?"

"Hi, Tiff. I'm meeting a friend. Can you bring us two Coors longnecks?" Thomas refused to make eye contact, keeping his focus on the patrons.

"Sure thing, Tommie." Tiff walked away in a huff. When Thomas worked here, he was a little flirty with looks and winks, but he treated all the female servers equally to keep the peace. *"Keep it light and everyone happy"* was his motto. Bars and nightclubs were fertile ground for hurt feelings and catfights.

"Why are you doing this, Thomas?" Kostas asked. They'd washed the blood from his face to make him presentable, but his eyes and cheeks were bruised and swollen from last night's beatings. They were primarily red, with a hint of dark patches starting to form.

With Viktor listening in the van, Thomas had to be careful what he said and not let on that he had a soft spot for the kid. "The old man is at odds with Sasha again. He wants to talk to him."

"So you kidnap and beat me to a pulp?" Kostas pressed two fingertips against his cheekbone and winced.

"Like I said, Anton needs to see his son." Thomas lied. Anton's instructions were to capture Sasha to stop him from helping the feds build a case against him. In Anton's world, that didn't necessarily mean talking.

If Sasha was dumb enough to throw off his federal protection and come here tonight, his only hope of staying alive would be to convince his father he'd been misleading the feds to set up the competition. However, from what Thomas had seen of him, Sasha wasn't conniving enough to pull off a lie of such magnitude with Anton. Since the big blow-up about Sasha being gay, Anton questioned everything he said and did.

"What did Sasha do? Is he running from his father?"

"I really don't know."

"Like I'm supposed to believe it." Kostas didn't appear the least bit convinced, so Thomas merely shrugged, hoping Sasha didn't show. If his father didn't kill him, he would send Sasha somewhere Kostas and the feds would never find him.

Tiff delivered their beers with an expectant look, as if hoping for one more shot, but this was not the time for games. Thomas raised his beer silently in appreciation and returned his attention to the crowd, watching for Sasha. Tiff left in a huff more pronounced than the first.

The loud, thumping music transitioned from one song to the next while people danced on the center floor. Two people moved from table to table, and Thomas recognized the type. They were selling party favors or negotiating for the price of a lady's or man's company for ten minutes in the restroom.

Thomas continued to scan the room. The email they'd sent said to meet Kostas at the Comet at nine. It was fifteen minutes past. He heard Viktor through his earpiece. "It looks like he's not going to show. Pack it in, Falco."

"Give it a few more minutes," Thomas replied in the microphone hidden in his jacket lapel. "Sasha was never on time a day in his life."

Kostas laughed. "His mother once told me he was eight days overdue as a baby, setting the tone for his life."

A group of six or seven men gathered at the wall counter. Some had their backs to Thomas, so he couldn't see their faces. Tiff showed up, took the new group's drink orders, and gave Thomas the side eye as she left.

The man closest to Kostas turned around and grabbed him by the arm. "Kostas." It was Sasha in eyeglasses and a wig to mask his ultra-short hair.

Kostas played it smartly and didn't say Sasha's name to alert Viktor he was there. Instead, he pulled him into a tight embrace. It lasted long enough to see the love these two shared.

Thomas had worked behind the bar the night Kostas proposed to Sasha. Kostas had shown him the ring, seeking approval and reassurance that he wasn't nuts for proposing at the nightclub where they first met. The proposal had gone well, but "ask me after I come out to my father" wasn't the answer he'd expected. Thomas suspected Kostas now understood Sasha's reluctance.

Sasha pulled back and gasped, placing three fingers gently over Kostas' bruise. "Who did this to you?"

"It doesn't matter. You need to leave." Kostas gripped Sasha's upper arms tightly.

"Leave? You said you were sick. You beat it once before, and you can beat it again. I'll be there every step of the way. If we marry tonight, you can come with me and get the medical help you need."

Oh boy, Thomas thought. That was enough for Viktor to figure out Sasha was there. He alternated his stare between Sasha and the door to the back storage room, expecting Viktor to make an appearance.

"You don't understand. It was a lie. Thomas forced me here. This is a trap. Your father is searching for you."

Sasha turned his head toward him. "Thomas? I thought we were friends."

"Your father wants to talk to you." Thomas glanced at the door again. Viktor rushed through, holding a pistol against his thigh, and was approaching at a rapid pace. Thomas' gut told him both men would be dead by the night's end if he and Viktor brought them to the Boyko compound. He had a dilemma. Do nothing and let their fate play out. Or make a stand and blow up a year of hard work. The choice was easy.

"There's no way I'm talking to him."

Counting on the loud music to muffle his voice and Kostas' religious workout regime, Thomas leaned closer and whispered into his ear. "Hit me and run."

Kostas narrowed his eyes in confusion before throwing a massive punch to the jaw. The direct hit sent sharp shooting pain through the left side of Thomas' face. Kostas grabbed Sasha by the arm and rushed toward the main entrance. The thick crowd slowed their escape and gave Viktor time to close the gap.

Thomas didn't have to fake appearing stunned. Kostas had done a fine job of creating the real thing. He got his bearings and followed Viktor through the crowd and toward the main door. Several heads turned when Viktor plowed through two men who refused to move out of his way. They were only steps behind when Sasha and Kostas darted through the door. Thomas would have to slow Viktor down without making it look like he'd let Sasha and Kostas escape.

Parked cars lined both sides of the street, but there was no moving traffic. Sasha and Kostas ran from the club on the sidewalk and turned the first corner. Viktor was surprisingly fast on his feet and made the corner seconds behind them. Thomas turned next.

A car's taillights flashed several yards ahead as Sasha and Kostas dashed toward it. Kostas glanced over his shoulder. His panic-filled eyes widened when he focused on Viktor and Thomas. When Sasha opened the driver's door, Kostas's feet suddenly tangled, sending him tumbling to the asphalt. He rolled, clutching his knee. Sasha turned back to help, but Kostas shouted, "Go!"

Sasha hesitated and grabbed Kostas' hand. "I won't leave without you."

"I love you," Kostas cried. "Go. Save yourself."

Thomas could have seen the pain on Sasha's face from the moon.

Sasha turned, rushed into the car, and pulled out, spinning the wheels.

Viktor aimed his weapon at the speeding vehicle and fired once, shattering the back window. The shot echoed in the street. He clenched his fists and grunted to the sky. "Dammit." He spun on his heels and waved his gun at Kostas. "Get him."

Thomas lifted Kostas to his feet. The man winced when he put weight on his leg. After Thomas slung an arm over his shoulder, Kostas limped along, following Viktor around the corner to the van in the alley.

Viktor hurled the side door open, rocking the van on its wheels. "Toss him in and drive."

Thomas helped Kostas inside, and Viktor hopped in, shutting the door behind him. The microphone and earpiece still worked, and Thomas picked up Viktor's voice from inside while he circled the van.

"I warned you not to run."

A loud bang. It was the distinctive sound of a gunshot.

Thomas flinched. A sinking feeling of dread hung in the air. He was sure Kostas was dead but had to keep calm. Rolling his neck to gather his emotions, he jumped into the driver's seat. One glance into the back compartment confirmed his fear. Kostas was lifeless. Thomas could do nothing but play along. "Where to next?"

"Back to the compound."

After the privacy gate closed behind the van, Thomas parked between the Boyko main house and the stone workshop where Boyko's wife worked on her pottery. The property was dark and quiet with no one around—the perfect setting to get rid of a body.

"Help me with the body." Viktor stepped out and unlocked the workshop while Thomas opened the van's side door. He dragged Kostas closer to the opening by the feet and said, "Get the arms."

Great, Thomas thought. Working with the bloody end meant he would have to burn his clothes after they finished. He grabbed Kostas' arms, and he and Viktor carried him inside like a lamb carcass after the slaughter. "Where are we taking him?"

"The kiln."

Viktor's answer explained why Anton's wife had a pottery oven the size of a bathtub. Thomas wondered how many of Boyko's previous victims were cremated in this thing. They packed Kostas inside like a big sleeping bag into a tiny duffle bag and watched the flames envelop him through the small glass window on the chamber door.

When nothing but ash remained, Viktor walked outside and handed Thomas the end of a garden hose. "Wash it out and come inside."

Thomas took his sweet time rinsing Kostas' blood from the van, stalling for what awaited him inside the main house. Anton wouldn't be happy to learn Sasha had escaped and would be out for blood. Thomas would have to make himself indispensable.

He entered the mudroom through the side door, wiping his feet thoroughly on the mat. A dim light was on in the kitchen, beckoning him toward it. Mrs. Boyko was at the granite island, sipping her nightly double scotch. She looked up when he stepped farther in. The most recent bruise around her eye had finally faded some.

"Good evening, ma'am. Sorry to interrupt."

"Viktor looked pissed. You better watch yourself tonight, Thomas." She took a long sip and returned the glass to the countertop with a blank, distant look. It wasn't a mystery why she stayed with him. She'd end up in the kiln if she tried leaving.

"Thank you, Mrs. Boyko. I'll get out of your hair." Thomas went to Anton's office, knocked, and waited to be invited in. After hearing the familiar "Enter," he took a deep, calming breath and opened the door.

Viktor was close to the wall, flanking the door. Thomas kept an eye on his hands, expecting him to draw or come after him with a garrote. Anton stood by the fireplace, staring into the flames as they cast a flickering glow on his face. Thomas had seen him angry enough times to know Anton would speak to him when he was good and ready to. He remained silent, splitting his attention between Anton and Viktor.

"You disappoint me, Thomas."

"I know, sir. I disappointed myself by underestimating Sasha. He's your son. You trained him well. I should have known he'd have a plan and people to help him. He came in with a group of men. They acted as a buffer and surrounded me when Sasha approached Kostas. Too many people were in the club to use my gun, so I waited for Viktor to arrive. That's when Kostas slugged me and ran out with Sasha. I'd like another chance at finding him." Sensing Viktor didn't buy his story, Thomas glanced at him again. His arms were folded across his chest, so he posed no immediate threat.

Anton finally turned to face Thomas. "I reached out to my source after Viktor told me what happened tonight, but he's not answering my calls. How do you propose finding my son?"

"Who was your source? I'll get the information out of him."

"I'll send Viktor with you. You have two days. Wait in the hallway until he comes out."

"Yes, sir." Thomas stepped into the hallway, shut the door behind him, and walked several feet down to not be heard or seen when Viktor came out. He stuffed his hand into his underwear, fished out the burner phone hidden in his crotch, and typed a text message, hoping arrangements could be made in time.

9

Maxwell Keene's note not to bring her own car nor one with government plates had piqued Lexi's curiosity this morning. She'd expected him to reserve a small meeting room at the Dallas FBI building to discuss the Raven case, not send her fifty miles west of Fort Worth, where the average home lot was measured in acres, not square feet.

Cell phone reception had been iffy since leaving the interstate, but Noah's rental car thankfully had a built-in GPS. The spotty coverage plagued large swaths of rural Texas, explaining why Lexi bought only vehicles with an onboard navigation system.

When Noah made the final turn onto a long gravel access road, Lexi checked the reception on her phone. Five bars. A tower or signal booster must have been close by. Once through an open cyclone gate, three buildings came into view—a single-story craftsman-style house, a separate four-car garage, and a small, rickety wood barn with one side missing. A half-dozen cottonwood and mesquite trees circled the buildings and stood out among low-lying desert shrubs. He pulled into the open garage bay per Maxwell's instructions. Two other cars were there. One was an older sedan, and the other was a newer, dark SUV. Both had Texas plates.

"Is Keene always this secretive?" Nathan asked.

"Not really," Lexi said. Maxwell was never one for cloak-and-dagger stuff, so something big must have been at play. "Let's go find out what's up."

All four car doors opened. Lexi and Noah exited from the front, and Nathan and Kaplan did from the backseat. Lexi shielded her eyes from the bright sunlight when they stepped from the garage. The breeze was slight but enough to rustle the cottonwood leaves. Noah and Kaplan stepped away from the others and talked privately. A lot of nodding transpired, followed by smiles.

Lexi's phone buzzed with an incoming text. Maxwell's message instructed them to enter through the house's front. The door was unlocked. "It looks like we're letting ourselves in." Returning the phone to her cargo pocket, she led the group up the cracked, weed-laden concrete pathway toward the house.

Lexi's instinct kicked in. "Wait. Everyone, stop." She crouched as low as her prosthetic allowed to scan left and right, searching for signs of hidden mines and other explosives. The sun and breeze played tricks, casting moving shadows on their path and forcing her to focus harder. Noah bent both knees, crouching lower and following her stare.

"Do you see it?" she asked.

"Fishing line ten feet ahead, but it's not taut."

"Right. It looks tangled, so the wind likely blew it there."

Noah continued his inspection. "The group of three rocks on the left side of the path another two feet up. Is that anything?"

"Good eyes." Lexi smiled. "It's a manmade grouping. A pressure trigger could be at the center." Having Noah by her side felt natural like no time had passed. She'd relied on him, starting with the border bombing case in Nogales. Their unbreakable trust began when he acted as her overwatch while she disarmed a Gatekeeper's minefield, and it had been rock solid since.

She craned her neck toward him, locking gazes. "You can be my overwatch anytime."

Noah grinned, forming the vitiligo around his lips into the shape of a football. "I'd like that."

The front door opened, and Lexi and Noah snapped their stares toward it. Maxwell Keene stepped out, dressed casually. He chuckled. "You're becoming paranoid, Lexi Mills." He waved her inside. "It's clear. Get your butts in here."

The group entered the house. Maxwell shook hands with everyone and invited them to sit. The living room had all the basics but lacked decoration or a personal touch saying it was someone's home.

"What is this place?" Lexi asked. "And what's up with the incredible cell reception?"

"We'll get to that. Let's talk about the Raven. Tell me about the Brooklyn connection." Maxwell never held back information from her, but Lexi got the impression he was fishing, expecting her to fill in some blanks. She had to trust he would share whatever he could.

"This is my case now, Agent Keene," Nathan said. "How about telling us why you're interested in our new lead?"

Maxwell looked at him like he was his teenage son who had backtalked to his mother in front of him. Lexi had to give Nathan credit for his audacity. He stood up to the FBI deputy director, measuring his response before he gave anything away, but his mistrust was misplaced. As much as Lexi wanted to step in and clear the air, Nathan was in charge and would have to build trust.

"All right, Agent Croft," Maxwell leaned forward in his chair, resting both elbows on his knees. "We believe the Raven helped in a Brooklyn crime syndicate hit, so when Lexi mentioned you have a lead on the Raven's engineer in Brooklyn, she got my attention."

"And that interest brings us to a safe house in the middle of redneck country." Nathan briefly extended his arms as if surveying his surroundings. "Who are you hiding, Director Keene?"

"No one said this is a safe house." Maxwell leaned back in his chair.

"Please. This place is decorated like a Motel 6. Cameras were set up on the road and around the buildings. You have sheltered parking away from the road and boosted cell reception in the middle of what should be a telecommunications black hole. If this isn't a safe house, I'm Marilyn Monroe reincarnated. Tell me why you suspect the Raven was involved in the hit."

Maxwell laughed and focused on Lexi. "I like him."

"He grows on you," Lexi said, winking at Nathan. "And he's right. Are you hiding an informant? Can they give us the Raven's client?"

"It's a distinct possibility." Maxwell knocked three times on the wall behind him.

An interior door opened. Lathan Sinclair and Coby Vasquez stepped out. Someone an inch or two taller than Lexi was between them. They wore loose jeans and a sweatshirt with a hood covering their head. The person flipped it down, exposing her face.

Lexi gasped.

"Hello, Lexi," Delanie Scott said, stepping forward.

Lexi's head spun hard. She swam in shock so thick she couldn't stand, frozen in her seat.

Kaplan and Noah leaped from their seats with smiles on their faces. They greeted Delanie with hugs and peppered her with questions, but she answered none. Instead, she focused on Lexi and walked to her once the excitement settled down. She sat on the coffee table in front of Lexi's spot on the couch, facing her. "I'm sorry to put you through this."

"Me?" The revelation had finally sunk in, and Lexi felt worst for Delanie's family. "What about your mother? Your father? They were devastated."

"I know." Delanie's shoulders sagged. Her expression grew long. "It was necessary to sell my death. The syndicate we're investigating had someone at the funeral, so we had to be careful bringing you here."

"How long do you plan to keep them in the dark?" Lexi asked.

"Until this is over."

"What is *this*?"

"Director Keene," Delanie turned to him, "do you want to set the stage?"

"Sure," Maxwell shifted in his chair to better face Lexi and Nathan. "Fifteen months ago, the FBI sent an undercover agent to infiltrate the Boyko organization in Brooklyn."

"Boyko?" Nathan said. "I've heard of them. They're into prostitution and drug and gun running."

"And human trafficking," Maxwell said. "The UC's job was to find a weak link, work them, and get documentation to back it up. Ledgers, photographs, recordings, whatever. The problem was finding someone who could point the finger at Anton Boyko and would flip either through pressure or enticement."

"That's always the dilemma," Nathan said. "But I guess you eventually found someone."

"It took a year, but yes. We were about to pull the plug, but the UC suggested we work on Anton Boyko's son, who moved to Fort Worth a year ago to escape his father."

"Fort Worth?" Lexi said. "That must be where Delanie comes in." She turned to her old friend. "How did you convince him?"

"The truth. Anton has abused his son's mother since he left," Delanie said. "The UC befriended his wife and got her on audio and video. The images of her battered face were the kicker. The son told us about the entire operation. He knows his father keeps ledgers documenting everything but doesn't know where he keeps them. Keene's man stayed to find those damn books so the son wouldn't have to testify, but things blew up this week."

"I'd say so if you had to fake your death," Lexi said.

"It wasn't all a fake," Maxwell said. "The UC tipped us off about a hit on Delanie. Anton wanted to slow down the case. He said Anton hired the Raven to build a device to incapacitate her and had him and another man meet with the Raven to pick it up. I read the notes you added to the Raven case file. The man they met fits the description of his engineer, Robert Segura, the one you have an address on in Brooklyn."

"This guy sure gets around," Noah said. Everyone snickered.

"What kind of device did the Raven use?" Lexi asked.

"It was a packet placed in the air vent designed to release chloroform into her car and dissolve after hitting the water to make it look like an accident. It was genius. However, Delanie disabled it and left it for us in her garage. Then she faked her death, putting on a snorkel mask before driving into the lake. These two"—Maxwell gestured toward Coby Vasquez and Lathan Sinclair—"were driving behind her and stopped. They dove into the water to make sure she got out, hid her in the brush, and played witness."

"That was what you meant about her courage and willingness to take risks," Lexi said, pausing at his affirming nod. She turned to Delanie with an inquisitive look. Delanie shrugged as if her heroics were nothing.

"She was a badass," Lathan Sinclair said.

"A soaked to the bone badass," Coby Vasquez added.

"This is one hell of a story, Delanie. I should have had you on the task force, leading raids."

"No, thank you," Delanie said. "I've had my share of action."

When the compliments stopped, Nathan redirected the conversation. "You said Anton wanted to slow down your case. What was he buying time for?"

"Anton found out his son was helping us and wanted to flush him out from under our protection," Delanie said.

"Did he?" Nathan asked.

"Yes, but we have him now. The UC did all he could to help him get away. Unfortunately, Sasha's boyfriend was killed in the process."

"That's a shame," Lexi said. "Do you know who leaked the information to Anton?"

"We suspected it was someone in my office, so I called Director Keene for help days ago. His undercover agent confirmed it last night," Delanie said.

"We have Sasha in a safe location until we can go to trial," Maxwell said. "No one in the U.S. Attorney's office but Delanie knows where we're keeping him."

An idea germinated in Lexi's head, and she trusted her friend to tell her the truth. "Maxwell, besides letting us know Delanie is alive, I think you brought us here because you want to capture the Raven as much as we do. Am I right?"

"Yes, in my position, I'm privy to much information kept from the public domain. Do you understand?" Maxwell paused at Lexi's nod. He was speaking about the locust and the attack on the president the government had kept secret. "Capturing the Raven is a national priority."

"What do you have in mind?" Lexi asked.

"We join forces, leverage the Boyko syndicate, and bring in a madman." Maxwell had the same determined expression when he gave Lexi and Noah the order in Las Vegas to take the shot, whether justified or not, to ensure Tony Belcher didn't slip through their fingers.

Lexi nodded as several options came to mind.

"I recognize that look," Maxwell said. "What are you thinking?"

"I haven't worked out all the angles, but we should use the leak and your UC in tandem. Your team can release Sasha's location to Delanie's office. Say he has something important to add to his statement. Once the information gets back to Anton Boyko, your UC needs to work him. Convince Boyko the place will be fortified, and they'll need special help to get to him."

"This could work. Boyko gave Agent Kent the task of beating the information out of the leak. We could put the leak on ice until this is over, and Kent can say it came from him."

"Kent? He's your UC?" Lexi asked.

"Yes. He goes by Falco. He'll have to suggest bringing in the Raven again since his device worked so well on Delanie Scott." Maxwell glanced at her, forming an apologetic look.

"If Boyko sticks to his pattern," Lexi said, "he'll have Kent accept delivery of whatever weapon the Raven comes up with. We can be there when he does."

"And what if Boyko doesn't send Kent?" Nathan asked. "We'll have only one shot at this, so we'll need a scenario where the Raven or Segura has to be there when Boyko's men attack the safe house."

"I can think of only one weapon the Raven makes where he'll need a specialist to operate it."

"We need to talk in private," Maxwell said. "Lexi. Croft. You're with me." He led them out the back door past the clearing for the outbuildings, stopping underneath the canopy of an old-growth cottonwood tree. He surveyed the area, confirming they were alone. "I know what you're thinking, Lexi, but it's too risky to have the Raven break out the locusts."

"He has the technology, Maxwell. His man Segura perfected it, so it's a matter of time before he uses it. And when he does, we need to be there."

"Yes, we do."

"Then why not control the playing field? The conditions at this safe house are ripe for using the locusts. The neighbors are a mile away, and the lot has camera surveillance. Segura or the Raven would be close by controlling them."

"You make a sound argument," Maxwell said, "but what if you can't disable the locusts again?"

"I haven't worked with Lexi as long as you have, Director Keene," Nathan said, "but I trust her gut better than my own, especially regarding the Raven. If she says she can knock out the locusts, I believe her."

"It sounds like you've known her long enough," Maxwell said.

"We could track movement on the ground with drones," Lexi said. "Once we get a fix on the Raven's or Segura's location, someone will have to jam the locusts' signal. One team will repel the attack at the safe house while Nathan and I take down the Raven or whoever controls the locusts."

"Who is the someone on the jammer?" Maxwell asked. "The only ones who know about the locusts are the three of us. I have news for you. Outside of my phone, technology and I don't get along."

"Then I'll stay at the compound," Lexi said. Someone had to operate the jammer, and she was no longer in charge of the case. Her job was to follow orders.

"This isn't right," Nathan said. "You've earned the right to take down the Raven. Teach me. I'll do it."

"I can't ask you to take a back seat," Lexi said, turning to Maxwell, "but there is another option. How many people in the intelligence community know about the locust and what really happened to the president?"

"About a dozen," Maxwell said.

"Then what's one more? Let's bring in Kaplan Shaw. I trust her with my life."

"I agree," Nathan said. "She could operate the drone surveillance and the jammer, freeing up Lexi and me for the job we've waited months for."

"This whole thing is risky." Maxwell ran a hand through his hair, weighing Lexi's plan.

"Risky like having Delanie launch her car into a lake with her in it?" Lexi smirked.

"That was pretty crazy, but it worked."

"And so will this."

"We should loop in Agent Kent and warn him about the locusts," Maxwell said.

"Why?" Lexi asked. "Once Kaplan employs the signal jammer, the locust should be inoperable before anyone on the op sees them. He'll never know unless the Raven or Segura clues him in. And if they do, we'll brief him later to keep it secret."

"Okay," Maxwell said. "Let's do it."

Nathan pulled out his phone. "I'll let Willie Lange know what's going on, minus the locust angle."

"I'll have Kaplan come outside." Lexi fished her phone from her pocket and sent a text. Moments later, Kaplan stepped from the house and joined their group. "We have a plan but need to brief you on something the president has deemed top secret."

Kaplan grinned. "Does this mean you'll finally tell me what really happened in Napa?"

"Yes."

10

The bright lights of the twenty-four-hour truck stop guided Viktor to the row of pumps. Once he stopped and popped the tank lid, Thomas unbuckled his seatbelt and opened the passenger door. Viktor's hand grabbed his arm before he could step onto the gas station asphalt.

"Where are you going?" Viktor sneered. He had yet to show Thomas an ounce of trust in the year since they'd met, and Thursday night's debacle had turned his distrust into suspicion. He hadn't let Thomas out of his sight since they left the compound early yesterday morning, opting for drive-thru joints for food and roadsides to pee.

"To take a dump. We've been on the road for twelve hours, and I'm not shitting in a ditch." Thomas threw off Viktor's grip and walked toward the truck stop store at a fast clip. This was his first opportunity to contact his handler since he was in the hallway outside Anton's office, and he had to make it count. Once through the doors and out of Viktor's sight, he dashed to the men's restroom, entered the last open stall, and fished out his phone. He dialed his handler.

"Kent," Lathan Sinclair said. "Where are you?"

"Halfway to Texas. I'm texting you the address of the leak." Thomas typed quickly, praying he didn't fat finger a number.

"Got it," Lathan said. "We know who lives there. What's your ETA?"

"Twelve hours. Who will be there?" Thomas asked.

"Me, so make it look good."

"I'll try not to break anything." It would be challenging to pull back on punches while making it look convincing with Viktor looking over Thomas' shoulder, so he would have to make a few do some damage.

"Appreciate that," Lathan said. "Stop at the Big Buck Travel Center ten miles east of Dallas. Go into the farthest stall. We'll have what you need for the assault. From there, you'll be thirty out. We'll set up in both places before you hit town, but text us with the go time if you can. Be sure to sell Anton on the need for the Raven."

"I'll try."

"Make sure you're the first one through the door. We don't like getting shot."

"I'll do my best. I gotta go."

"I know you will. Good luck, Kent."

"Where the hell are you, Falco?" Viktor said loud and clear.

"Wiping my ass." Thomas returned the phone to his hiding place, flushed the toilet, and swung the door open. "I gotta wash up."

"Stay in here." Viktor went to a urinal but kept an eye on Thomas while he did his business.

With Viktor's short leash on Thomas, he doubted he'd get another chance to call Sinclair to confirm the assault time. He had a basic idea of the plan from their earlier messages when he was still at the compound but wasn't sure about the details. If everything went well, Sasha would be safe, his cover would be intact, and the FBI would have some high-value target in custody. All in a day's work.

Thomas took the wheel for the next leg of the trip and wouldn't give it up until this was over. Twelve hours later, the last road sign he passed said Dallas was fifteen miles ahead, his cue to put on an act. He shifted uneasily in the driver's seat and pressed a hand against his stomach, hoping Viktor wouldn't push back. If he didn't pick up the package, the assault could turn out badly. "I don't know about you, but that last burger didn't sit well with me."

"It *is* sitting like a rock," Viktor said.

"There was a sign for a truck stop a few miles up. I'll stop there."

Without objection, Thomas pulled off the interstate and followed the signs to the Big Buck Truck Stop. He parked in the lot, walked inside with Viktor, and headed for the restrooms at the back of the store. He tried to be first through the door, but Viktor took longer steps and beat him to it.

Thomas thought, *please, please, don't choose the last stall*. But, as luck would have it, Viktor headed for the one toilet Thomas needed to use and closed the door. "Dammit," he whispered. Thomas considered waiting, but Viktor might get suspicious if the other toilets were available and usable. Out of options, he went into the first stall and peed, so it wasn't a wasted trip. He waited until he heard a flush from the other end, flushed his toilet, and exited to join Viktor at the sinks. They washed up in silence and walked out.

"We should get some water and snacks in case this guy isn't home and we have to wait," Thomas said.

Without responding, Viktor headed to the store's refrigerated section. This guy clearly didn't like him. His instincts were good. If he knew Thomas' real identity, he'd put a bullet in his head.

Thomas picked out a large water bottle and a bag of chips and headed with Viktor to check out. After paying, he faked a stomach cramp like he did in the car. "Oh, man. I gotta head back to the shitter. Can you take this? I'll be right out." Thomas handed Viktor his bag without waiting for a response, hoping his own issues with the fast-food meal meant he wouldn't make a fuss or follow.

Thomas walked quickly and hunched slightly to play the part. After turning down an aisle out of sight of the register, he ran down the restroom corridor at top speed and flew through the door. He darted to the last stall, closed the door, and reached around the underbelly of the toilet, feeling for a plastic baggie taped there. Bingo! He grabbed it, made sure the tracker was there, changed out the bullets, and stuffed it into his pants near his phone. It was getting crowded down there, so he adjusted things until they felt somewhat comfortable.

The stall door vibrated when someone pounded on it. "Get the hell out of there." He recognized Viktor's voice, flushed, and opened the door.

"Christ, Viktor. You gotta let a guy take a shit." When Thomas stepped out, Viktor slammed him against the wall, holding him in place with a stiff arm to the throat. He frisked him, groping his waistband and every pocket, thankfully avoiding the bottom of his crotch.

Once satisfied that Thomas had nothing on him besides his phone, gun, and wallet, he narrowed his eyes. "Don't ever try a stunt like that again. Got it?"

"Got it," Thomas repeated. "Then you'll have to put up with the smell when I crap my pants."

"I don't like you, Falco. Never have. One false move, and you'll end up in the kiln."

After last night, Thomas had no doubt the threat was a promise. When Delanie Scott issued an indictment and this undercover assignment was over, the forensic lab guys would be busy for months, sifting through the remains.

"Then we better get going." Thomas returned to the van—the same one in which they'd hauled Kostas's body across town—and followed the GPS directions to the apartment of the person who leaked Sasha's name. He kept one step ahead of Viktor while crossing the courtyard to ensure he was in position to push through the door first when Sinclair opened it.

Thomas reached the door first and took a position at the knob with Viktor directly behind his right shoulder. He knocked and counted the seconds in his head when a dilemma hit him like a ton of bricks. What if the real leaker was there, not Sinclair? He hadn't discussed the possibility with his handler and didn't know how far he should take it. Should Thomas rough him up or abandon his undercover position? He had Viktor dead to rights for Kostas' murder and a hundred other felonies he'd witnessed. *The latter*, he thought. This had gone on long enough, and Viktor had taken things too far with Kostas. If Sinclair didn't open the door, Thomas would call an audible, knock Viktor out, and call for help.

The door opened when Thomas reached the count of ten. He tried hiding his response from Viktor but released a breath of relief before rushing Sinclair like a bulldozer and pushing him deep inside the apartment.

Sinclair backpedaled, flailing his arms. His shocked look was priceless. It lasted through Thomas' wink and ended when his head thumped against the hallway wall. "What the hell?" he said.

"You should have picked up the phone when Anton called." Thomas used his best menacing voice while gripping the fabric of Sinclair's shirt in both hands.

On cue, Sinclair widened his eyes with clarity. "I couldn't. Everything went crazy after Sasha threw off his protection detail. Everyone in the office was questioned."

Thomas threw a punch to his stomach. "When you accepted Anton's money, it made you his for life." A second punch and a third. Both missed a rib or vital organ but released drool from Sinclair's mouth. "Tell me you understand."

Sinclair groaned and gagged on his spit before croaking out, "I understand."

Thomas' handler was average height but was in good enough shape to take more than a few hits. A few belly punches wouldn't convince Viktor that Thomas had put the fear of death into Sinclair without drawing blood. He pulled back his fist and launched it at Sinclair's face, landing it on his cheek with a loud thwack. Pressure and pain radiated through Thomas' knuckles as blood and spit flew from Sinclair's mouth, spraying the worn beige carpet. Whoever rented this place after the asshole leaker would have a hard time getting the stain out.

Thomas sneaked a quick glance at Viktor. The right corner of his lips was raised, and his right eye was narrower than the left. It was his sinister look that meant he was pleased.

Sinclair fell to his knees with a dazed look, raising a hand above his head to beg Thomas to stop. "Okay, okay. What does Anton want?" He stayed on his knees without looking up.

"Where are you holding his son?"

"The FBI has him." Sinclair gave an accurate but not readily believable answer. Every mobster knew the U.S. Marshal's office headed the Witness Protection Program. The only option was to make a show of beating the truth out of him.

Thomas let loose with a kidney punch but pulled back some to reduce the amount of force. Sinclair buckled flat on the floor. "If you lie again, I start breaking bones."

"I'm not lying." Sinclair shimmied against the wall to protect against another hit to the kidneys. "Justice was spooked, so they called in a special FBI unit. These guys are former special forces. No one is getting past them."

"Where?"

"A safe house in the sticks west of Fort Worth. I have the address on my laptop."

Thomas lifted him to a sitting position, using a choking grip on his neck. "Where is it?"

Though Thomas' hold was light, Sinclair gagged and pointed straight ahead. "Coffee table."

Thomas gestured for Viktor to retrieve the laptop and used the time to make sure Sinclair was okay. He mouthed, "Sorry." Sinclair's breathing was labored, but he winked, telegraphing he wasn't hurt badly.

Viktor returned with the laptop and threw it on Sinclair's lap. "Find it."

Blood trailing from his mouth to his chin, Sinclair trembled while typing in the computer passcode and bringing up a file. He flipped the laptop around, showing Thomas and Viktor a scanned government document marked classified on official Department of Justice letterhead. It had the signature of Deputy Director Maxwell Keene.

"I know this name," Viktor said before snapping a picture of the address where the FBI Special Response Team—a fictional unit—was keeping Sasha Boyko for pre-testimony protection. He slammed the laptop shut, pulled his firearm from his shoulder holster, and leveled it at Sinclair. Viktor was a cold-blooded killer and wouldn't hesitate to shoot.

Thomas saw the panic in Sinclair's eyes and hit Viktor's arm downward with his forearm. "Not here. Too many people are around. Besides, we may still need him." He turned his attention to Sinclair. "We'll kill your entire family if you go to the cops."

Sinclair shook his head silently, looking terrified. "I won't say a word."

Thomas hovered over Sinclair and connected one last punch to his jaw to sell the act before turning to his partner. "Let's go scout and report back to Anton."

Viktor looked unhappy but holstered his weapon and walked out of the apartment. The first part of the plan was complete, with only a few bruises. When this was over, he'd have to buy Sinclair a drink.

A preview of the address Sinclair passed along on Google Maps revealed the property encompassed several acres and was in a rural part of a small town west of Fort Worth. Activity around the three buildings would not be visible from the road, but Thomas had suggested buying a radio-controlled drone equipped with a camera from a hobby store.

Three hours later, he and Viktor were parked along the fence line of the neighboring property. Thomas unpacked, set up the drone for flight, and set its onboard camera to record. He offered the controls to Viktor, knowing he would decline. He considered video games and this sort of technology the bane of society. "Want to give it a try?"

"Don't be a smartass."

Thomas silently chuckled. This unit was similar to the one he'd trained on during his field investigation course and came with a comparable controller that included a video screen. He shouldn't have trouble operating it, but he feigned two failed attempts getting it off the ground.

"Are you sure you know how to work this thing?"

"Give me a minute. It's been a while since I've played with one." Thomas manipulated the toggles again and sent the drone soaring above the treetops. He flew it over the property and scanned the area, focusing on the security measures in place. "Those are cameras and motion sensors," he said before flying it toward the buildings, circling them above the trees.

"Take it lower, so we can see inside," Viktor said.

"I'll set off the sensors if I do. It's better to hover and wait. We have an hour of juice. Then, I can change out the battery pack." Thomas kept the drone stationary, hoping the unmarked sedan that had followed them from Dallas called in their presence, so he wouldn't have to stay there too long.

Forty minutes later, the back door opened, and three men stepped onto the back patio. Two were dressed in tactical outfits, not traditional casual FBI clothing, and were armed with semiautomatic sidearms. The other was thin and blonde, carrying a plate. He resembled Sasha Boyko. Thomas zoomed in while Sasha opened the gas grill, fired it up, and placed the burgers over the fire.

"It's him."

Viktor nodded. "Good. Anton will be pleased."

Thomas recalled the drone, packed it in the van, and drove a block away. The second part of the plan was complete. The final step to draw out whoever the FBI wanted to snare could come in hours or days. The ball was in Anton's court.

11

Anton sat in his office alone, sipping his finest scotch and sensing the walls closing in. Viktor had said in his last message they had a location, would check it out, and get back to him. That was three hours ago.

His mind drifted to his son and how far gone he'd become. Anton had such high hopes for Sasha when he was young. In deference to his mother, he'd waited until Sasha finished high school and turned eighteen to introduce him to the family business, but his son was no fool. He had eyes and ears and picked up on things growing up.

Sasha's curiosity had begun with a poignant question the day he turned eight. He'd asked why his uncles and older cousins wore guns when they visited. Not all the men were related by blood, but it was easier to explain their presence by calling them Uncle Viktor or Cousin Alonzo. Anton had answered with a version of the truth. "If there is one word to describe the members of the Boyko family, it is loyal. We keep each other safe. They protect us when we sleep and you and your mother when I'm away."

"Will I get a gun when I'm older and protect the family, Papa?" Sasha had asked.

"I promised your mother that your job is to go to school until you become a man. But once you do, the choice will be yours."

To his father's delight, precisely ten years later, Sasha picked up a gun for the first time. He was a natural with a pistol and walked with an extra swagger when he wore it under his arm. For the next five years, Anton taught him every aspect of the family business and who he could trust with his life. Sasha had become his most trusted lieutenant until the truth came out after the second beating he took at a nightclub. The night Thomas Falco had rescued him from severe injury suddenly made sense.

Anton had long suspected his son wasn't right in the head with his affinity for other men. He'd attributed it to his mother babying him for most of his life and shielding him from the realities of the world. Anton had tried to reverse what his mother had done, but his growing up to be less of a man was inevitable. It was a closely held secret until a repeat of the night Falco had brought him home ended with Sasha in the emergency room and a police report. Afterward, everyone in Brooklyn knew what type of man Anton Boyko had raised and earmarked to be his successor. That was the last day he'd seen his son.

Anton would have had no regret if he'd gone to his grave without seeing Sasha again—if not for his betrayal. A treachery like his deserved to be met with death, but Anton wanted him alive so he could provide answers. He needed to know why Sasha would do such a thing, knowing the consequences. In the past, those who had dared to go the dangerous route did so for power, money, or to avoid a lengthy prison sentence. Anton had kept tabs on his son until he disappeared, and none of those motivations seemed to fit. Something else was at play, and he was on the precipice of unearthing it.

Anton rechecked his phone for the third time in the last hour but hadn't missed a message. His stubborn life anchor was silent. He'd become overly dependent on the damn contraption and rued the day he'd agreed to carry it. He swigged the last of his scotch and prepared to throw his anchor into the fire when it rang. The caller ID said he was about to get answers.

"Did you find my son, Viktor?"

"Yes, Mr. Boyko. Sasha is there, but the location is guarded with cameras, motion sensors, and an elite tactical unit. We'll need more men to take him."

"We'll need more than men." Anton recognized Falco's muffled voice.

"Put me on speaker," Anton ordered and paused until Viktor did so.

Falco had yet to earn his unconditional trust, but everything he'd done so far to capture his son made him more trustworthy. "Explain, Mr. Falco."

"I've seen defensive systems like this when I was in the army. We'll need to disable their electronic surveillance first, but from what I could tell, it's multilayered. If we miss one, we're dead in the water. We'll need help to take it out."

"What do you recommend?" Anton asked.

"I don't know," Falco said. "It's beyond my expertise. I could study it, but it might take time. The guy who built the chloroform device we used to knock off the U.S. Attorney might know how to defeat it."

"That's not a bad idea, Mr. Falco."

"Does he work quickly? The FBI might move Sasha."

"I'll reach out. Until I work something out, I want you to sit on my son's location. I can't chance losing track of him again."

12

Robert opened the door to his underground lab and stood in the entryway, remembering the first day Starshiy had brought him there after graduating from MIT. The room was barebones then, with countertops, cabinets, two sinks lining the walls, and a large island workstation in the center. The ventilation system was in dire need of upgrading, but the grid of fluorescent ceiling lights was sufficient once he added a dimmer to control the intensity.

"I want you to fill it with everything you'll need to build custom products for my clients," Starshiy had said, *"but order only the best."* He'd given Robert an initial budget of a million dollars for equipment and materials. Robert didn't think he would need so much, but after a preview of the type of bombs and weapons he would build for the Raven, Starshiy's underworld persona, he realized it wouldn't be enough. Over the years, the lab required several redesigns, and adding items had become commonplace. The storage room, where he neatly kept specialized, rarely used equipment, was an engineer's dream marketplace.

For seventeen years, Robert had sat on a stool beneath these bright lights, designing everything Starshiy had asked of him, yet it wasn't enough to undo his mistakes. Proudly embedding parts of a raven feather in every product he produced for Starshiy had left a trail for the authorities to track.

He'd broken Starshiy's trust, and Starshiy had been cold since he learned of it last month in California, interacting only when business called for it. The change was heartbreaking. His oldest and dearest friend, his orphanage brother, no longer confided in him. No longer spent days with him in their lush garden, tending to their beautiful plants. The situation was nearly untenable, one he hoped to salvage.

Robert stepped inside and threw his jacket over the back of his chair. He had another ghost gun to manufacture from the 3D printer and several 9mm rounds designed to explode on impact to piece together before he went to bed. He turned on his desk lamp, woke up his computer with a jiggle of the mouse, and brought up the printer application for his favorite 3D blueprint.

Robert was proudest of the undetectable all-plastic gun he had designed for a client of the Raven. It was simple after MIT scientists early last year perfected his initial research into developing a plastic stronger than steel. He'd explored the technology eighteen years ago in graduate school but didn't earn as much as a footnote in the findings reports. *A bunch of narcissists*, he thought. Rampant egos in the field of science were why he happily worked for Starshiy, developing unique toys for him. He didn't have to deal with anyone but his friend.

After loading the design he'd tweaked last night to shorten the barrel by a half inch per the client's parameters, he loaded the printer with the 2DPA-1 plastic he liked to call Daphne. Besides the play on the letters, the polymer reminded him of the lovely biracial femme fatale Daphne Monet in Walter Mosley's novel *Devil in a Blue Dress*. The heating process altered its pure white color, making it appear slightly darker but a shade still considered white. And once Robert formed it into his unique design, the plastic was deceivingly lethal, just like Miss Monet.

He monitored the printing process while infusing TNT into the body of six hollow bullets and sealing them with pre-scored outer jackets.

The lab door opened. Robert snapped his stare toward it. Starshiy appeared at the entryway, dressed as the Raven. The black suit, tie, and shirt contrasted against his pale skin, making him seem mysterious. However, the blood-red contact lenses added a demonic look. He'd left his collar-length stringy black hair pulled back into a ponytail—the style

Robert preferred on Starshiy—but would let it down before leaving the house.

"Good evening, Robert. Do you have the bullets? I need to deliver them tonight."

"Yes. I sealed the last one a few minutes ago." Robert gestured to the palm-sized metal case on his workstation and returned his stare to the printing chamber. "I'll have the ghost gun ready for you in a few hours."

"Good work." Robert expected Starshiy to leave without further conversation but heard him slide a stool at the island work area. He continued, "I received another call from Anton tonight."

Robert froze and slowly craned his neck to look Starshiy in the eye. "I understand why you dislike the man, but you're playing with fire, my friend."

"I worked for him. He got greedy. He stole the weapons I'd sourced and tried to kill me, Robert. What he did was unforgivable." Starshiy's cheeks flushed in a rare moment of anger. His contact lenses glowed eerily.

"That was twenty years ago."

"Revenge has no expiration date, my friend. The locusts have shown me the weaknesses of his compound. This is an opportunity to even the score."

Robert remembered seeing the wheels turn in Starshiy's eyes after Anton had reached out two weeks ago for the Raven's special services. The request had made Starshiy leery of his intentions, but it had become clear Anton didn't know the Raven and Starshiy were the same man. Starshiy had accepted the job, seeing it as an opportunity to learn more about his old enemy.

The reconnaissance mission to Anton's Brooklyn fortress he'd sent Robert on proved he was out for revenge, which put their partnership in uncharted territory. Every job Starshiy had taken on was without emotion, even when he tied up loose ends for those clients who violated his rules for doing business with the Raven. He was indifferent to killing, acting as if it was merely an aspect of his job. However, Starshiy risked making mistakes going after Anton Boyko if he didn't have a clear head.

"What does Anton want?" Robert asked.

"He needs to overtake a federal safe house and capture a witness FBI agents are protecting. The property is remote, well-equipped with electronic defenses, and guarded by an elite tactical team. He needs to knock out their defenses to send a team inside to scoop up his target."

"What did you tell him?"

"I said we have a tool for the job, but it would come at a steep price."

"You're referring to the locusts. How much?"

"I know Anton. He's desperate and would pay nearly any price. I told him two million." A slight grin formed on Starshiy's lips.

"You're squeezing as much money out of him as possible before turning the locusts on him."

"You know me well, Robert."

"If he wants the witness killed, we could send in a single locust with an explosive pack undetected to reduce our costs and risk. Sensors wouldn't pick it up, and cameras would see it as a fly. I could easily train one of Boyko's men in a day to control it."

"He was specific. He wants this person alive. The job will require at least a dozen units to disable the security system and serve as recon and containment."

Robert rubbed the back of his neck in frustration. "He's outlined a complicated mission. It would take weeks to train an operator."

"You don't understand, Robert. He wants it done tomorrow. You'll need to operate the controls in person."

"In person? Then why in the hell did I spend all of my free time upgrading the satellite link to enable operation from anywhere in the world?"

Since their falling out, this would make the fourth time Starshiy ordered Robert to engage with a client. He understood why he had to deliver the dissolvable vibration-triggered chloroform deployment system to Boyko's man at the barbeque stand in Arkansas. Viktor had been a part of the organization for twenty years and might have recognized Starshiy. The same held true for this job, but Robert got the sinking feeling Starshiy was looking for ways to put him in harm's way.

"Settle down, Robert. Anton insists on having someone on site in case something goes wrong. If it does, you can make adjustments on the fly."

"Or he can have someone to blame and put a bullet in my head."

"Would it make you feel better if I was close by to cover your back with more locusts?"

Robert flipped the scenario on its head. Starshiy could easily use the extra locusts against him to end their animosity once and for all. Either way, Robert sensed this was a one-way mission and would have to devise a protection plan of his own. "Let me think about it."

13

Kaplan Shaw zipped up her pants, stepped out of the porta potty the FBI delivered yesterday, and poured a blob of sanitizer into her hands before heading to a cot. After donning her bulletproof vest—using the toilet with that thing on was nearly impossible—she peeled open a military-style meal ready-to-eat and pounded down the vegetable crumble with pasta. Eating fast was unhealthy, but she had to return to her station.

She'd been cooped up in the garage on the safe house property with Maxwell Keene and Noah Black for the last twenty hours. Her job was to keep the reconnaissance drone surveilling the surrounding area and operate the signal jammer when the assault began. Noah kept the bank of drone batteries charged and served as her backup for breaks. She was tired but loved every minute of this operation, even when her bulky ballistic vest cut into her armpits.

Agent Keene sat across from her atop the second cot, looking on with awe. "You can take your time, you know. Noah has you covered."

"I know, but I don't want to let you or Lexi down. I don't get many opportunities to work in the field these days."

Not since Kaplan's days on Task Force Zero Impact under Lexi's leadership had anyone called on her to assist in a field investigation. Why Agent Willie Lange and other team leaders hadn't taken advantage of her proven abilities as a field agent was a mystery and insulting. Having an intelligence officer augment a team was a force multiplier with real-time fact-finding. Like any other field agent, Kaplan had gone through the same basic FLETC course and had to maintain her weapons qualifications yearly. She was an agent in every sense of the word. However, Lexi Mills had been the only one to treat her as one.

"It's a shame," Agent Keene said. "The ATF is wasting your talent. You're a capable field agent."

"Thank you, Director Keene."

"I think we're past the formalities, Kaplan. When it's just the team or us, please call me Maxwell."

"All right, Maxwell."

"If you want more field experience, consider applying to the FBI. I could always use someone with a talent like yours."

"I'll keep that in mind, Maxwell." Kaplan hadn't considered leaving the ATF until Lexi brought her onto the task force. Those months working in the field proved she was much more than a data source at the end of a phone line so other agents could close a case. Frankly, the only reason she stayed in the ATF was Lexi Mills. Lexi had a gift for the job. Working with her was like working with family. Tossing aside a strong connection such as theirs would be difficult.

"I better get back to work." Kaplan swallowed the last of her pasta, tossed the packaging into the garbage sack, and walked to her makeshift desk of a wood plank stretched across two stacks of upturned garbage cans. "I got it now, Noah."

He gave up his seat and stepped aside, inviting Kaplan to sit. "I heard you talking with Maxwell. Are you considering leaving the ATF?"

"I don't know. I enjoy my job, especially working with Lexi, but he's right. They underutilize me. The only times I've felt truly useful were the task force and now."

"I know what you mean," Noah said. "The team had something special."

"Would you ever consider moving back to the Dallas area?" Kaplan's question was more hopeful speculation than curiosity.

"I've been thinking of it since my plane landed."

Kaplan tried to force back a grin but failed. "Really?" Maybe the kiss they shared on their last day on Task Force Zero Impact was more than an emotional goodbye. She'd refused to let herself think of it as anything more back then since he was leaving, but his return to Dallas would open the possibility.

"Yeah. The things I've seen and the people I've caught give me nightmares. Lexi put the thought in my head about relocating here. It might be good for my aunt and me."

"Where would you work?"

"I'm leaning toward the Texas Rangers. Maybe work with Sarah Briscoe."

"Why not the ATF or FBI?" Kaplan asked.

"They could bounce me around the country to work on a case. The idea of staying put appeals to me."

"Texas is a big state. I wouldn't exactly call it staying put."

"You're right," Noah laughed. "At least I'd be closer to the people I care about. Including you."

"Hmph." Kaplan gave Noah a wink before he went to the cots to join Maxwell.

She returned her attention to her laptop, showing the live camera feeds surveilling the compound's interior and perimeter. Out of habit, she focused on the block displaying the road across the street, where a white panel van had been parked since yesterday. Nothing had changed.

She'd identified Agent Thomas Kent as the driver and Viktor Liski as the passenger within seconds of arrival. The van hadn't moved since, but Kent and Liski had left the van periodically to pee along the shoulder. Keene and Lexi had anticipated Anton Boyko's move. He didn't want his men to lose sight of his son until reinforcements could get there to take him by force.

Her focus drifted between the feeds, watching for people and cars. Still nothing. They had enough food and water to last three more days, but Kaplan's gut told her they were close to something happening.

She kept her vigil on the screen until her mouth turned dry. Kaplan reached blindly for her water bottle, but her fingers touched nothing but air. A scan of her work area confirmed she'd forgotten the container at the cot. She pushed back her chair and retrieved her bottle. Returning to her workstation, she noted a change in the live feed. Two SUVs appeared on camera eight and parked on the shoulder. Moments later, Agent Kent and Liski exited their van.

"This is Team One. We have movement. Pigeons are on foot. Feed eight. Standby."

Maxwell and Noah jumped to their feet and joined Kaplan.

She watched Kent and Liski turn the corner and disappear from the screen, expecting several seconds to lapse before the next camera picked them up. "We've lost sight," Kaplan said over the radio. "They're in a blind spot. Moving in the drone."

This was it, she thought. It was go time.

14

The charade was working, Thomas thought.

No one had come or gone from the safe house compound since he and Viktor camped out down the street yesterday after spotting Sasha on the back patio grilling hot dogs. The same two agents in tactical uniforms had filtered in and out of the house several times for smoke breaks and hourly perimeter checks of the buildings. They'd kept a predictable schedule to lull Viktor into a false sense of security. It was almost too conventional for a trained tactical unit supposedly guarding Sasha. Thomas would have smelled a setup hours ago, equating these guards to a bunch of rent-a-cops guarding a corporate industrial building. However, Viktor wasn't the brightest of Anton Boyko's thugs. He sounded convinced only two or three federal agents lay inside, and once they knocked out the security system, taking Sasha would be simple. Thomas had Viktor precisely where he wanted him, but one question remained. Would they get the Raven in the same position?

If the agents waiting inside were half as tired and achy as Thomas felt, they were anxious to get this thing rolling. Except for one slip of the tongue, Viktor hadn't shared the details of his calls and text messages with Anton since staking out the compound. Thomas had no way of telling how close the Raven was or whether he was even coming. He only knew they were supposed to sit on the compound until Anton could get three more men in place. Thomas had texted the tidbit to Lathan while he pissed along the roadside several hours earlier but had returned the flip phone to its hiding place before receiving a confirming text. He wasn't sure if the message had gotten through but had to trust it had.

Viktor's cell buzzed again. He read the screen and returned the phone to his jacket pocket. "They're here." He exited the car and walked toward the back of it. Since Viktor didn't tell him to wait, Thomas took it as a sign to follow. He slid his index finger between his belt and his slacks' waistband, confirming the tracking device Lathan had given him at the truck stop was still there. He'd get only one chance to place it, so he had to be ready.

They walked twenty yards to the edge of the property and turned the corner. A black Escalade and another dark SUV were parked together on the shoulder. A small, thin man wearing a baseball cap, dark-rimmed glasses, and preppy casual clothes stepped from the Escalade. The men exited the other SUV, and everyone met on the shoulder. This wasn't the ideal meeting place for secrecy, but in the eighteen hours they'd spent sitting stakeout, only three cars had passed them. The location was secure enough for Viktor's purposes.

"Your name must be Viktor. It's good to see you again," the thin man said. It was the same Raven's man Thomas and Viktor had met at the barbeque stand in Arkansas.

"I'm told you can disable the security systems so we can go in and get our man back. How will it work?" Viktor asked.

"A nano drone equipped with an explosive charge will simultaneously land on each camera and sensor. I will detonate them. At the same time, I'll have four drones equipped with cameras flying reconnaissance in the compound. I'll send you a link to the live feeds so you can follow the action with only a two-second delay."

"How big are these drones?" Thomas asked. "Commercially available drones are still big enough to set off the sensors. Their system is as high tech as they come."

The thin man popped the tailgate to his Escalade and opened a metal suitcase in the rear compartment, revealing a custom foam insert containing a sophisticated remote control. Next to it were sixteen small glass windows embedded in a display case in four rows of four. He picked up the controller and pressed one of its buttons. The sixteen glass windows retracted simultaneously, exposing two-inch square compartments. After typing a command and flipping several toggles on the controller, an object flew from one of the compartments and landed on the man's shoulder.

Thomas strained to focus, deciding it looked like a horsefly. "What the hell is that? A fly?"

"It's called a locust, the newest technology in micro-warfare. It's designed to infiltrate an enemy's defenses undetected, provide reconnaissance, and carry a payload of offensive measures."

"What kind of offensive measures?"

The thin man stiffened his spine as if Thomas' question had offended him. "Currently, I can equip them with an explosive charge, electrical pulse, fire spark, or chemicals in solid or gaseous form. For today's operation, I've packed eight with enough TNT to disable the devices."

Holy shit, Thomas thought. This technology was incredible and incredibly dangerous. It could penetrate any place previously considered "safe" and eliminate any protectee and security detail before a single guard could squeeze off a bullet. Lathan had said in a text that his team had a way of defeating the assault, but seeing the locust's capability, Thomas didn't see how it was possible. He now understood why capturing the Raven was a national priority.

"I have four containing knockout gas in reserve," the thin man said. "I know our task was to knock out the security system for you to go in, but if you prefer, I can send the reserve units in advance of your assault and render everyone inside unconscious."

"Yes, that will work," Viktor said. "I want this going down without the chance of taking a bullet in the chest, so you stay here. If we have to fight our way out, I want you to send more of those buggers in."

"My employer was specific," the thin man said. "I'm to get you inside safely, not out."

"Well, this is part of the deal. Plans change. And I want you around in case things change on the ground."

Change of plans, my ass, Thomas thought. Viktor wanted him within the range of his pistol if the locusts failed to yield them Sasha. And the thin man's puffy exhale suggested he sensed it too.

"As you wish," the thin man said. Thomas didn't believe for one minute that he planned to stay put. This man would be long gone once Viktor's team entered the house.

The man pulled out his phone. "I'm texting you the link for the live feed. I'll send you a second text when it's clear to breach the compound."

"Fine. Give us two minutes to get into place." Viktor pivoted to Anton's men. "You're with me. I'll need you in the lead to ram the chain-link gate. Once the gas deploys inside, we'll drag out our man while you make sure there are no surprises. Do you understand your role?"

"Yeah, we got it," one said.

No surprises? What did he mean? Thomas thought. Whatever it was, it was information Viktor didn't see fit to share. He held every detail regarding this mission close to the vest like it was a national secret, and Thomas didn't have clearance until the situation hit him like a charging bull.

"Follow us around the corner," Viktor said. While Anton's three men stepped toward their SUV and the thin man fiddled with his gadgets, Viktor gestured for Thomas to come with him and took off toward their van.

Thomas slipped his hand into his waistband, retrieved the hidden GPS tracker, and activated it. As he passed the front tire of the Escalade, he tacked it inside the wheel well without hitching his stride, and then he slid his hand around the grip of his sidearm. If someone saw him, he'd have to kill five men with the fifteen rounds in his magazine. But then his breath hitched. The first two rounds were blanks. Thomas was supposed to fire them at the agents as the first one through the door to maintain his cover. If any one of them called him out, he was screwed.

Thomas took one step, squeezing his pistol tighter and pulling it from its holster. He could squeeze off two rounds as he turned, setting up a live bullet by the time he faced Anton's men.

Second step. A dog barked nearby, making Thomas flinch and every muscle tighten.

Third step. Car doors slammed, and an engine started.

Thomas glanced over his shoulder and breathed easier when the SUV pulled away from the curb. He was safe.

The next two minutes required perfect timing.

By now, Lathan's team should have a bead on the man with the Raven's toys, and Sasha should be secured. Supposedly, they had a handle on the locusts, but Thomas wasn't holding his breath. In the best case, he would be the first to go through the door armed with the blanks to fire on the agents. Then, after failing to find Sasha, Viktor and his team would speed out of there. In the worst case, the FBI team would be forced to kill Viktor and his men, leaving Thomas to explain to Anton how it happened if he hoped to find the ledgers hidden somewhere in the Boyko criminal compound.

15

Lexi glanced to her left, confirming Nathan was still asleep in the front passenger seat of their unmarked government SUV. Kaplan had guessed the Raven or Segura would set up a mile or two away from the safe house to control the locusts, so they'd moved around the radius for the last twenty-four hours, parking for no more than two hours at a time. They'd taken turns sleeping and making food and bathroom runs to a nearby Dixie Mart, the only spot where cell phone coverage was slightly reliable. However, their tactical radios and the agency satellite smartphone kept them in contact with Keene and the rest of the team at the compound.

She shifted in her seat and wiggled her left leg to relieve the pressure on her residual limb. Prolonged sitting with her prosthetic always took a toll on her. Changing the liner and a double layer of socks had helped some, but she'd applied the remedy six hours ago, and the benefit had worn off.

The last time Lexi had this problem on a stakeout, her task force was on the trail of the remaining Gatekeepers and Red Spades following the failed attack on the Texas governor at his home in Spicewood. Long hours in a car or on a casino floor, waiting for their target to show, was commonplace, but each time she had Noah Black by her side to keep her eye on the prize—Tony Belcher.

Despite having most task force members involved in this operation, today felt different. She was waiting for a different madman with a different partner. Nathan Croft was an exceptional agent. They respected one another but had yet to develop a shorthand of tactics and way of speaking that well-paired partners typically had down after several cases together. She and Noah had it walking away from the carnage at the governor's Spicewood mansion—their first case together. Maybe it would develop over time between her and Nathan. At least he didn't snore.

Lexi checked her rearview mirror when motion in her side view caught her attention. A dark sedan parked fifty yards behind them. The stretch of road they were on wasn't a traditional hotbed for parking, so Lexi's antennae were up. A woman wearing casual clothes and a light jacket exited the driver's side, stuffed her hands in her coat pockets, and walked toward their SUV.

When the woman was halfway, Lexi recognized her. "What the hell?"

Nathan stirred and sat upright, blinking his eyes rapidly to clear the fog of sleep. "What?"

"Willie Lange is here."

"What the...?" Nathan adjusted the rearview mirror to focus on their approaching boss.

"When did you check in last?"

"When I went inside the Dixie before my nap."

Lexi had worked with Lange long enough to know she didn't come into the field without good reason. Either she didn't trust Lexi's judgment, or something was wrong. Lexi unlocked the doors, letting Lange inside. She sat in the backseat behind Nathan.

"How's the stakeout coming?" Lange asked.

"Still nothing," Nathan said. "What brings you out on a Sunday?"

Lange turned her attention to Lexi. "Mills, everyone is fine, but I received a call from your wife."

Lexi's heart pumped harder at the possibilities of what may have happened. Nita never called when she was in the field. Lexi held her breath for further explanation, trying not to jump to any of the dozen wild conclusions swirling in her head.

Lange continued. "Nita said she tried reaching you this morning. I explained you were out of cell phone range and told her I would relay her message."

Just get to the damn point, Lexi thought. The anticipation was killing her.

"Your father had an accident in his garage, and she took him to the emergency room. He received eight stitches over his right eye and was diagnosed with a mild concussion."

Lexi closed her eyes, recalling the concussion her mother had received at the hands of Tony Belcher's thugs. She died weeks later. *Mild*, Lexi thought, willing herself to remain calm. Her mother's head injury was severe, but that wasn't how Lange described her father's. *This is good. This is good. It's not the same thing*, she told herself.

Lexi took three deep breaths, her practice to calm her nerves before disarming a bomb, and asked, "Did Nita say what happened?"

"He was working on a car engine when the hood collapsed."

It must have been the Camaro. Lexi and her father hadn't realigned the hood yet. "I need to call her."

"That's why I'm here," Lange said. "If you need to go home, take my car. I'll take your spot on the op." Lexi wasn't sure how to read her boss's concern. Was Lange worried about her well-being or afraid she might create another embarrassing incident and tarnish the agency again?

Lexi started the engine and buckled in. "I need to get in cell range."

Lange briefly touched Lexi's shoulder from behind before dangling a key fob beside her. "Use the sat phone. You can use my car for privacy."

"Thank you." Lexi turned the engine off, grabbed the satellite phone from the center console, and jogged to Lange's sedan. She tapped the fob and slid into the driver's seat. The change collection in the cupholder, the cell phone holder clipped to the vent, and wadded-up plastic grocery bags in the door storage pocket made her realize this was Lange's personal vehicle.

Lexi punched Nita's number into the phone. The call connected.

"Lexi, I've been trying to reach you."

"How's Dad? Lange said he hit his head on a hood and needed stitches."

"He's home and resting. Dad went to the garage after dinner like always but returned to the house minutes later, bleeding something awful. He was groggy, and I couldn't close the cut, so I took him to the ER."

Lexi envisioned her father stumbling across the yard, blood gushing from his temple. She tried reining in the horrible memories, but the image of her mother lying on the kitchen floor of their home in a puddle of blood popped into her head in high definition and bathed in bright light, so every detail was crystal clear. It was an image no one should ever have of their mother.

"How bad is his concussion?"

"It's mild, Lexi. I know what you're thinking. This isn't anything like what happened to your mother."

Lexi rubbed her forehead to hold back the fear of putting another parent in a grave. "I can't lose him too, Nita."

"And you won't. The ER took head scans, and everything looked fine. But Lexi, he's forgetting things more and more. He forgot to chock the wheels on the Camaro, it rolled, and the hood fell."

"He's getting old. Isn't it to be expected?" Lexi didn't want to say the word that had been on her lips since she and Nita moved into the Ponder home. Seeing her father daily for the last several months had clarified a disturbing reality. Her father could remember what position he started in the field for his first and last NASCAR races, but on some days, he had trouble remembering what he had for breakfast.

"We both know it's more than age," Nita said. "I think it's time we have him see a doctor about it."

"I know." Lexi sighed. Two years with him after fifteen years of estrangement wasn't nearly enough time with her father. She'd only gotten to know him again since her mother died, and the thought he might not remember her was too much to take after losing her mother.

"It might not be Alzheimer's or dementia. I've had patients with short-term memory loss caused by stress, medication, sleep apnea, and even a vitamin B-12 deficiency. Heck, it could be his thyroid."

"Okay." Lexi took a deep breath to reel in her sense of dread. "But I should be home."

"We were up most of the night, so I'm sure he'll sleep the rest of the day."

"Then I should be there when he wakes up."

"Stay. If the Raven got away and you weren't there, I know you'd never forgive yourself," Nita said in a supportive tone without any hint of frustration. She wasn't the type to hold back or downplay something as important as her father's health, but something in Lexi's gut told her this wouldn't solve itself today. They would have to deal with it for some time to come.

"You're sure," Lexi said.

"Yes, I'm sure."

Lexi listened for a sign of hesitation but heard none. "Okay but call me on this number if anything changes."

"I will, Lexi. Now, catch that man, so we can all rest easy."

Lexi ended the call, worried about what faced them in the long term but reassured that her father would be fine for now. After returning to their SUV, she handed Lange her car fob and explained her father's condition.

"That's good to hear, Lexi," Lange said. "Do you want to head home?"

"No, I'm staying."

Nathan gave her a wink as if he expected her to stay.

"Would you mind an extra gun? I brought a tactical radio." Lange said. "It's been a while since I've worked the field. Besides, it's Sunday, and I need an excuse to not do laundry."

"Umm." Lexi stalled to find the right words for why Lange shouldn't join the operation, but she couldn't think of any. Kent had gotten off a message saying the attack force would be five people strong. Three-person teams on the good guy side were optimal to repel the attack while keeping the number of people who might learn about the locusts at a minimum.

Coby Vasquez and two trusted FBI agents were inside the house awaiting the assault. Maxwell, Noah, and Kaplan were in the garage at the compound, controlling the drone surveillance and jammer and would help fight off the attackers. Lathan Sinclair was nursing his injuries from the beating Agent Kent had given him and helping guard Sasha and Delanie in the safe room. Nathan and Lexi's team was one person down. A third person in a second car would be optimal.

Lexi whispered into Nathan's ear. "I think we should." He nodded his concurrence.

"That would be great," Nathan said. "We could use the second car."

The car's tactical radio chirped. "This is Team One." Lexi recognized

Kaplan's voice. "We have movement. Pigeons are on foot. Feed eight. Standby."

"Team Two, Copy," Lexi acknowledged over the radio.

She brought up the live camera feeds on the satellite phone and clicked the correct link. She positioned the phone so Nathan and Lange could see. They watched the undercover agent and Viktor Liski turn the corner and disappear from the screen.

"We've lost sight," Kaplan said. "They're in a blind spot. Moving in the drone."

Lexi switched over and picked up the action. Kaplan kept the drone at the treetops along the edge of the property line to avoid detection. The distance was too great to get a close-up view, but Lexi made out four men exiting two SUVs parked close together on the side road. Heat flushed Lexi's face as frustration mounted. They were impossible to identify. Watch and wait were her only options.

Kent and Liski joined the four men gathered at the back of an SUV, but Lexi didn't have the right vantage point to see what they were doing. Minutes later, the men separated and headed toward their respective vehicles.

"I have a hit on the tracker," Kaplan said.

Agent Kent had activated the tracker Lathan Sinclair left for him in the truck stop restroom, which meant one thing. The Raven or Robert Segura was here. Or maybe both.

Lexi picked up the radio mic. "Team One, this is Team Two. Wait to hit the jammer until the fence is breached. We want the Raven complacent." She switched to the tracker feed. It was stationary. "Got you."

16

Sasha adjusted his position on the mattress and leaned against the headboard. He had one word to describe himself today—live bait. He'd never willingly put himself in harm's way, but revenge was a powerful motivator. When Delanie Scott and the FBI big wig, Keene, explained more was at stake than the case against his father, Sasha wasn't convinced to put his life in the line of fire. But when Scott showed him pictures of Kostas' body and told him Viktor, the man who put a bullet in his lover's head, would be lured into the trap, Sasha wanted payback.

Scott exited the bathroom, returning to the bedroom where she and Sasha waited for the action to begin. Their protective cocoon in the bullet-proof safe room for when the attack started was steps away. She gave him the side eye as she passed to her side of the bed.

"I said I'm sorry, Ms. Scott." Sasha had spent two weeks cooped up in a Dallas hotel with U.S. Marshals, unable to go anywhere or contact Kostas, and he'd hated every minute of it. It was stupid, but when he thought the love of his life faced cancer again, he had to go. Maybe now that Delanie was in the same boat after faking her death, she would know how confining and demanding witness protection really was.

"Sorry doesn't cut it, Mr. Boyko. You should have told the marshals about Kostas' email the moment you opened it. I'm not sure if I can trust you." She placed her hands on her hips, lowered her head, and exhaled before staring him in the eye again. "But agreeing to help us lure in the Raven goes a long way in rebuilding our broken trust, so thank you."

"You're welcome."

Sasha drifted his stare to the corner of the room where an armed FBI agent sat, reading a book. He focused on his discolored cheek. "How'd you get those bruises?"

The agent ran a hand along his jawline. "Your friend, Thomas."

Scott sat taller on the mattress. "Which should tell you how far we're all willing to go to protect you and put your father behind bars."

"It does." A pang of guilt screamed in Sasha's head. "I promise to see this through."

Learning from Scott today that Thomas was an undercover agent had thrown him for a massive loop, but it also cleared up many oddities. It explained why Thomas was so friendly to him and Kostas when the other bartender merely served them drinks before moving on to the next customer. It explained why he came to his defense in the club's restroom when two men pummeled him in a homophobic attack. Explained why he easily wormed his way into his father's organization. Why he let him and Kostas escape from Hailey's Comet Thursday night when Viktor was on their tail.

"I hope you do," Scott said. "Your father needs to spend the rest of his life in prison for his actions."

"On this, we can agree," Sasha said. His father had committed reprehensible crimes to gain and hold on to power through his crime syndicate. However, beating his mother with the regularity of Big Ben and killing the man Sasha wanted to marry were unspeakable. "So, what comes next? What happens if Thomas can't find my father's ledgers? Will I need to testify?"

"After this is over today, we'll get you into a hotel under U.S. Marshal protection. Since your father has tried to get to you twice, we're accelerating things. Yes, you'll need to testify at the grand jury. We'll prep you Monday and Tuesday, and following the announcement of my miraculous resurrection, you'll testify on Wednesday. We'll go with Thomas' corroborating testimony if he doesn't find the ledger by then."

"But you said we needed irrefutable evidence. Will that be enough?"

"It will have to be. This has gotten too dangerous. We can't wait any longer."

Sasha gulped. Testifying against his father had been merely a possibility, not a certainty. He'd banked on Scott recovering the ledgers and other corroborating testimony, but now he was about to become the poster child for his father's prosecution. He hated his father for what he'd done to his mother and Kostas, so a son's love wasn't holding him back. However, so far, his father only suspected what he might have told the authorities, which explained his desperate attempts to capture him. Testifying on the record would confirm his betrayal. The gloves would be off, and his father would pivot from trying to stop him to killing him.

The agent's radio chirped. A woman's voice came over the air. "This is Team One...We have movement...Moving in the drone...We have a hit on the tracker."

The agent tossed the book to the floor and sprang from his chair. "Time to take cover."

Sasha and Scott scurried to get off the bed and followed the agent.

The bedroom door flew open, and another agent rushed inside. "Did you hear, Lathan?" the man asked.

"Yes." He entered the walk-in closet and entered a code into the wall-mounted security panel. A hidden metal door swung open. He ushered Sasha and Scott inside the safe room the same size as the closet. One light hung from the ceiling. The small space was stocked with water, a bucket, and flashlights, giving Sasha the idea that the FBI expected them to hold out there for some time. The room was ample enough for the three to sit comfortably on the floor, but they would have to take turns lying down to sleep. And what the hell was the bucket for?

Let's hope this doesn't take too long, Sasha thought.

"I hope Kent is the first one through," the other agent said.

"He hasn't let us down yet. Good luck," Lathan said. He hit the palm-sized paddle button on the wall inside the safe room. The door swung shut,

Viktor's phone buzzed. He flipped it open. A smile sprouted on his lips when he read the screen. He pointed an index finger upward and twirled his wrist in circles as if telling the men in the other car to round up the herd.

The SUV's engine gunned, and the car sped toward the compound. It continued to gain momentum while the engine roared ferociously at everything in its path. Viktor followed but more slowly. The SUV charged faster and faster until its front end collided with the chain-link gate in one loud crash and a cacophony of clanks, sending the two panels flying on their hinges in opposite directions.

The SUV plowed through, clearing a path for Viktor and his van. Gravel crunched beneath its wheels and sprayed out the back when the vehicle came to a skidding halt between the house and the garage. Viktor stopped behind them.

The two men jumped out from the passenger side, each with military-style automatic rifles held at the ready position. The driver remained at the wheel. One man dashed to each garage door and inserted wedges at the top between the door and trim. Meanwhile, the other man looped a thick metal chain around the SUV's side mirror and ran to the side door with the chain. He twisted the other end around the door handle and issued a thumbs-up to the driver.

The SUV rolled back until the chain was taught without an inch of slack. This was Viktor's meaning of no surprises. If anyone was inside the garage, they were trapped. A glance at the dilapidated barn with a side missing thirty yards away confirmed it was unoccupied. His men had limited the threat from federal agents to those inside the main house.

Meanwhile, four locusts appeared in front of the van's windshield and hovered. They must have been the ones with the gas. They made another loop as if showing off for the customer, but instead of flying off toward the house, they dropped to the ground like...well...like flies.

Finally, Thomas thought. Lathan's team had broken the Raven's toys.

"What the—?" Viktor yelled. He flipped open his phone and dialed. "What the hell happened?...What do you mean jammed?...You better hope I never find you." He slammed the phone shut and slipped it into his pocket, his face flushing red with hot anger. "We're on our own. Let's go."

Viktor slipped out of the van. The house was on his side, so Thomas had to hurry to beat him to the door. If Viktor was the first one through with guns blazing, an agent or two could be killed.

A pounding noise started inside the garage, like someone was desperately trying to break out. The men fanned out, watching its perimeter.

Viktor stomped toward the building at a furious pace. Thomas trailed by five or six steps but put his legs into high gear and closed on him fast. Viktor reached the door and put his hand on the knob.

"Wait!" Thomas yelled.

18

The live drone feed, camera number eight, and the GPS tracker block on Kaplan's laptop screen showed activity. Things were happening fast. Too fast for Noah. Being on an operation with Lexi again had brought clarity, showing him what and who really mattered to him, but he didn't like being separated from her. He focused more on the tracker than what was happening yards outside the compound, exposing a salient truth. If he couldn't be paired with Lexi to have her back, he preferred going at it alone like he had at the border for the last six months.

Lexi Mills was an explosives expert. It was in her blood, and she would never give it up. Noah Black was a cop. Serving justice was also in his blood, and he would not quit, either. Unless he joined the ATF or they were on a joint operation like this one, he'd never get back the one partnership that ever clicked. But moving closer to the one place in the world that mattered to Lexi was the first step. His aunt might not like the idea of moving away from the only place she'd known for the last forty years, but Noah had to convince her. He couldn't—wouldn't—move without the woman who raised him.

Noah refocused on the screens, zeroing in on the drone feed as it settled on a side street across from the safe house property. A black Escalade was parked on the shoulder. He flashed back to the security video from the day

Kris Faust was killed. A similar vehicle was seen driving away moments after the prisoner van she was riding in exploded. "The Escalade. It's the Raven."

Kaplan keyed her radio. "Lexi. We think the Raven is here, driving a black Escalade."

"Copy. Heading to your location," Lexi replied.

Every camera feed viewing the compound's interior went offline, displaying static. The drone and exterior feeds from the hidden cameras were still visible.

"What the hell happened?" Noah asked, adjusting his bulletproof vest.

"It's started," Kaplan said before keying her radio again. "Lexi, do you have him?"

"Not yet. He's on the move. Wait."

Noah watched the marker on the screen speed down a street and make a turn.

"Got him," Lexi said. "Hit the jammer."

"You got it. We'll be comms out. Good luck." Kaplan said.

Noah suddenly felt like the odd man out. Everyone knew what was going on but him. "Comms out? A signal jammer? What the hell is going on?" Noah turned to Maxwell. "What haven't you told me?"

"Do you trust me?" The solemn look in Maxwell's eyes said something else was at play.

"Yes," Noah said, but trust wasn't the issue. He'd put his life in Maxwell's hands before and would again. He trusted everyone from the task force without question—Lexi, Maxwell, Kaplan, Lathan, and Coby— but Lexi keeping him out of the loop felt odd. If she couldn't share all the details with him, something bigger than he imagined was happening.

"Lexi and I will tell you everything soon." Maxwell drew his weapon, ready to go on the offensive.

"I'll hold you to it." Noah pulled his pistol from its holster and focused on the camera eight feed.

The dark SUV lined up with the white van they'd been watching since this began. It lurched forward and barreled down the street, collapsing the gate panels like toothpicks—a planned outcome after Maxwell's team replaced its heavy-duty chain with a weak one.

The unmistakable sound of gravel crunching under tires seeped through the tin garage doors. The noise got louder and louder and stopped close to the garage. The doors at the front rattled, and something clanked on the side door. When Noah snapped his stare toward the drone feed, a sense of dread infected his sense of calm.

"What the hell was that?" Maxwell asked.

Kaplan popped her head up from the screen. "The sound of everything going to shit. They've wedged the front doors and chained the side door. We're trapped."

"How many targets?" Maxwell asked.

"Two. No. Three men from the SUV with automatic rifles. Kent and Liski are still inside."

"We'll see about being trapped," Noah said. He dashed to the side door but couldn't pull it open even by putting each of his one hundred seventy-five pounds into it. Pressing the opener attached to the wall near the door frame yielded only a flashing light on the ceiling-mounted motor. He unlatched each garage door opener rail and tried pulling up on the doors, but they wouldn't budge. Each door was made of metal and was impossible to kick through.

"Think, dammit. Think," Noah told himself. How would Lexi get herself out? She could MacGyver her way out of anything with the right tool. "That's it." He snapped his fingers. He needed tools. If he couldn't pull the left side of the side door open, why couldn't he open it from the right?

Noah dashed to a workbench against the back wall, rummaged through a tray until he located a claw hammer and a flathead screwdriver, and rushed back to the door.

Maxwell darted over. "How can I help?"

"Just wait." Noah tapped at the three hinges with the hammer and flathead until each metal pin fell to the concrete floor. The remaining trick was getting the door from its frame while the chain held it in place. "I need to pry it loose."

He slid the screwdriver's tip between the door and the jamb, halfway between the top and middle hinges, but the tension from the chain on the other side kept the door tight against the frame. It would require a synchronized effort to counter it. "Dammit. It's too tight. I'll need that help now."

"Is there another screwdriver?" Maxwell asked.

"No."

Kaplan stood from her chair and approached. "How about a crowbar from the Blazer?"

Noah stepped closer to her. "You're brilliant." He cupped his hands over her cheeks and drew her in for a brief yet passionate kiss. Kaplan was smart, witty, fun, and cute as a button. Why he kissed her and moved back to Nogales the next day was a mystery—the dumbest thing he'd ever done.

Within a month of working together, he'd gotten the vibe she was attracted to him, and the feeling was mutual. However, going there while they were on the task force would have endangered the entire team. They had to approach their work without emotion. Office romances were always messy. When he returned to Dallas, he'd have to choose between working with her or being with her.

Noah popped the tailgate of their SUV, opened the tire compartment, and fished out the tire rod. He was shorter than Maxwell, so he took the screwdriver and lower half of the door, leaving the crowbar and top half for him.

After using the hammer to wedge both tools tightly into the gap, Maxwell asked, using a low whisper, "You and Kaplan, huh? When did that start?"

"About two minutes ago."

"Bold. I like it."

"On three?" Noah counted down, and they applied pressure simultaneously. The door loosened enough to get their hands around the edge. After much pulling and straining against the tension, they wobbled the door askew.

Maxwell turned to Kaplan, drawing his firearm. She'd pulled out her service weapon and appeared ready to charge outside. "We're going to need comms back," Maxwell told her. "Stay here until I give you the all clear to cut the jammer."

Kaplan rolled her eyes. "Fine."

Meanwhile, Noah inched his phone past the door opening and snapped several pictures. One showed a man behind the front fender of the SUV with his weapon trained on the side door. Noah showed it to Maxwell.

Remembering how Lexi got the drop on a Red Spades guard at the governor's mansion, he said, "I have an idea. I'm more agile, so I'll go first."

Maxwell didn't object.

Noah picked up the hammer, identified a wood pile ten yards away between the garage and the broken-down barn, and wound his arm over his shoulder. He never thought a couple of evenings of axe-throwing at the business near his aunt's restaurant would come in handy. The pile was six feet wide and four feet tall, so it was ample enough for him to hit unless he overshot or bounced the tool in.

He let the hammer fly. As it rotated in the air, spinning end over end, he drew his weapon and held it in the ready position. The hammer crashed against the pile, creating a loud ruckus.

Gunfire erupted in rapid succession—Noah's cue.

He emerged from the opening and located his target, his heart thumping fiercely and reverberating in his ears. The sun was high enough in the sky to not be a factor. The man fired at the wood pile. Noah would get only one shot before he lost the element of surprise. He leveled his weapon, lined up his sights as best as possible, and pulled the trigger once, twice, one second apart.

A hit to the head. Blood sprayed as the man collapsed on the hood.

Noah struggled to keep his mouth closed and breathe through his nose to maintain normal respiration. He changed the grip on his pistol and held it in the compressed ready position with the muzzle level with the ground, his arms bent, and elbows pressed against his rib cage. He would need to be steady and shoot in a fraction of a second to face two more armed men with superior firepower.

Noah moved lightly on the balls of his feet toward the front of the garage. Footsteps at his back meant Maxwell was behind him. Motion appeared at the corner of the building. Someone was there. Noah didn't wait to determine friend or foe and fired.

A hit. A man in dark clothing, holding a rifle, fell to the ground.

A shot rang out from behind.

"Oof!" Sounded from his back.

Noah dove to the side, rolled on the ground, and came up facing the rear of the garage. Maxwell was lying flat, moving slowly. There was blood.

He'd been shot, but Noah couldn't tell how badly. The third attacker was there, side shuffling with his gun pointed in his direction.

Noah aimed and fired twice but missed. He was unprotected in the open and had three choices for cover. He could hide behind the vehicles, but Kent and Liski were on the other side, and Kent only had two blank bullets. The wood pile was another possibility, but the thug was closer to it than Noah and was heading there. His final option was the old barn several yards away. It wasn't perfect, but it was his best choice.

Noah took off, firing in the thug's direction on the fly. *Where in the hell were Sinclair and White?* he thought. The backup would have been nice, but they likely had their hands full with Liski to maintain Kent's cover.

Ten more yards. He fired.

Five more. He fired.

Two yards. His clip was spent.

Noah dove through the opening, hoping he didn't land on a sharp implement like the pitchfork with the tongs facing upward he'd glimpsed while in the air. He prayed inertia would carry him over. He landed a foot past it with a thud and rolled on his shoulder.

Gunfire pierced the broken planks of the barn wall in a constant barrage, sending splinters flying.

Silence.

There were three explanations: the gunman was dead, he'd run out of ammunition entirely, or his clip was empty and he was reloading.

The unmistakable sound of metal on metal told Noah the reason for the momentary silence was the last option. A second hail of gunfire began much closer than the first. The man was advancing on his position, but he was pinned down. Noah changed out his empty clip for a fresh one full of ammo and remained flat on the dusty, musty, hay-strewn floor with his weapon aimed toward the source of the shots. Sensing the gunman's aim getting more accurate, Noah returned fire blindly, hoping one shot might find his target.

His heart thudded wildly out of control. He was outgunned and running out of bullets. The smell of moldy hay turned into the rancid smell of death. The sense that the end was coming hung over his head like a stubborn rain cloud in the dark of the night.

The race was on. Who would run out of bullets first? Or who would be the first to hit their mark? Conserving ammunition was Noah's only hope. He stopped firing. The end was getting closer and closer. Louder and louder.

Silence.

Silence.

Silence.

Too long to reload.

"Noah?" Though it was barely above a whisper, he recognized Kaplan's voice. "I got him," she said a second before appearing at the opening with her weapon ready to fire again.

"Thank goodness." Noah exhaled in relief and got his bearings. "Maxwell." He took off toward him and was relieved to see him sitting against the garage wall. A belt was wrapped tightly around his upper right arm. Maxwell was conscious, holding his weapon in his left hand, but appeared in tremendous pain. "We need to get you inside."

Noah lifted Maxwell by his left arm with Kaplan's help and guided him to a cot inside the garage. He was weak and unable to sit up unassisted, so they laid him down, leaving on his bulletproof vest.

"Is your bleeding under control?"

Maxwell nodded. "Kaplan tied it off."

Noah met her gaze. She'd saved both their lives. He added a new word to this woman's long list of incredible qualities: badass. Kaplan Shaw was a cute, brilliant badass.

"I gotta make sure Kent gets away so we can get an ambulance for you," Noah said.

Maxwell nodded. "Go."

Kaplan reached out, grabbing Noah's hand before he could leave. Worry was in her eyes. "Be careful."

He gave her hand a firm squeeze. "I will."

Noah dashed from the garage expecting another firefight, hoping what he was about to do was just for show.

19

"Lexi, we think the Raven is here, driving a black Escalade," Kaplan said over the radio.

They were close, so close Lexi's skin tingled with excitement from head to toe. The last time she had a bead on the Raven or anyone within his inner circle, she'd let them slip through her fingertips. She'd had her gun shoved into the back of the Raven's weapons builder without any idea of his identity before letting him go to chase one of the Raven's perfectly layered misdirections. But it wouldn't happen again. She and Nathan knew who they were looking for and tracked his movements in real time.

Lexi picked up the radio microphone from its cradle on the dashboard. "Copy. Heading to your location." She craned her neck toward Agent Lange in the backseat. "Follow. We'll text the tracking link once we're in cell service."

Lexi shoved the satellite phone into the dash-mounted holder and counted each agonizingly slow second while Lange dashed toward her car. Those were precious seconds she could have...should have been racing toward the blip on her phone screen.

One. Two. Three. Four.

Nathan threw on his seatbelt.

Unlike in California, she wouldn't let the Raven or his emissary slip through her fingers. Not again.

Lange's headlights flashed. She'd unlocked the car.

Five. Six. Seven. Eight. Nine.

Lange hopped inside. The second the headlights turned on, Lexi threw her SUV into gear, stomped on the gas pedal, and peeled out to finally get the son of a bitch. The Raven had killed Kris Faust, supplied the weapons and explosives that killed countless men and women, and promised to come after Lexi for killing his people. His days of flying loose in the world would soon end.

According to the map, the tracker was a mile from Lexi's position, a quarter mile from the safe house on a side street. She pushed her speed well past the limit but estimated she wouldn't reach his location for another seventy seconds. They would be close enough to the compound in forty-five to text Willie Lange.

"I have service," Nathan said. "Sending her the link."

The blip shifted position on the screen, telling Lexi whoever was there to control the locusts was rolling and traveling away from her. "No, no, no," she whispered.

"Lexi, do you have him?" Kaplan asked over the radio.

Lexi picked up the radio mic. "Not yet. He's on the move. Wait." Lexi split her attention between the road and the phone screen. *Turn, turn, turn, you son of a bitch*, she thought. "Yes!" She pressed the mic again as she stared down the taillights of a black Escalade three blocks away. "Got him. Hit the jammer."

"You got it. We'll be comms out. Good luck." Kaplan said.

Lexi flashed back to video recordings from the parking lot across the street from the FBI building when Kris Faust had been killed. A car from the scene seconds after the explosion that day matched the one she was chasing. Every fiber in her being told her the Raven or someone close to him was in the SUV ahead of her.

Lexi gunned the engine. She closed in on her target for several seconds, but then the car increased speed, and the distance between them remained constant. She smelled his fear. He knew Lexi was on his tail.

Too many country roads were feeding off this street to predict a specific getaway route. However, his northwestern direction told her he might try to hop on the interstate and lose her in traffic. If that were the case, there were few paths to take whether he intended to head east or west. The farther west he traveled, the thinner the traffic would become until they hit Abilene. However, going east toward Fort Worth, the number of cars would multiply like locusts.

How fitting, she thought. "Call Lange. I think he'll head east on the interstate. She can cut him off if she heads north."

Nathan studied the map on the phone and pointed to an intersection about eight miles ahead. "There. We should funnel him there." Following Lexi's nod, he dialed and guided Lange toward the perfect chokepoint.

Meanwhile, Lexi continued her pursuit, frustrated by her lack of progress. He kept up his speed on the straightaway, but an opportunity to make up ground rapidly approached—a sixty-degree curve. Lexi had three years of experience test-driving racecars on speedways and knew how to take turns at the optimum speed and angle to minimize deceleration.

The Escalade entered the turn, but the driver slowed at the precise moment Lexi would have and took the same angle she had in mind. She followed, closing the gap by only half of what she'd hoped. Whoever was driving the Escalade was as skilled as Lexi was behind the wheel or was more afraid of getting caught than dying in a rollover crash. Or maybe a little of both.

They rapidly approached the chokepoint, but the area had spotty cell phone coverage. "Is Lange in place?" Lexi asked. If the Escalade got onto the freeway, she could quickly lose him in traffic and not realize if he took an exit. They had to make him turn west a half mile short of the on-ramp.

"I'm not sure. I lost the call," Nathan said.

Trust, Lexi told herself. The success she'd enjoyed while leading the task force and during every harried situation she'd found herself in was rooted in trusting the people around her. Lange's faith in Lexi's abilities might have been weakened by a hidden truth about the locusts, but Lexi had no doubt her boss would come through. Willie Lange had become the first woman to lead an ATF Special Response Team for one reason: she was damn good at her job.

They were four car lengths behind, with one more curve to negotiate before reaching the critical juncture. Lange may have been good, but what if she ran into traffic or blew a tire? Lexi had to devise a plan B if her boss wasn't in place. If Lexi could cut the trailing distance between her and the Escalade, she could catch up on the next straightaway and clip his inside fender while he made the sharp turn to enter the on-ramp.

Lexi gripped the leather wrap on the steering wheel tighter and pressed the gas pedal harder, forcing the needle on the speedometer into triple digits. The SUV they were in was built for hauling capacity, not stability at high speed. The higher profile meant it was more vulnerable to rollover with a sudden jerk of the wheels, and at the faster rate, she and Nathan likely wouldn't survive. He appeared tense in the passenger seat and had a stranglehold on the roof strap.

Lexi grinned. "I got this, Nathan."

"I trust you behind the wheel," he said, "but I don't trust *him*."

Nathan's instincts were spot on. If the Escalade spun out or flipped, Lexi would have a second to react. And if she over-steered, they would join the party with a bang, a fate every NASCAR driver faced after the drop of the green flag. Lexi recalled what her father had said twenty years ago when she asked him if he was ever afraid of getting into a wreck. He'd said the thought was always at the back of his mind, but he had to believe the machinery and his skills were enough for him to let him walk away. Once the hesitation was gone, he knew he belonged on the track and started driving like the best of them. She had to trust she was good enough.

The car ahead slowed, entered the next curve, and hit it with precision for the second time. Lexi came out the other side and got back up to speed, only two car lengths behind. She'd cut their trailing distance in half, giving her a decent chance of preventing the driver from escaping.

Lexi drifted left to see what was ahead. Straddling the center line brought a smile to her lips. Willie Lange had parked her car across both lanes of the country road at the critical intersection and was standing in front of it. Lexi couldn't be sure at this distance, but Lange appeared to have her service weapon aimed at the oncoming vehicle.

A pit maneuver was an ideal way to stop the Escalade, but not at the intersection. Lange was too close. Lexi couldn't possibly come to a standstill in time to avoid hitting her. She'd have to get him after the turn.

Her residual limb throbbed rapidly in her prosthetic socket to the rhythm of her heart. This was it. Lexi drifted right as far as possible. The next turn was as dangerous as any bomb she'd disarmed. If she slowed too much, she risked losing the driver. Too little, and she would miss her mark, overshoot the one-lane gravel road, and jettison into a drainage ditch at high speed. The result would be disastrous.

Dammit, she thought. Her SUV had an automatic transmission. If it had a manual, she would downshift as she braked to generate more torque while coming out of the turn. An automatic handled the function internally, but Lexi trusted her reaction time and instincts more than a computerized machine. *Trust*, she reminded herself.

She applied the brakes a half second after the Escalade's taillights came on and trusted the transmission to do its work. The Escalade made the turn but fishtailed while coming out of it. This was Lexi's chance. She executed the turn almost perfectly, overshooting the road's center by a wheel width.

Nathan glanced out the passenger window and whistled. "That was close."

Lexi winked. "We got him."

By the time the driver had corrected his zigzagging, Lexi had gained on him. He had drifted a little to the left side of the road, so she remained on the right and rammed the SUV's grill guard into his back bumper while accelerating. The push angled the Escalade left, sending it over the shoulder. It broke through a barbed wire fence, bounced through a rocky area, and went nose-first into a soil conservation pond.

Lexi slammed on the brakes. The wheels crunched rocks and pebbles and created a dusty cloud. She and Nathan unbuckled and exited their doors simultaneously. While he circled the SUV, Lexi drew her weapon and ran toward the pond. The rocky terrain forced her to slow. Uneven ground was not a leg amputee's friend. Slipping abruptly at sharp angles could shift and misalign her prosthetic.

Nathan caught up. He also slowed at the rocks but could take them using a faster pace with two natural legs. He passed Lexi before she reached the edge. They watched the Escalade's front end bob as its tail drifted until the car settled parallel to the shore five feet away. The water level reached the bottom of the driver's side windows. The vehicle was stuck and quickly took on water.

"I can't jump in with my prosthetic," Lexi said.

"Well, I'm not unless I have to. Water and I don't get along." Nathan stood at the pond's edge with his hands on his hips, arms akimbo. "I say we wait him out."

The driver's window started to lower. Lexi and Nathan drew their weapons simultaneously and trained them on the opening.

"Federal agents. Show us your hands," Nathan yelled.

The driver stuck his hands out the window and turned his head toward them. "I can't get the door open."

Lexi instantly recognized the face haunting her for weeks. She had nightmares of the day she'd had the Raven's engineer at gunpoint yet had let him go. "It's Robert Segura," Lexi said quietly to Nathan.

"Robert Segura, are you armed?" Nathan shouted.

"Yes."

After getting Segura to toss his weapon into the water, Agent Lange arrived in her vehicle and joined Lexi and Nathan at the water's edge. "Is everyone okay?" Lange asked.

"We're fine," Nathan said.

"Then what are you waiting for? Get him."

Nathan sighed, handing his pistol and jacket to Lexi. "Hold these." At the first step in, he sunk shin deep. "Aww, geez. I hate this part of the job." He waded in waist-high water to the car, pulled Segura out the window, and handcuffed him before peering into the center and rear compartments. "There's no one else."

When they returned to the shoreline, Lexi pulled out Segura while Lange helped Nathan. Their soaked clothes hung onto their bodies like rags.

As Lexi ushered Segura through the rocks, he said, "I suspected it was you behind the wheel."

Once at the cars, Lexi flipped Segura around to stare him in the eyes. They weren't cold and evil like the Raven's, but they were calculating. "You're not getting away from me again, Robert."

20

Too many moving parts, Thomas thought. His year-long undercover assignment went to shit when Anton Boyko learned his son was a witness against him before the FBI and U.S. Attorney could gather enough evidence to corroborate Sasha's story. Part of that blame was his. Thomas had yet to locate the business ledgers. Sure, he had Viktor dead to rights for killing Kostas, but Viktor was loyal and would rather die by a thousand cuts in agony than betray his oldest and dearest friend. The unshakeable truth was why they'd winged it from faking Delanie Scott's death to helping Sasha escape his father's trap at the Comet to setting up this elaborate plan to maintain Thomas' cover while setting a trap for this Raven character.

Thomas understood the importance of capturing the arms dealer, but it sure as hell made his job a thousand times more complicated. He felt like he was twelve again when his mom and dad got divorced, and each parent pulled him in different directions every other week when it was their turn to have him. It had made his childhood shitty beyond belief and left him unsure who to trust. As a result, he learned to only trust himself. Natural leeriness had served him well as an undercover operative while living in the belly of the beast this past year.

His gut told him to do anything necessary to continue the ruse and ensure the operation's success. As he watched Viktor storm toward the safe house's front door, no one could have convinced him to do the dumbest thing he'd done in his life. Only he could. If Viktor was the first one through, the agents inside would have no other choice but to open fire on him. Once Anton learned of his death, he would be out for blood, and Thomas would be the first kill on his list. Despite Thomas' preference to have Viktor die painfully today, the best hope of all the good guys surviving today was to beat him through the door, even if it meant risking Viktor putting a bullet in his back.

"Wait," he yelled, catching up to Viktor. "I'm the one who lost Sasha at the club. I should be the first to stick my neck through the door."

Viktor shoved his gun's muzzle deep into the flesh of Thomas' chin with fire in his eyes. "Why should I trust you?"

"Because I fix my mistakes, no matter what it takes."

Viktor gave him a doubt-filled glare but lowered his pistol. "If they don't shoot you, maybe Anton will." Practicality had finally penetrated his skepticism.

Thomas now had to make his entry appear believable. Like him, the agents had two blank bullets in their firearms. The rest were live rounds, so they had to put on a good show. He twisted the knob and counted down from three in his head to give the agents on the other side time to set their positions.

"Well?" Viktor barked.

Thomas pushed through the door, quickly assessed the orientation of the furniture and agents, and dove behind a recliner, using a tuck-and-roll technique. Gunshots sounded from the far end of the room. They should have been blanks, according to the plan. In one continuous motion, Thomas rolled to his knees, aiming his gun at the first agent. He fired. A red dye pack exploded under the agent's shirt, simulating a shot to his chest. Thomas was a good shot but not that good on the move. He quickly pivoted, firing his second blank at the other agent in the room. A dye pack burst mimicked a hit to his abdomen. Now, that was a shot he would make every time.

Viktor darted in once the so-called bullets stopped flying. He glanced at the agents lying still, face down on the floor, and continued to the hallway. Gunfire erupted outside, but Viktor remained focused and searched the bathroom and two bedrooms while Thomas searched the kitchen and laundry room. Viktor returned with an expression scarier than when he'd had his gun to Thomas' throat.

"Anything?" Thomas asked, knowing the answer. Sasha and Lathan were barricaded in the hidden reinforced safe room.

Viktor didn't respond and blew past Thomas. Following a fruitless search of the kitchen, he clenched his free hand into a fist, tensed his arm muscles, and growled like a ferocious animal. "He's not here."

"But we saw him with our own eyes," Thomas said, trying to appear shocked.

"They must have sneaked him out the back." Viktor dashed out the patio door and turned toward the gunfire. Thomas followed, keeping his gun ready to fire on Viktor if needed.

The gunshots stopped before they turned the first corner. They jogged to the front of the house. The three men Anton had sent weren't in position. One lay lifeless at the fender of their SUV. Viktor went toward him and was met with gunfire.

"Pull back," Thomas yelled, laying down a cover fire near the garage while ensuring he missed whoever was shooting at them.

Viktor returned fire, taking cover behind the fender where Anton's man lay dead. "We can take him."

More gunfire came from the other side of the garage. Whoever was shooting gave Thomas the perfect excuse to usher Viktor out of there. "Sasha isn't here. We'll be boxed in if we don't leave now. Throw me the keys!"

Viktor hesitated, but when a bullet whizzed past his head, he changed his response in a fraction of a second. Thomas caught the key fob in midair, ran to the van, and spun it around, allowing Viktor to hop in the open side door. He pressed the button to close it, punched the gas pedal, and sped through the exit. On the way out, he clipped a broken gate panel and bounced Viktor around in the back hard enough to leave a few bruises. Thomas grinned.

Once on a straightaway, Viktor crawled forward and slipped into the front passenger seat. He looked like he'd been through a beating. "Anton isn't going to be happy."

"I got the leak to give us Sasha's location once. We can do it again. If not him, we can find someone else." Thomas twisted the steering wheel extra tight to make it appear he was bloodthirsty. "Those assholes almost killed me. They won't get close enough to try again."

Several minutes of silence passed. Thomas wasn't sure if Viktor had bought his act or was deciding on the perfect location for them to pull over to finish the job. Finally, Viktor asked, "Where did you learn to shoot like that?"

"Afghanistan." Which wasn't a lie. Clearing buildings in Kandahar had taught him to expect the unexpected and develop the element of surprise even when they knew you were coming. "Too many house-to-house searches, more than I care to remember."

Viktor fell quiet again, raising the tension inside the van. Thomas considered resting his hand on the grip of his pistol, but it was holstered under his left armpit. He couldn't get it out, turn, and aim before Viktor got a shot off. He then drifted his left hand to the storage area on the driver's door, feeling for anything sharp to serve as a weapon. The only sturdy thing was a writing pen, so he clutched it like a dagger. A piece of plastic against a 9mm semiautomatic gun was like Popeye without his spinach taking on Bluto, but it gave Thomas a sense of comfort, nonetheless.

When they reached the interstate to head back to Brooklyn, Viktor said, "I smell a rat."

21

Lexi stood outside the basement holding facility in the Dallas FBI building, waiting for Noah's call before she went inside. Her heart had nearly stopped after throwing the cuffs on Robert Segura when Noah called her from the safe house compound, telling her Maxwell Keene had been shot. A hit to the arm could have been life-threatening if the bullet had nicked an artery. Noah's last message said he was in the ambulance with him but gave little other detail. Her head wouldn't be straight until she knew he was out of danger.

Nathan Croft remained patient beside her, despite Kaplan's earlier message saying Segura was processed and ready for their interrogation. The squeeze of his hand on hers in the car after hearing the disturbing news was enough for Lexi to know he wouldn't rush her.

Her phone buzzed in her hand, the ringtone telling her it was Noah calling. Every muscle tensed when she swiped the screen. "How is he?"

"Maxwell is fine," Noah said. "The shot was a through-and-through on his upper arm, hitting only the flesh. The ER doc patched him up, and his wife is here to take him home. I'm going with her to make sure he gets settled in."

Her muscles relaxed, shoulders drooping in profound relief. "Thank goodness. Please give him and Amanda my love."

"Will do," Noah said.

"As soon as I'm done here, I'll drive to their place and pick you up."

"I know there's no talking you out of it, so I'll see you later."

Lexi finished her call with Noah and dialed Nita to give her an update. During their brief call earlier, Maxwell's prognosis was still unknown.

"Lexi, how is Maxwell?"

"He's doing fine." Lexi explained about Noah and Amanda. "So, I'll be home late. Is Dad resting?"

"He had supper and is watching TV. I'll make sure he goes to bed by ten."

"Thank you, Nita. I couldn't do this without you." Following *I love yous*, Lexi slipped the phone and her smartwatch into a plastic tray on a table near the door. "Thanks for waiting."

"He's family to you. I get it." Nathan pushed off the wall and added his electronics to the bin. "Ready to squeeze this guy?"

Lexi considered responding with, "*You have no idea*," but he was the one person in the world who knew exactly how she felt. They'd chased the Raven for months over multiple states. Capturing his engineer was the closest they'd come to ending his reign. She simply answered, "Yes."

They walked inside the secure facility reserved for special high-value prisoners. Its added layers of protection and configuration were more sophisticated than supermax prisons and more secure than a top-secret sensitive compartmented information facility in the Pentagon. No electronic signal could penetrate its walls, and the only way out was through a single door.

When she first saw it last year after taking over leadership of Task Force Zero Impact, she'd conjured visions of Tony Belcher's future. One was death. The other was slamming the cell door shut on him and losing the key. She had a similar vision today about the Raven but couldn't decide which future she wanted more for him. Death would be swift, but a lifetime behind bars in a place like this, with a guard as his only human contact, would be maddening. Conversely, the Raven had untold resources and capabilities. Escaping wasn't out of the realm of possibilities.

Her blood still ran hot for him killing Kris Faust, a fellow ATF explosives expert under her command. However, her fury didn't seep to her bones like it had with Tony Belcher after he had come after her family, killing her mother and nearly killing her then-fiancée. A pang of guilt tugged at her conscience when she glanced at Nathan. The fire in his belly over Kris' death never wavered, and tonight, his eyes narrowed in pure hatred for the man inside the cage. The idea of capturing the Raven kept him going night and day, often without enough food or sleep, and drove him with the same intensity as it had the first day they met.

Lexi returned her gaze to Robert Segura on the only chair in his cell. The room was spartan, filled with a metal cot, a chair, a toilet, and a showerhead in the corner. Thick, unbreakable, clear plexiglass provided a see-through view on three sides, affording Robert not a sliver of privacy. The only obstruction was the metal bars at the entrance layered with retractable plexiglass, offering a pass-through for food and a slot to handcuff him before opening the door. The walls muffled sound so those on the outside could hold private conversations.

Robert was dressed in a federal orange jumpsuit and black flip-flops and had on his personal eyeglasses. He had a white bandage on his forearm that was not there when he arrived at the facility under Lexi and Nathan's escort.

Kaplan stepped close and showed them a clear plastic evidence bag. "I found this inside his arm, and he consented to have a medical technician remove it." The bag contained a small bloody metal device slightly larger than a grain of rice.

"What is it?" Lexi asked.

"A tracking device, which is why I had him moved to the basement. It connects to cell towers and has a lithium battery. If I had to guess, I'd say it had been there for years."

"Then it's a good thing we employed a signal jammer until we got him down here. Did Segura know it was there?" Under any other circumstance, a subcutaneous tracking device would have been bizarre, but Lexi had come to expect anything associated with the Raven.

"I don't know. Beyond consenting to the medical procedure, he's not talking."

"Did he give you any trouble?" Nathan asked.

"Not at all," Kaplan said. "He wasn't the least bit smug and did as he was told."

"Thanks, Kaplan," Lexi said. "By the way, I heard from Noah. Maxwell is fine and is going home to recuperate."

"That's good to hear. I was worried I hadn't done enough."

"Come now. You stopped Maxwell's bleeding and saved Noah. You did plenty," Lexi said. "But I always knew you had it in you."

A grin appeared on Kaplan's lips. "Thanks, Lexi."

"After we're done here, I'm heading to the Keene's. You're welcome to join me."

"I think I will. While you're chatting up our guest," Kaplan raised the evidence bag in her hand, "I'll head to the lab to see if the techs can get anything useful off the tracker."

"Depending on how this goes, I might need you tomorrow." Lexi trusted no other intelligence officer to provide her real-time backup during an interrogation.

"Of course." Kaplan exited the secure area, leaving Lexi and Nathan alone with the prisoner. Multiple hardwired cameras mounted on the walls would monitor and record everything said and done.

It would be strange interviewing a suspect without Kaplan in her ear, but after finding the tracking device, Lexi couldn't chance giving the Raven any advantage. He was tracking Robert and may have known he was here, so limiting the ways in which he could listen to the interrogation by using this unique cage was imperative.

Lexi and Nathan pulled two metal chairs in front of Segura's cell.

She pressed a button on the cage wall, retracting the plexiglass panel covering the steel bars at the entrance, and sat. She spoke to him through the bars. "How is your wound, Mr. Segura? Do you need anything for the pain?"

"Your associate was kind enough to offer an analgesic, but I declined. The numbing agent administered before the extraction is still working. Thank you for your concern, Agent Mills."

"You're facing multiple charges," Nathan said. "Tell us where we can find the Raven, and we can cut you a deal."

Robert briefly glanced at Nathan but said nothing before returning his attention to Lexi and making it clear the Raven was off limits, or he would only speak to her. Or both. She whispered into Nathan's ear, "He's responding to me. I'd like a shot at him."

Nathan nodded his concurrence.

"Mr. Segura, we found the locusts and controller in your car and others at the safe house," Lexi said. "How did you get them?

"I built them, but you already knew I was the designer."

"Yes, we know you were on Falcon Industries' payroll, and Benjamin Foreman paid you to work on the Locust Program. We don't know why he hired you when he had an army of engineers and scientists at his disposal. I know he flew you to Mexico City several months ago. What did you need there?"

"You're smart enough to figure it out."

One thing came to mind—the metal alloy required to make the locusts operational. It made them unique and valuable. "You needed to source a supply of graphene to make it lighter and stronger."

"Very good. The design was solid, but its construction material was too heavy. The original engineers couldn't add a payload without draining the battery rapidly. Consequently, its available flight time shrank from hours to minutes, defeating the project's purpose. The solution was obvious."

"For someone of your caliber, I'm sure it was."

"You were doing so well, Agent Mills. There was no reason for platitudes."

"I wouldn't categorize recognition of fact as false reassurance. Benjamin Foreman had developed some of the most advanced weaponry in the world, but you succeeded where his staff had failed. You must have quite a reputation in the engineering world." Lexi was careful not to refer to illegal weapons or the criminal world. Robert seemed eager to discuss his work, so Lexi would steer the discussion accordingly.

"I've made my mark." Robert shrugged.

"Is the locust the pinnacle of your designs?"

Robert cocked his head to one side as if weighing Lexi's question. But was he considering a response or doubting her motivation? He remained silent, so Lexi moved on.

"I've followed your work for six months, but my partner has had the pleasure for years. He was impressed with the ghost gun you developed, saying you'd solved the problem of needing certain parts to be made of metal to make it reliable beyond a single use." Lexi leaned forward to knock a memory loose. "What was the name of the plastic? It was stronger than steel."

"You're referring to 2DPA-1. It's twice as strong as steel."

Lexi snapped her fingers. "That's it. Using the material made the gun undetectable through the metal detectors. It will completely revolutionize the ghost gun manufacturing process."

A self-satisfied grin sprouted on Robert's lips. "I'm sure it will."

"As an explosives expert, I was enamored with the dirty bomb at the Bellagio. The construction was nearly perfect."

"Nearly?" Robert's head jerked back. Lexi had clearly hit a nerve.

"The secondary trigger and power source were genius. The explosive configuration to shape the charge inward toward the plutonium pit to generate maximum energy was good, but..." Lexi intentionally trailed off her voice to pique his curiosity and bait him into another response.

"But what?"

"Placement of the blasting caps wasn't optimal. The bottom of the sphere had none. Without a counter explosion from the bottom, much of the energy would have been forced downward. If anything, the energy should have been forced upward to increase the radiation ceiling. And don't get me started about its location. Inside the casino was a poor choice. A strong wind could have carried the radiation for miles if it were outside. In my opinion, the design was seriously flawed."

Robert shifted uncomfortably in his chair. He didn't take well to having his work criticized. "Everyone thinks they can design a better mousetrap. You know enough about explosives to dismantle but not design them."

"I understand a lot better than you think. Every engineer with a degree from MIT thinks their work is impeccable and there's no improving upon it."

"A client's parameters always limit any design."

Lexi was steering him slowly toward acknowledging his part in building illegal weapons and explosives for the Raven. Now she needed to pivot and personalize the conversation. "Like Tony Belcher insisting the bomb had to go off inside the casino auditorium to take me out with it."

Robert laughed. "Talk about flawed. That man sacrificed effectiveness for revenge."

"And I'm still standing. Revenge is a reckless motivator."

"No truer words." Robert lowered and shook his head—his first emotional response. Revenge was the right tactic.

"Letting revenge fuel my fire cost my mother her life and nearly my wife's too. I'll never make that mistake again."

"I wish everyone could learn that lesson before it's too late." Robert shook his head.

"Too late for what?"

"Ruining everything we've built." Robert had said, "we." He was slipping. Now was the time to leverage what she'd learned from speaking with his cousin.

"You're talking about Starshiy." Other than serving as Robert's protector during his orphanage days and as a young adult, Lexi didn't know who Starshiy was nor if he was still in Robert's life, only that he was an older boy from the orphanage. Her gut told her he was the Raven, and Robert's sudden eyebrow arch said she was on the right track. Starshiy had to be the Raven.

"Is he making mistakes to keep his promise of coming after me?" she asked.

Robert laughed again. "You are full of yourself."

"If not me," Lexi said, "Then who?"

"I'm tired." Robert stood and went to his cot. His loyalty to this man went deep. She had to drive a wedge between them.

"Did you know Starshiy stopped your aunt from taking you in after your parents died in the fire?" Lexi paused, gauging his response. His body went stiff, so she continued. "Your aunt went to the orphanage months after the fire, but Starshiy scared her off. He said it was his job to protect you, not hers. She thought he would cause trouble and wanted nothing to do with you afterward. He's the reason you grew up without a family."

Robert leaped from his cot and marched to the bars with fire in his eyes. "Starshiy is my family. He might not be blood, but he is my brother. You killed one of our brothers on a Texas highway, so you must die. Starshiy has been too patient with you. You should have died at the bank."

"So that was you," Lexi said, recalling the bomb disposal she went on during her honeymoon when a sniper's bullet nearly took her out. "I should have guessed. The explosive was sophisticated, but the operation was half-assed. I'm surprised he didn't fire you or worse because of it."

"Starshiy is my brother. He would never hurt me." Robert spun on his heel, marched to his cot, laid down with his arms raised over his shoulders, and rested his head on his overlapping, upturned palms. "I'm not talking to you anymore."

"My partner was right. We can cut you a deal if you give us the Raven."

Robert rolled over, placing his back to Lexi and Nathan. "I'm done."

Lexi rose from her chair, and Nathan followed her out the door. They retrieved their electronics from the plastic container.

"Well, that was disappointing," Nathan said.

"I've dealt with my share of loyal fanatics from the Gatekeepers and the Red Spades. I'd call it progress."

"How do you figure?" Nathan asked.

"He hasn't asked for a lawyer yet."

"Good point."

"We have twenty-four hours before we have to take him for arraignment, so let's get some sleep, regroup, and give it another shot tomorrow." Lexi checked her phone for messages. Kaplan had texted that the lab was working on the tracking device and would meet her at Maxwell's home.

"Kaplan is meeting us at the Keene's. Do you want to come with me to check on Maxwell?"

Nathan looked at his phone. "Shit."

"What's wrong?" Lexi asked.

"My son. He drove up early for his week with me."

"I thought you told him to wait until Tuesday after we got sucked into Delanie's and Maxwell's case."

"I did. Now he's complaining the internet isn't working in my apartment. I better head home before he has a meltdown. God forbid a seventeen-year-old goes without service for an evening."

Lexi chuckled and patted Nathan on the back. "You better save him from his misery. I'll meet you back here at nine."

22

If Nathan Croft had known single parenting would be as difficult and complicated as it had turned out, he would have fought harder to stay in Houston to work on the Raven case. Hell, he would have fought to save his marriage. At least his son would be eighteen soon and off to college in the fall, ending the nerve-racking shuttling between households. And if Nathan were lucky, his son's deep-rooted resentment for their broken family would take a rest. That was the optimist thinking. The pessimist thought he wouldn't hear from his son for months unless he needed money.

He pulled his car into the parking lot of his apartment complex next to his son's pickup and rode the elevator to the third floor. His doctor would tell him he should have taken the stairs, but his aging knees said the elevator was a much wiser choice.

Stepping down the hallway, he thought it was a shame Lexi and her wife had moved out a month after he moved in. Living this close to each other would have made working their cases much more manageable. Scratch that. Living and breathing his job seven days a week was the core problem in his marriage. If he had any chance of repairing the damage, he needed to put his son first, starting today.

He unlocked the door, discovering the lights were on in the hallway, the second sign his son had arrived. Farther inside, he noticed dirty dishes on the counter and the unmistakable smell of something greasy having been baked recently. It was amazing how quickly his son could make himself at home. Too much. He opened the fridge, retrieved a can of soda and a slice of leftover pizza, and studied the mess. He released a puffy breath and realized he was responsible for most of the dishes. Chewing out his son would have to wait until he kicked himself in the butt for setting such a poor example.

Pizza in one hand, soda in the other, Nathan followed the trail of lights to the living room, where the television was on, displaying the intro screen for a video game. An hour of watching his son navigate a computer-generated world, collecting guns, ammo, and wood to build shelters, wasn't his idea of fun, but at least they would be in the same room together.

He drifted his gaze to the ratty backpack on the floor behind the couch, remembering the day he took Wesley to Target the summer before his freshman year. His wife's orders were to buy a backpack and nothing else. However, they'd left the store that day with a new glove for his son to try out for the junior varsity baseball team and a mini fridge for his room so he didn't have to traipse to the kitchen in the middle of the night when he got thirsty. Nathan would like to think Wesley had since refused to accept his parents' offer for a new backpack for sentimental reasons, but he knew his son. Like him, Wesley hated change. He wore a pair of shoes until they fell apart and would use his bag until the bottom fell out.

Nathan scarfed down his pizza and swigged half the can of soda before resetting the wi-fi router next to the entertainment center. A minute later, he checked his phone and confirmed a full-strength signal. Now, where was his son?

The hallway light was on, and Nathan braced himself for a higher power bill at the end of the month before walking to his son's bedroom. He knocked on the door and waited for a response. The room was strangely quiet. Wesley played music day and night at home, especially while doing homework. He'd said it was too hard to concentrate in a quiet room. At first, his explanation made little sense, but then Nathan remembered his wife often took him to her hair salon when he was a toddler. He frequently fell asleep in a hair dryer chair with the warm air blowing on him and a half dozen stylists chatting with their customers at their workstations. Those formative years had conditioned him to sleep and thrive in an environment with white noise. And his taste in music certainly qualified as noise.

He knocked again. "Hey, Wes. I got the wi-fi working." His son still didn't answer, so Nathan did the one thing every parent in the world would think reasonable, but every teenager would consider an invasion of the highest order. He opened the door without an invitation.

Geez, what a mess. According to Nathan's calculation, his son had been in his apartment for less than four hours, and it already looked like a tornado had whipped through. The bedding was askew. Jeans, shirts, and hoodies were draped over every surface that could remotely double as a clothes hanger. Wesley wasn't there, but his laptop was. The stickers of potential colleges on it had multiplied like rabbits since he was here last, but Nathan liked the one from Texas Tech the best. He would crawl out of his skin with pride if his son attended his alma mater.

Nathan retraced his steps to the hallway bathroom, but his son wasn't there either. The last time his son visited, he had his eye on the cute high school senior at the end of the hall. He might have gone there, so Nathan pulled out his phone and texted him, saying he was home and the internet was fixed.

A ringtone chimed from the living room, so Nathan followed the sound, but it stopped. He had no other cell phones in the house, so it must have been Wesley's. He dialed his number, and it rang from the couch. After fishing it from between the cushions, worry swept through him. Wesley had a symbiotic relationship with his phone and was never more than five feet from it. He slept with it in bed, brought it into the bathroom, and if he could, he would shower with it. His son would not forget his phone, nor would he willingly leave without it. Something was amiss.

A noise came from the back of the apartment toward the bedrooms. Nathan didn't consider looking in his room for Wesley because he had no reason to be there. Then a thought came to mind. Maybe the full-sized bed in his son's room wasn't big enough for certain activities if he had a guest. The idea of his son having sex in his bed was nauseating and infuriating. Growing up, Nathan never considered taking a girl to his parent's room. He would have conjured up an image of his mom and dad getting it on and thrown up on the spot. If Wesley had a girl in there, he was a thousand times gutsier than Nathan was at the same age. But his son's temerity wasn't the worst of the situation. Since moving to Dallas, Nathan had yet to invite Willie for an overnight stay. She had a key and had left a few things in case she stayed, but they'd always done sleepovers at her place since it was closer to the office. He hated to think his son had christened the new bed before he could.

Nathan marched down the hallway, expecting to find his son naked atop the neighbor's teenage daughter. After kicking them out, he'd have to change the sheets and spray an entire can of Lysol on the mattress. "Dammit, Wesley, you better be dressed by now."

He turned the knob and pushed the door open. His fight-or-flight instinct kicked in when he discovered a large man sitting on his bed. He reached for his sidearm in his waist holster. When his palm touched the grip, he felt something hard and cold pressed against the back of his head and froze. Instinct told him it was the muzzle of a semiautomatic pistol.

"I wouldn't do that," the man from behind said. "Put your hands behind your back."

This was new territory. During Nathan's twenty-year career, no one had gotten the drop on him. His training told him to headbutt the perp, but then he realized the man on the bed had a gun aimed at him. By the time he incapacitated the guy behind him and pulled his service weapon, the man in front of him would have put two slugs in his belly. His best choice was to cooperate until he was out of options.

Nathan inched his hands slowly behind his back. The man placed a plastic flex cuff around his wrists, cinched it tight, and pulled him back down the hallway. Nathan struggled to keep his balance as he backpedaled. The man from the bed followed, keeping the business end of his gun aimed at Nathan's chest.

When they reached the end of the hallway, the man spun Nathan on his heel. Seeing a third man in his apartment sucked the air from his lungs. The dark clothes, long stringy hair, and blood-red eyes were unmistakable. He said, "Where is my son, Raven?"

The Raven stepped close. The woody scent of his body soap tickled

Nathan's nose. "I have plans for the two of you." The Raven's voice wasn't as deep as he expected, but it still contained a sinister quality.

Something struck the back of Nathan's head with enough force to make a cracking sound and roll his eyes to the back of their sockets. His knees buckled, sending him to the floor. His surroundings faded to black.

23

The last time Lexi saw guards in front of Maxwell Keene's family home, she was in the backseat of his SUV with Nita in her arms after rescuing her from Tony Belcher's death trap—a bomb he'd meant for them both. The added security that night was there to keep her mother and Nita safe while Lexi and her team chased the people responsible for hurting them. The guards' presence perplexed her tonight until she remembered Delanie Scott had relocated here until the federal grand jury met later in the week.

Lexi doused her headlights and pulled up to the two SUVs blocking the entry gate to Maxwell's home. Two FBI agents dressed in tactical uniforms leveled their automatic rifles at Lexi's car. The darkness made distinguishing the agent's faces challenging, so she approached cautiously. Lexi came to a creeping stop, lowered her window, and displayed the leather case with her ATF badge and credentials.

"ATF Agent Lexi Mills. Director Keene is expecting me."

The agents lowered their weapons and approached her window. Lexi recognized the shorter one. "Evening, Agent Mills," he said before glancing over his shoulder and twirling an index finger in a small circle above his head. A second later, both SUVs pulled apart, creating a path up the driveway.

"Forgive me," Lexi said. "I've forgotten your name, but you were on the tactical team outside the FBI building the day we laid a trap for Tony Belcher."

"It's Burns, ma'am. That was a good day."

"Yes, it was," Lexi said. They'd used Jamie Porter as bait and captured Belcher's fix-it man. The operation's success had led them to Las Vegas in time to prevent Belcher's attack with a dirty bomb and end his reign of terror for good.

Regret swam in Burns' eyes. He lowered his head. "I wish we would have been set up outside the day the prisoner transport was hit with the IED." He was referring to the day the Raven cleaned up loose ends of the people who could identify him. Killing Kris Faust was collateral damage.

"I do too." Lexi joined him in a moment of silence, recognizing missed opportunities to save lives. If Lexi had kept her guard up after they took down Belcher, Kris might have been alive today.

She continued up the driveway and pulled around the circle behind Kaplan's car. The moment she stepped from her SUV, the front door opened, pouring light from the entry room onto the porch. Amanda Keene appeared at the opening and leaned a shoulder against the door jamb with her arms crossed over her chest. She clutched the fabric of her sweater with both hands.

As Lexi stepped closer, she saw Amanda's eyes were red and puffy. She said no words and simply pulled Amanda into a comforting hug. The tightness of Amanda's grip said she was still upset, so Lexi kept a firm hold.

Pain was in Amanda's voice when she whispered, "If not for his vest, he would be dead."

Not realizing Maxwell had taken a bullet to his vest, Lexi held her tighter and let her friend dictate when the embrace should end. It lasted longer than Lexi expected, telegraphing how deeply disturbed Amanda felt. When it finally ended, Amanda had sadness in her eyes. "Thank you for coming."

"We're family. Thanks aren't necessary. Nita sends her love. She would be here too, but my father had an accident in his garage this morning and needed stitches above an eye. He's fine, but we didn't want to leave him alone tonight."

"This seems to be the day for trips to the hospital for the men in our lives."

"Let's hope we don't have a day like this again any time soon," Lexi said. "How is Maxwell?"

"Grumpy. He's never been a good patient. He doesn't do well when he's out of his routine at home."

"Why doesn't that surprise me?" Lexi laughed. "I won't stay long. I'll grab Noah and head home."

"You might want to play your departure by ear." Amanda's playful grin suggested something good was percolating.

"Why is that?"

"Noah might appreciate more time with Kaplan."

"Really?" A light went on in Lexi's head. Before Noah returned to Nogales when Lexi was planning her wedding, he'd mentioned possibly bringing a plus-one as his date but never mentioned who. She'd thought it might have been someone he'd met at his apartment building or the café he frequented when he lived in Dallas, but she hadn't considered Kaplan. Though, the more she thought about them, the more she liked the idea of them becoming a couple. They had the same drive and several common interests, and the idea of Lexi's best friends falling in love made her heart melt. After all, they were already family from their time on the task force while putting their life into each other's hands and chasing wanted, crazed zealots for six months. Developing feelings for one another was a natural byproduct.

"Maxwell said they kissed today, and I say it's about damn time," Amanda said.

"You saw this coming?"

"From a mile away," Amanda said. "They hid it when you were around, but I caught them several times sneaking looks at each other during our Saturday cookouts. They'll make a great couple, and I couldn't be happier for them."

"I am too. We better head inside."

Amanda led Lexi to the great room, where Maxwell was on the couch with his feet propped up. Anyone else would be comfortable with a blanket covering them from the waist down, but Maxwell was fidgety as if his shoes were two sizes too tight. Noah, Kaplan, and Delanie were seated close by and chatting.

Lexi approached Maxwell from behind and kissed him atop the head. "Hello, my friend." It was frightening to think she'd come close to losing him today. During the task force days, he was the first to insist on safety over bravado and to take every precaution to ensure everyone went home at the end of the day. Following his own edict saved his life today.

Maxwell patted a section of cushion next to him. "Sit with me, Lexi."

She circled the couch, hugging the others briefly on her way by. She kept one eye on Noah and Kaplan. "Segura hasn't given up the Raven, but he hasn't asked for a lawyer yet, either."

"That's positive," Maxwell said.

"I had him talking about his work and his past."

"Which shut down the conversation?" Maxwell asked.

"His past. That's my wedge," Lexi said. "Any word on your undercover agent?"

"Not yet, but we're tracking his phone. He's still moving east toward Brooklyn."

Lexi turned to Delanie Scott. "Do you have enough to make your case against Boyko?"

"Having his ledgers would cross every T and dot every I, which is why we're giving Kent one last chance to find them," Delanie said. "No matter what, I'll present the case to the grand jury on Wednesday."

"When is your resurrection?" Lexi asked. "Your parents will be relieved and angry beyond belief after grieving your supposed death."

"I know," Delanie sighed. "I'm dreading that part."

"Which is why I laid the groundwork after the funeral," Maxwell said. "I gave your parents my card and told them sacrifices aren't always as they seem. They had questions, but I said nothing other than I would call soon. When the time comes, I'll break the news and tell them everything."

"Thanks, Maxwell," Delanie said. "I might need you as a buffer." Her breathy exhale said explaining to her parents why she faked her death would be the favor of a lifetime.

"I should be going," Lexi said. "We're taking another crack at Segura in the morning before we have to take him for arraignment."

"Tread lightly, Lexi," Maxwell said. "Otherwise, nothing you get from him will be admissible."

Lexi understood why he issued the warning. He could never prove it because everyone there kept to their stories, but he rightly suspected Lexi had beat information out of a suspect when Nita's life hung in the balance. However, understanding didn't equate to liking it.

"We need to bury the technology Segura and the Raven have," Maxwell added.

"Yes, we do." Something clicked in Lexi's head. The locusts were why her motivation for capturing the Raven had changed. She'd gone from chasing Kris' killer to hunting the country's biggest threat. The ramifications if the technology got into the wrong hands were too great to ignore and took precedence over finding justice for Kris.

Lexi patted Maxwell on his leg before approaching Noah. "I'm heading home. Do you want a ride?" She glanced at Kaplan and winked before returning her attention to Noah. "Or should I expect to see you later tomorrow?"

Noah stood, casting his stare toward Kaplan. "I should head back with Lexi. I'd like to have lunch with you before I fly back tomorrow evening."

Kaplan fought back a grin. "I'd like that, but I'm not sure when I'll be available. I'm working on the Segura interrogation with Lexi tomorrow."

"We could use an extra pair of eyes and ears in the observation room," Lexi said, turning to Noah. "Would you like to watch the interview?"

"I thought you'd never ask."

––––––––––––

Once on the highway and settled into the familiar drive to Ponder, Lexi turned off the radio and waited for Noah to speak. He was the type who wouldn't talk about his feelings until he was good and ready. Ten minutes passed. Twenty. Then thirty. The silence was uncomfortable.

When she took the offramp to Ponder, Noah finally said, "I guess you have questions."

"Should I ask them, or would you prefer to tell me the parts you want me to know?"

"We kissed. Twice. The attraction is mutual, and I'd like to see where it could go."

"Fair enough," Lexi said, intentionally not probing.

Minutes later, he said, "She sees *me*, not my condition."

Lexi remembered when she and Noah went to the Beebo Club and several women eyed him like he was the evening special. They saw his vitiligo as a spectacle and threw themselves at him for the novelty of having sex with an oddity. Meeting someone who saw who he was behind the mask was rare. Finding someone who saw that and wanted a romantic relationship was a unicorn in the wild.

"I'm happy for you, Noah. Kaplan is an incredible woman."

"You don't have to tell me, but I couldn't go there until I got my head straight." Coming to terms with crossing the one line he'd sworn to never flirt with could not have been easy. If Lexi had crossed it and taken that shot, she likely would never be the same again.

"And is it now?" she asked.

"I'm getting there. Being here with you and the old team has helped."

Lexi reached across the center console and squeezed Noah's hand. "We're family. We help each other."

"We save each other's lives in many ways," Noah said.

"Yes, we do."

The headlights of Lexi's SUV guided them down the Ponder house access road. She parked in the back next to Nita's car, exited her SUV, and walked toward the house with Noah. "Expect Nita to gush after I tell her about you and Kaplan."

"And you wonder why I haven't said anything." He gave her a playful shoulder shove.

"I'll wait until we're in bed."

"Thank you."

Light flickered through the kitchen window, signaling someone in the house was still awake. Lexi pushed through the porch door and discovered Nita at the kitchen table on her laptop, nibbling on a slice of pie. She looked up, locked stares with Lexi, and smiled with her eyes.

Nita placed her fork down, walked to Lexi, and wrapped her arms around her in a brief hug. She then moved on to Noah, but his hug lasted much longer. "I'm so glad you and Kaplan weren't hurt. When are you two going to finally get together?"

"Ummm." Noah needed rescuing.

"Where's Dad?" Lexi asked before Nita could sling another question.

"He went to bed an hour ago and was doing fine."

"It was a long day. I should get to bed." Noah yawned.

"We leave at eight."

"Mind if I cook breakfast?" he asked.

"Be careful what you ask for, Noah," Nita said. "We could get used to your cooking."

"That's kind of the point if I move back here."

"Really?" Nita's smile lit the room.

"He's only considering it," Lexi said. "We should all get to bed. You can chat him up in the morning."

Nita pulled out her best pouty lips all the way upstairs and while getting ready for bed. When Lexi invited her under the covers, Nita gave her the side-eye.

Lexi lifted the blanket. "Get in here, woman. I have something to tell you about Noah and Kaplan."

24

"I'm disappointed, Mr. Falco. Or is it Kent? I know you're frightened, but I must send a message to those who might want to betray me." Anton appeared unemotional, which was more terrifying, considering he now knew Thomas' true identity. At the snap of his fingers, two men simultaneously held him by the arms. Thomas glanced over his shoulder to see two more men holding a thick plastic tarp between them. The plastic was large enough to roll a man into without leaving a trail of blood. Returning his focus to the man he feared most, Thomas watched Anton pull a pistol from under his suit coat and slowly screw a metal silencer to the end of the muzzle.

Viktor stood behind Anton, licking his lips as if tasting the blood about to be spilled. "I told you not to trust this guy. I suspected he was a fed from the start. Why else would he bring Sasha here and not leave him to bleed on the restroom floor? Why else would he find every opportunity to chat up your wife? He played you from day one."

"You were right, Viktor. I should have listened, but I'll remedy my short-sightedness right now." Anton leveled his pistol at Thomas, its silencer calculated to not disturb his wife in the next room. The more intensely Thomas focused on the firmly attached silencer, the broader and deeper the hole in its center grew. It became so large it was the only thing he could see. Became the only thing in the room.

"Goodbye, Mr. Kent."

A bright flash. A firm jolt.

Thomas woke with a start, sprang his eyes open, and looked out the small window on his left. Their plane had landed at JFK International Airport and was taxiing toward the gate. He shook off the disturbing dream and glanced at the aisle seat in his row. Viktor removed his phone from his coat pocket, swiped the screen, and turned off airplane mode. It dinged several times with incoming messages. Thomas did the same with the phone Viktor knew of, but he'd missed no messages.

"Anton wants to see us." Viktor seemed less suspicious of Thomas since the elaborate show the FBI had put on in the safe house compound, but Thomas refused to let his guard down. Less suspicious didn't mean Thomas was in the clear. He rarely had nightmares, so he guessed his subconscious was telling him something.

"I figured. I'll have to hit the head before we drive to Brooklyn."

Once off the plane, Thomas chose the men's restroom closest to the gate, estimating it would be the busiest to limit the chance of Viktor using a stall next to him. He'd predicted correctly. The place was packed. Viktor went to an available urinal, placing his duffle on the floor behind him while Thomas waited for an available stall so he could check his secret phone for messages. The race was on for a stall to open before Viktor finished and rushed them out.

Viktor zipped his fly and stepped away from the urinal. He eyed Thomas on his way to the bank of sinks when a stall became available. Thomas raised an index finger, telling him he'd be a minute. Once inside the stall, he placed his duffle bag on the floor, lowered his trousers to complete the ruse, and dug out the FBI burner phone he'd hidden in his bag to get through security. He had one unread text message from Lathan Sinclair. *Grand Jury Wed. Find ledgers or come in from cold by Tues afternoon.*

This was it. He had one day to find the documents to end the Boyko syndicate and put Anton and his men behind bars for the rest of their lives. If he failed, the case against Anton would fall apart, and the year he'd spent undercover would have been wasted.

Thomas typed a reply. *Understood.* He finished his business, returned the phone to its proper hiding place in his skivvies, and pulled up his pants. He opened the door and discovered Viktor leaning against the bank of sinks directly across from his stall with his duffle between his feet. His arms were folded across his chest, and his sour expression had returned. He was impatient. Thomas acknowledged him with a jut of his chin but ignored his pushiness while washing up.

"Our ride is here," Viktor said.

Thomas threw the crumpled paper towel in the trash and grabbed his bag. "Then we shouldn't keep them waiting."

Walking through the terminal toward the pick-up area, a news story on the television screens between the gates caught Thomas' attention. He slowed.

"Get your ass moving, Falco."

"Hold your horses, Viktor." Thomas gestured toward the screen. "Check it out."

The screen showed the property he and Viktor had staked out for nearly a day from the same perspective. Several network news vans and police vehicles were parked in front. The text on the screen's right side highlighted the story's main points. *Texas Shootout. 3 Assailants dead. 2 Federal agents shot, 1 dead, 1 serious condition.*

The newscaster described a report from a neighbor about a chaotic exchange of gunfire on the fenced-off property in a small rural town west of Fort Worth, Texas. Law enforcement officials provided no information about the property, limiting their remarks to the assailants. Officials said the attack was related to an ongoing federal criminal investigation. After discovering the suspects' getaway vehicle abandoned on the outskirts of Fort Worth, they also believed the suspects had fled the state. They withheld the victims' names pending the conclusion of the investigation. The story ended with a report about the injured federal agent being at a local hospital in critical condition.

Viktor smirked at the screen with a hint of pride in his smile. "We gotta go."

Silence marked the drive from the airport, but so were most of the trips with Viktor and the driver Anton had sent. It was hard to predict whether

Anton would chop their arms off for failing to bring back Sasha or pat Thomas and Viktor on the back for making the best of a horrible situation.

When the driver pulled into the Boyko compound and parked close to the building with the human-sized kiln, two of Anton's men stepped from the main house and approached the car. Thomas masked his nervous gulp by faking a yawn after noting the workshop door was open. At this early hour, it should have been closed. It was mid-morning in New York, hours before Mrs. Boyko traditionally started her day. And since she never left her shop door open overnight, Anton's men must have pulled it open. This was a disturbing turn of events.

Thomas placed his left hand on the door handle and slid his right under his left jacket flap to grip the butt of his pistol. He was ready if Anton's men flanked him, similar to his dream. Leaving his bag in the car to keep his strong hand on his gun, Thomas pushed the door open and stepped out before the men got too close to defend against.

They stopped several yards short of the car. One focused on Thomas and asked, "Was that your handiwork on the news?"

"Yeah. I did what I could."

The man harrumphed and offered a slight nod. Unfortunately, his resting angry face made it impossible to discern whether he thought what went down in Texas was good or bad. He and the other man continued to the workshop, putting Thomas somewhat at ease.

Thomas grabbed his bag and joined Viktor at the trunk while he retrieved his duffel. "Ready to get our asses handed to us?" Viktor asked.

"Lead the way, boss."

They entered through the kitchen. Anton's wife was at the island, drinking coffee, and she looked like hell. Darya was dressed in her pottery work clothes, which were stained and wrinkled—their normal state. However, her hair was a mess, which it never was, and her face was unusually void of makeup. It was clear she'd been crying. She locked gazes with Thomas as he walked past, and the vacant look in her eyes told a story about a mob kingpin's wife who was done with this life. Of a mother who wanted her son back. Of a woman who knew the only way out was by suicide. *She* was the FBI's ticket to convicting Anton Boyko. If Thomas' search for the ledgers tonight and tomorrow morning proved fruitless, he would talk with her privately and offer another way out before he left. A reunion with her son should be the push she might need.

Viktor dropped his bag at the mouth of the hallway leading to Anton's office. Thomas did the same. Viktor knocked the appropriate three times and waited for a verbal invitation to enter before opening the door.

Anton was at his desk with a plate of half-eaten breakfast in front of him. Sipping his coffee, he fixed his stare on the television above the stone fireplace. He raised the remote control and pressed a button, bringing up a video detailing the shootout at the Texas safe house.

"Explain how my son slipped out of this compound if you watched it every second before my men arrived." Anton's tone was firm and slower than his regular cadence, telegraphing his disappointment. It bordered on disdain.

"No vehicles came to or left the compound after we arrived," Viktor said. "Thomas flew the drone every hour to keep an eye on things. They must have sneaked him over the fence in the back when it was dark."

"This is my fault, Mr. Boyko," Thomas said. Taking blame was an enormous risk, but he hoped Anton would see it as a sign of loyalty. "If we had gone in after seeing Sasha like Viktor wanted, we might have captured him. I saw the advanced security systems and superior weapons the agents carried and thought going in was a bad idea. Maybe I was wrong. Maybe we could have taken them."

Anton slowly wiped the corners of his mouth with a cloth napkin and returned it to the desk before fixing his sights on Viktor. "You were outgunned even with five men. It would have been a suicide mission with no chance of success with only two. Waiting for reinforcements was a wise choice. Though it appears I didn't send enough manpower in the first place. The FBI would not have scurried off with my son if I had."

"Snatching Sasha alive from the feds was a longshot," Viktor said. "Your lawyers will have to tear him apart on the stand."

"I can't take that chance." The veins on Anton's neck pulsated. He smashed his lips together tightly. When he squeezed the coffee mug in his hand tighter, it shattered into pieces. "We need to kill him at the courthouse before he testifies. A source tells me the Northern District of Texas Deputy

Attorney General is assembling the grand jury on Wednesday. We have to be ready by then."

"His mother will be devastated." Viktor lowered and shook his head but didn't disagree. Anton Boyko, the head of the most powerful crime syndicate in the five boroughs, was about to put out a hit on his only child.

"I suppose she already suspects," Anton said, wrapping the napkin around the small cut on his palm. "She spent all night in her workshop and asked for help collecting dirt to make more clay."

"I can help, sir," Thomas said. "I could use the exercise and distraction after the last few days."

Anton focused on Thomas, scrutinizing him for several beats. "Viktor said you went in first, putting yourself in harm's way before taking out the two agents."

Thomas averted his eyes to appear reluctant, not cocky. "Yes, sir. My training while in the sandbox kicked in."

Several silent moments passed. Anton appeared to be assessing Thomas, his performance, and the depth of his loyalty. If he decided Thomas wasn't worthy of his trust, Thomas expected him to pull out his pistol, attach the silencer from his dream, and put a bullet between his eyes.

"I want you to pull the trigger in Dallas," Anton said. "Until then, keep my wife busy, so I won't have to deal with her crying."

"You got it, Mr. Boyko." Thomas left the room, thinking he had twenty-four hours to find those ledgers or prepare Sasha's mother for a new life.

25

The fog of sleep slowly lifted, bringing into clarity the cold, hard, damp concrete floor under Nathan. His first thought was of his son. He called out, "Wesley! Wesley!" but received no response, just like the last four times he'd tried after waking in the semi-darkness of a small basement room. For the first time in years, he wanted to cry. He was the Raven's prisoner and wasn't sure if his son was, too. Wesley was missing. Was he there and conscious? Or was he dead, lying in some alley? No matter his condition, Nathan doubted if he could ever forgive himself. He was Wesley's father. His job was to protect him from harm. Yet he'd invited the Raven into his life by hunting him for years. No case, no career was worth this.

If he had any chance at survival or giving his abductor his just due, Nathan needed to figure out the Raven's endgame. The lack of food and water wasn't a good sign, but still being alive meant the Raven had plans for him. He was likely a goner if this was a tit-for-tat thing for taking Segura. But Nathan might have a chance if he was the object of a prisoner exchange. Until then, he needed to continue working on his only way out.

Nathan opened his eyes and struggled to focus. He no longer saw double—an improvement. The only light came from two sources. The gap between the floor and the bottom of the metal door provided a thin sliver. Also, an old incandescent bulb hanging from the ceiling appeared to have a fraction of the required electricity to function fully. Neither illuminated the room effectively enough to discourage the cockroaches. However, Nathan could tell the room was eight-foot-square with cinderblock walls and ceiling. Besides him, its only contents were his chains and a metal pail to piss in.

He had no accurate way of gauging how long he'd been there nor how long it took to get there since he was in and out of consciousness during the drive. He remembered being brought downstairs through a door in the garage, but everything was blurry afterward. His splitting headache from being knocked out dissipated after sleeping for a while. If he had to guess, he'd been locked up for at least half a day, so the sun should be out.

While he was unconscious, someone had replaced the plastic straps around his wrists with metal handcuffs, placing his hands at his belly. The cuffs were chained to the shackles around his ankles, and the length between his ankles was secured to an eye bolt on the wall with a six-foot-long thick chain.

The padlocks on his restraints were too hefty to break through, so he'd focused his energy on the anchor. If this was anything like the bolts he'd installed on the patio beam at his mother's house for a porch swing, it must have been at least four or five inches long. It would take some time to work free. The block securing it appeared to have been laid in the mid-twentieth century, and damp conditions over the decades had softened its firmness some. He'd spent every waking hour tugging on the section of chain closest to the bolt, forcing it left, right, up, and down to chip away the block from the inside. Before his arms and back gave out, he'd made significant progress, boring a hole several inches deep.

His muscles no longer ached, so it was time to get back to work. Nathan rolled to his knees and pushed up on the leg with the least tender joints. Weathering the pain, he rose to his feet, stretched out the stiffness from sleeping on the hard floor, and resumed tugging—up and down, left and right. Soon, his arms felt like rubber again and his back had stiffened so tightly it was difficult to bend at the waist. Nevertheless, he pushed through the pain. His son's life depended on his steadfastness.

A clanking noise of someone unlocking the door came from the other side. Nathan dropped to the floor and leaned against the wall with his forearms resting on his raised knees. The door swung inward, drawing in light from the corridor. The silhouette of a tall, thin man appeared in the doorway, but the light made him difficult to make out until he stepped farther in.

He was the Raven. His eyes glowed the color of blood in the semi-lit room, but Nathan wasn't intimidated. He wasn't afraid of the man he'd dreamed about catching for years. He'd imagined confronting this faceless man so many times he was numb to the persona he projected.

"What have you done with my son, Raven?"

"He's unhurt, but that can change if you don't tell me where Lexi Mills is holding Robert."

Lexi's instincts were right after they captured Segura. She'd wanted to take every precaution transporting him to the FBI facility and employed a signal jammer the entire way to Dallas.

"Your man was easy to find, and we found the tracking device you embedded in his arm. That's just sick."

"Where is he?" The Raven's facial muscles rippled as he set his jaw tighter. Whatever Robert was to him beyond his engineering skills and a shared history at a Brooklyn orphanage, Nathan and Lexi had struck a nerve by capturing him.

"He's at a place where you can't get to him. We had a nice chat with Robert. He had a lot to say about his work. He was particularly proud of his effort in developing the locust for Benjamin Foreman." The Raven harrumphed, making Nathan think he wasn't convinced his man would give up information so easily. He needed to take this to a personal level. "Robert also told us about his time at the orphanage, Starshiy. He knows you scared off his aunt and robbed him of a life with family."

"I am his family." The Raven's eyes narrowed but glowed a darker red. Nathan was on the right track.

"You mean you engineered his life and manipulated him into believing you're his family. In truth, you've groomed him since childhood to do your bidding. The GPS tracker in his arm proves you consider him property, not family."

"It's a bond of trust, not unlike the tracker you activated on your son's phone. It says something when your loved one welcomes you to see their location at any moment. Though I doubt your son would say the same about your arrangement." The Raven showed Nathan the screen on his phone. It displayed a live video feed of a man with a black hood over his head bound to a chair in a similar cell as Nathan's. His breathing shallowed after he focused on the West Houston High School sweatshirt. It was from his son's school. Nathan shifted his stare to the Converse high-tops. He'd gifted those shoes to Wesley for his sixteenth birthday.

Nathan stood clumsily and tugged on his chains. Heat built in his belly and threatened to erupt in a flashpoint. "If you hurt him, I guarantee you a painful death."

"This doesn't have to be difficult, Agent Croft. If Robert is in a place where I can't get to him, you have nothing to lose by telling me where he is. Otherwise, I'll have to give you more incentive to cooperate." The Raven pulled his phone back and pressed something on the screen. Screams filled the corridor. When he stepped closer, the woody smell of his body soap wafted forward. He showed Nathan the screen again. The hooded man was writhing in pain.

"Stop." Nathan breathed too fast and shallowly. He made himself dizzy.

"Where is Robert?"

"The basement of the Dallas FBI building. Now, stop hurting him."

The screams stopped.

"Now, that wasn't so hard, Agent Croft."

Nathan tugged on the chains so hard he felt the bolt give way. "Your locusts won't work there. It's like a supermax facility in a Faraday cage. He won't leave there until he's convicted or acquitted. He's ours, and there's nothing you can do about it."

"Then I might need you after all." The Raven pocketed his phone.

It was now or never. If Nathan's guess was correct and it was daytime, the light would make it difficult for him to evade his captors outside these walls, but this might be his only chance of escaping.

Nathan lunged at the Raven, flinging the chain length with the bolt attached toward his head. A glancing blow sent his captor tumbling to the floor. The shackles around his ankles made running impossible, but he snatched the key from the lock and waddled into the lit corridor with some momentum. The chains at his feet echoed loud enough to announce his getaway to the next county.

His heart thudded wildly. He was unsure where to look for his son. Two other metal doors similar to the one holding him hostage were in view. He first tried the one on the left, using the key. He flew the door open, but the cell was empty. Darting across the hallway, he undid the lock, pulled hard on the door, and stood still in shock. The room was lit. A chair in the middle faced a camera mounted on a tripod, but the chair was empty. His son's clothes and shoes lay in a crumpled pile on the floor.

"It was a fake," he said, numb at what this likely meant. Two possibilities came to mind. The Raven never had his son and dug through his closet for his things to make torturing a man behind a mask appear real. If that were the case, why wasn't his son in the apartment when Nathan came home? His car, backpack, and phone were there. Nathan hated to think it, but the cold, hard truth drove him to his knees. The man was fake, and the torture was simulated because his son was dead. It was an elaborate ruse to entice Nathan into giving up Segura's location.

Nathan clutched his son's high school hoodie, brought it to his face, and soaked it with tears. His only child was likely dead, and the last memory he had of Wesley was arguing at the end of his previous visit and Wesley yelling "asshole" before slamming the door to drive back to Houston. Gut-wrenching thoughts filled his head. Which college would he have chosen? Who would he have married? How many children would he have brought into the world? But Nathan would never know the answers because he'd brought the Raven into their lives. He was why his son was dead.

A crack on the back of his head forced Nathan to the floor, landing with his hands trapped beneath his chest. Blow after blow to his back and ribs came from both sides, bringing unbearable pain. Two men were striking him with their feet and maybe a pistol, beating him into submission.

"That's enough," a voice said. It sounded like the Raven's. "Take him back to his cell."

The men lifted him by the armpits with an abrupt jerk, aggravating what felt like one or two cracked ribs. They pulled him out the door, dragging his feet along the concrete floor. Nathan struggled to crane his neck to glimpse the Raven, but the pain was too great to twist far enough.

The men dropped him in the center of his cell, each giving him a solid kick in the ribs before walking away. Nathan crawled toward the back, each arm or leg movement creating terrible agony. He propped himself against the wall, inventorying his injuries beyond the ribs. He had a more severe concussion for sure, and maybe a fractured upper arm.

"That was unnecessary and stupid, Agent Croft."

Nathan looked up. The light peeked through the door enough to highlight the gash on the Raven's cheek dripping with blood. *My son is dead*, repeated in his head. White hot anger stripped Nathan of his humanity. Images of ripping each limb from the Raven before gutting him with a buck knife to prepare him for the evening's meal formed in vivid detail.

"What did you do to my son?" His loud words dripped with spit.

"If you try that again, I might show you and find someone else to trade. But if you behave, I'll offer Lexi Mills your life for Robert's."

"Lexi will never agree to it. She'll come for you, Raven."

"We'll see about that." The Raven closed the door behind him, recasting the room into darkness. He made it sound like Nathan was a pawn, but Nathan's gut told him he was bait. He and Lexi had killed his men, and Robert had gotten caught. The Raven was preparing to clean up loose ends.

26

Nita opened the bedroom door, letting in the strong scent of frying bacon from the upstairs hallway. Lexi rushed forward, blocking her wife's route, and trapped her in place by resting both palms against the wall on either side of her head. "No peppering Noah with questions. He and Kaplan are still figuring things out."

"I won't." The corners of Nita's lips were upturned, hinting she had no intention of keeping her word.

Lexi leaned her head closer until their mouths were inches apart. "I mean it. I don't want to put any pressure on him. This move would mean changing careers and uprooting his aunt from the only place she's lived in the United States."

"Can I at least acknowledge the elephant in the room?"

"When haven't you?" Lexi smirked.

Nita pushed Lexi back with her palms and playfully swatted her chest. "That wasn't nice."

"I'm sorry." Lexi kissed her before turning to go out the door. "But it's true."

Nita chased her downstairs, giggling. Lexi discovered a heartwarming, unexpected scene when she turned the corner at the landing. While Noah cooked a delicious-smelling concoction at the stove, her father sliced cantaloupe on the granite island. In her thirty-six years, Lexi had never witnessed her father fixing breakfast. Noah must have had magical powers the women in her father's life lacked.

"Good morning, Dad. Hey, Noah." Both replied the same. "Can I help?" Lexi asked.

"We have everything under control," her dad said.

"Shouldn't you take it easy, considering you have a mild concussion?"

"The headache is gone, so I couldn't miss the opportunity to have Noah teach me how to make his special omelet."

"That's great, Dad." Lexi inspected the stitches over her father's brow. "Those look painful. We'll have to fix the hood hinges on the Camaro before we move on to anything else."

"I could have sworn I'd chocked the wheels before popping the hood. I must have had a senior moment."

Lexi hated to think it, but he'd experienced too many forgetful moments since his wife passed away to attribute to aging. Nita was right. Something else was at play. When things settled down at work, she and Nita should talk seriously with him about getting screened for dementia.

Noah plated the omelets, bacon, and fruit and brought everything to the table. "Breakfast is ready, everyone." He sat in his traditional chair.

Nita poured two cups of coffee and handed one to Lexi. She kissed Noah on the forehead. "I'm happy for you."

Nita kept her word, and everyone ate, chatted, and laughed. It felt like family.

An hour later, Lexi pulled into the parking garage at the Dallas FBI building, expecting to see Nathan's car in the visitor's section. While walking to the entrance with Noah by her side, she scanned the area, but the car wasn't there. *Strange*, she thought. Nathan was always the first to arrive, but then she remembered his son was in town. Wesley must have thrown a kink in Nathan's morning routine.

She and Noah met Kaplan in the basement outside of the secure area.

Lexi greeted her with a hug and whispered so only Kaplan could hear. "I'm happy for you." Kaplan blushed.

Noah kissed her on the cheek.

"Have you seen Nathan?" Lexi asked while drifting her attention to the screen on the workstation outside the secure door. Segura was awake in his cell, sitting in his chair, inspecting his fingernails. The log on the neighboring screen showed when Segura used the bathroom and was served breakfast down to the precise second.

"Not yet," Kaplan said. "Should I set up?"

"Let's wait until Nathan is here. We still have hours before we have to video arraign Segura." Lexi checked her watch. It was two minutes after nine. She'd give him fifteen minutes before calling. After sitting at the workstation, Lexi endured several awkward-filled silent minutes between Noah and Kaplan. "Will you two finally discuss the kiss and go on a real date? Not just lunch."

Kaplan gave her the "what do you think you're doing" look before fixing her gaze on Noah. "Can you stay longer?"

"I have a ton of vacation days coming, so I can stay the rest of the week," Noah said, refusing to break his stare.

"I'll put in for the time off." Kaplan's chest rose and fell faster, making Lexi feel like a voyeur.

"All right, can you two wait to get a room until Segura gives us the Raven?" Lexi glanced at her watch. It was nine-fifteen.

She dialed Nathan's number, but the call went to voicemail. After another fifteen minutes, she called again, but he still didn't answer. She called the phone in their shared cubicle at the ATF building, but the call also went to voicemail. Concern pricked the back of her neck, so she dialed Ronald, the logistics clerk whose desk was next to Lexi's cubicle.

"Hey, Lexi. What's up?" Ronald said.

"I'm looking for Nathan. Have you seen him this morning?"

"Sorry, Lexi. I haven't seen him since last week when he was with you. Do you want me to check around?"

"If you don't mind. We're supposed to interview a suspect this morning. If you find him, please have him give me a call."

Lexi finished the call and dialed Agent Lange's number. She picked up.

"Good morning, Agent Lange. Have you seen Agent Croft? We're supposed to interrogate Segura again."

"No. When were you supposed to meet?"

"Half an hour ago," Lexi said, "and he's not answering his phone."

"That's not like him." Concern cut through Lange's voice. "When did you last see him?"

"Last night, after we wrapped up with Segura. He received a text from his son saying he'd arrived, so we agreed to meet back here at nine."

"Wesley arrived last night? I didn't think he was due until Tuesday." Lange's familiarity with the schedule of Nathan's son was interesting, but this wasn't the time to dig deeper.

"Nathan was surprised, too. Wes had texted him, saying the internet was down in his apartment, so Nathan went home. I have a bad feeling about this, Agent Lange. We're heading there now."

"So do I. I'll meet you in his parking lot."

Lexi disconnected the call and turned to Kaplan. "I need you to stay here. Call me if Nathan shows up."

"I'm not letting you go there without backup," Noah said.

"I wouldn't have it any other way."

Pulling into the apartment parking lot was like traveling in a time machine to the past. Lexi had lived in the complex for two years after moving from Kansas City to rehabilitate after losing her leg. It was where she and Nita first kissed and fell in love. Where Nita recovered from being shot in the shoulder at the Beebo Club massacre. Where she and her father started their long road to reconciliation. This apartment complex would always hold meaning for her.

"I didn't know Croft lived in your old building," Noah said.

"Yeah, I helped him get the place, then Nita and I moved to Ponder a month later." Lexi parked in the visitor section closest to Nathan's apartment and stepped from her car. "His reserved spaces are on the other side. Let's see if his car is here."

Turning the corner, Lexi discovered Agent Lange was there, peering into the windows of Nathan's car. "Agent Lange," Lexi said. "Anything interesting?"

"Nothing strange." Lange popped her head up and focused on Noah.

"Agent Lange, this is Detective—" Lexi started.

Lange extended her hand to Noah. "Detective Noah Black. You did excellent work taking down the Red Spades and Gatekeepers on Lexi's team. It's a pleasure."

"Likewise." Noah shook her hand. "I hope you don't mind me tagging along, but I was with Lexi when she grew concerned about Nathan."

"Are you carrying?" Lange asked. He nodded. "Then we could use the backup." She turned to Lexi. "The pickup is Wesley's. I tried both their numbers, but neither answered."

"Let's go to his apartment," Lexi said.

Lange turned on her heel and made a direct line to Nathan's apartment. She pulled a set of keys from her pocket and unlocked the door. A picture had started to form. Agent Lange had the phone number of Nathan's son, knew the car he drove, was privy to his comings and goings, and had a key to Nathan's home. The signs pointed to them having an affair, but Lexi didn't want to jump to conclusions without knowing the facts. She kept her suspicions to herself.

Lexi was in Nathan's place several times while still living down the hallway but hadn't returned since moving to Ponder. The apartment had two bedrooms, two bathrooms, a laundry area off the hallway, one living room leading to a small balcony, and a galley kitchen.

They drew their sidearms, holding them close to their bodies at the compressed ready position for optimum maneuverability in the enclosed conditions. Lange eased the door open silently. The interior was well lit and silent. Lange pushed down the entry hallway. She peeled off right to the kitchen. Lexi was on her heels and continued to the living room and patio. Both were unoccupied. Noah slid down the hallway and entered the bathroom. Lange and Lexi followed. Lange continued to the end of the hall to the larger bedroom since the door was open. Lexi stopped at the secondary bedroom door, turned the knob slowly, and gripped her pistol more tightly before pushing the door inward. She trained her weapon left, center, and right, looking for targets. Something lumpy was beneath the bed covers but posed no immediate threat. She went farther inside, stood beside the closet, and slid the door left. Nothing.

Lexi returned to the bed, lowered the covers, and shouted, "I have Wesley." She heard "Clear" twice before Noah entered the room. Wesley was motionless with tape over his mouth and his hands and feet bound with plastic straps. She pressed a palm against his chest and felt it lower and rise in a gentle breathing pattern. "He's alive."

Noah dialed 911 as Lange entered the room. She rushed to the boy's side with worry in her eyes. "Wes."

Lexi fished her Leatherman tool from her cargo pocket and cut the bindings from his hands and feet while Lange peeled the duct tape from his mouth. He started to wake and thrashed his arms and legs violently on the bed.

Lange gripped him by the shoulders to calm him. "Wes. Wes. It's Willie. You're safe." Once he stopped and gained his senses, she asked. "What happened?"

Wesley pushed to a sitting position and grimaced, pressing a hand against his temple like he had one hell of a headache. "These big dudes were at the door and forced their way in when I answered the bell. They took my phone and tied me up. After they unlocked my phone using facial recognition, a scary-looking, thin guy dressed in all black with these devil-like red eyes came in. Then they gave me a shot of something to knock me out."

"The Raven," Lexi whispered so only she could hear.

"What about your dad? Was he here?" Lange asked.

"No." Panic filled Wesley's eyes. "Did they take Dad?"

"We're not sure, but we can't reach him on his phone."

Wes stood but wobbled. Lange steadied him. "We have to find him, Willie."

"We'll find him, Wes," Lange said. "The important thing right now is to make sure you're okay. We have paramedics coming to check you out."

Wes buried his face in his hands. "This is my fault. I shouldn't have answered the door."

He towered over Lange by half a foot, but Lange gripped him by the shoulders again. "It's not your fault. You had no way of knowing."

"Who took him?" The boy's eyes welled with tears. "Who was the guy with the red eyes?" He was seventeen but was well on his way to filling out as a fully grown man. Seeing him crying broke Lexi's heart.

"An evil man," Lange said. "Noah, can you stay with Wes for a minute?"

"Of course," he said.

"Lexi, there's something you need to see." Lange led her through Nathan's bedroom, stopping in the private bathroom. A message was written on the mirror in lipstick. The shade matched Lange's color. The text started with a phone number and the directions, *Call when you're ready to trade.*

27

Thomas entered the hallway, closing Anton's office door. Viktor was occupied with the boss behind the door, making this Thomas' best opportunity to search a part of the house off-limits to Anton's men unless by invitation. He ascended the stairs quickly. Going up there alone was risky but looking for Mrs. Boyko to start work as her helper was the perfect cover.

Thomas reached the top, discovering four doors. This was his first time exploring this level, so he wasn't sure of its configuration. He suspected the floor plan included the owner's suite, a shared bathroom, Sasha's bedroom, and the guest room he'd heard mentioned several times.

He doubted Anton would hide the company books anywhere someone might stumble upon them, so the owner's room was his target. Guessing its location, Thomas opened the door at the end of the hall. The room was unoccupied, but its small size suggested it was a secondary bedroom, not Anton's. He retraced his steps and entered the room closest to the top of the stairs. The king-sized bed, large-scale furniture, and paisley bedding screamed the Boyko's. Anton liked everything big, like his gated compound in the middle of Brooklyn. His wife preferred ornate furnishings. The rest of the house was decorated in similar bold patterns. Also, her pottery pieces contained intricate designs from hours of detailed work. This had to be their room.

One nightstand was littered with a lotion bottle, a tissue box, a phone charger, and a pair of headphones. Deciding it was likely the wife's side, Thomas focused on the other stand. The two books on top drew his attention. A closer inspection, however, revealed they were crime fiction novels. *It figured*, he thought. The drawer contained a loaded pistol with the safety off, pens, a notepad, and cold medication, but no ledgers.

Thomas moved on, peeking behind portrait frames on the wall, but found no hidden safe. Stepping toward the walk-in closets, he heard a door slam downstairs. His pulse picked up at the thought of being caught in Anton Boyko's private bedroom. He glided quickly but silently toward the hallway, closed the door, and knocked on it to maintain his cover.

He called out. "Mrs. Boyko, it's Thomas. I'm supposed to help you today."

Thomas knocked again, took a deep breath, and descended the stairs. Footsteps on the main floor alerted him to someone in the hallway. There was no escaping without being seen. Expecting resistance, he slipped his right palm over the butt of his gun hidden inside his jacket and continued his downward climb. Each step thumped his heart harder and faster at the prospect of fighting his way from a compound fortified by a half dozen armed men. A nasty one, Viktor, looked for any excuse to shoot him.

A bead of sweat dripped from his brow.

The footsteps grew louder. Closer.

He tightened his grip under his jacket, reminding himself to use discipline, aim center mass, and conserve ammo. His breathing labored.

Then.

Mrs. Boyko appeared at the bottom of the stairs. "Thomas?"

Every muscle relaxed in relief. "I've been looking for you, ma'am. Mr. Boyko assigned me as your helper today. I understand you need more dirt."

"Yes, I do."

"Then let's get to it."

Speed was critical to avoid getting caught. Thomas reached the bottom and steered Mrs. Boyko down the hallway toward the central part of the house. When they came to the end, he heard the door to Anton's office open at his back. Thomas didn't slow. Getting the hell out of there while still breathing depended on Mrs. Boyko not letting on that she found him upstairs. He turned the corner, pulled out his weapon, flipped off the safety, and held the pistol close to his thigh. He was prepared for a close-quarters battle.

"Darya," Mr. Boyko called out.

"Yes, Anton," the wife replied.

"I sent Thomas to help you today."

This was it. Her response would determine whether Thomas would have to shoot his way out.

"Yes, I found him. We're heading to the workshop now."

Thomas blew out a breath of relief. Over the next two hours, he filled the wheelbarrow with red dirt he'd dug up from a pit at the back fence of the compound and added each load to a pile in the workshop's corner. After bringing in his fifth haul, he stopped to wipe the sweat from his brow with a forearm.

"That should be plenty, Thomas," Mrs. Boyko said. "Thank you."

He eyed the pile of dirt. "I'm curious, ma'am. How do you turn this into clay?"

"It's a process of adding water, letting the sediment sink to the bottom, and pouring off the excess. I pour what's left into a cloth sack and let its moisture drain for several days."

"It sounds complicated."

"Not really," she said. "It just takes patience. What else do I have to do?" Her question gave the impression she considered herself a prisoner in her own home.

"Well, it's interesting."

"Would you like to help? she asked.

Thomas looked more closely at Darya's bruised face. It was a shame. She was a kind woman and, from what he'd seen, a good mother to Sasha. She didn't deserve Anton treating her as his personal punching bag. "Sure. Show me what to do."

After settling into a rhythm of pouring and draining, Thomas decided that resuming the search for the ledgers today was a bust. But after a year undercover, he refused to fly back to Texas empty-handed when he had yet to search Anton's office.

One more shot in the morning, he thought. Then, even if his search was unsuccessful, Thomas would fly home and work with Delanie Scott to convict Anton Boyko and his men for their many crimes.

28

Stepping into the conference room at the Dallas ATF building, Lexi took comfort in the faces around the table. Lathan Sinclair with his collection of undercover bruises. Coby Vasquez with a look of determination. Kaplan Shaw with her new sense of purpose in the field. Noah Black with his sense of calm. And Willie Lange, despite her pale expression of fear. FBI Agent Daniel White was an unknown, but he was part of the deception at the safe house, and Coby had said he would trust him with his life.

Lexi needed one more person to complete the circle of people she trusted to bring Nathan Croft home. The conference room door opened, and Maxwell Keene stepped inside, wearing casual clothes, not his traditional tailored suit for the office. His left arm was in a sling. He had his service weapon holstered at his hip and the same determined look as Coby.

"Glad you could make it, Director Keene." Lexi pointed at his weapon. "Do you think you can use your gun if you have to?" She was sure he'd tell her if he was on pain meds. She couldn't afford to have anyone on the prisoner swap who didn't have their head in the game.

"Yes, but only as a last resort. I'll be your mover and shaker."

"All right then." Lexi turned to her boss. "Agent Lange, do you want to get things started?"

"I'm too close to this one," Lange said, shrinking in her chair. Worry was overshadowing her typical in-charge demeanor. "You've headed operations like this before, Mills. I need you to take the lead."

"All right, Agent Lange." Lexi took a position at the head of the table and outlined the situation, including the Raven's message. "Kaplan, any luck on the phone number the Raven provided?"

"It's a burner phone bought in Venezuela. The service provider refused to release records, but they gave me the International Mobile Equipment Identity number. That was enough to get a court order for the major cell tower providers. It's a long shot, but I had them set up a trigger to message me in real time when the IMEI connects to a tower. The Raven is smart, though. He could use call forwarding to a different phone to receive our call."

"Any other ideas?" Lexi directed her question to the people around the table.

"I sense the Raven is desperate to get Robert back," Noah said. "Otherwise, why would he have taken Croft? We should leverage his weakness if the tower tracking doesn't work."

"Meaning we control the narrative," Lexi said. "*We* pick the location and dictate the terms. Noah. Kaplan. Can you two work on selecting a location?"

"We're on it," Kaplan said. She and Noah exited the room.

"Now," Lexi said, "the Raven is expecting a prisoner exchange, but too many things can go wrong. Too much is at stake to risk losing our only link to the Raven."

"What are you saying, Lexi?" Lange's face went pale. "What's more important than Nathan's life?"

"There's more at play here than capturing a weapons dealer."

"Like what?" Lange stood, flapping her arms. "I should have followed my initial instincts about you. You care more about making a name for yourself than the people around you."

Lexi lowered her head. She could see how Lange could think her so callous.

"That's enough, Agent Lange," Maxwell said, turning to Lexi. "We should tell her." She nodded her concurrence.

"Tell me what?"

"Gentlemen, we need the room," Maxwell said. After Lathan, Coby, and Daniel exited, he locked the door. "Agent Lange, we need to tell you about a top-secret project called the Locust Program." Maxwell described the technology and detailed how the nation dodged a catastrophe in California with the locusts. "Without Lexi's quick thinking, everyone there, including the president and her husband, would have been killed. Benjamin Foreman hired Robert Segura to perfect the design. Now the Raven has the locusts. The president considers capturing the Raven the highest priority and has authorized us to do anything necessary to safeguard the technology. Agent Croft knows what's at risk, and I think he would agree we can't let Segura go. He has the knowledge and expertise to endanger the entire world."

"Jesus," Lange slumped in her chair. "I had no idea." She turned to Lexi. "I owe you an apology."

"No, you don't," Lexi said. "We need to concentrate on finding a way to get Nathan back home and not lose Segura."

"What about a decoy?" Lange said. "We could send someone with the same height and build dressed in his clothes. If we control the exchange, we should make sure it's at night in an area with poor lighting."

"That could work," Lexi said. "But who? We can't risk bringing in more people. Otherwise, information about the locusts will get out. Noah is close in size, but he's our best marksman. We'll need him as overwatch."

"Use me. Segura and I are the same build and are close in height. If I wear glasses and a hat and hunch over, I can pull it off."

"Maxwell?" Lexi looked at him with questioning eyes.

"It's our best option," he said. "Though, if the Raven dictates the location and time of day, your identity might be harder to hide."

"Then we better make it look good," Lange said.

A knock on the door. Lexi opened it. Kaplan and Noah wore satisfied expressions like they'd solved a puzzle.

Kaplan smiled. "We have a location."

Lexi opened the door wider and let everyone back inside. "Let's hear it."

Kaplan retrieved a remote from the table and brought up an aerial image on the wall-mounted flatscreen monitor at the room's far end. It showed the edge of a housing community. A freshly graded grid of unimproved streets was to the south and east.

"I remembered a new housing community under construction at the south end of Dallas near my house. Only the model homes and the club-house are under construction. They're almost done, so it's a prime remote location with some cover. The chance of a random vehicle or pedestrian wandering in is almost zero." She pointed to a graded street on the aerial image. "This street is freshly paved."

"What about access points?" Lexi asked.

"It's not perfect," Noah said, "but it's the best thing we could come up with on short notice. The north and west back up to existing housing with a solid cinder block fence, which is good. However, a temporary cyclone fence forms a perimeter to the south and east. They're flimsy and would only slow down a vehicle, not stop it. Road access is limited to two paved entry streets blocked by a chain-link gate."

"Okay. We would need a team outside the fence in case something goes haywire. What about lighting?"

"The construction sites have basic lighting to deter theft," Kaplan said. "And the street leading into the community has ample lampposts."

Lexi scanned the faces in the room. They all appeared satisfied with the location. "Okay. I'm sold. Where should we set up positions?"

"We should conduct the exchange on the road between the model homes and the clubhouse," Noah said. "The best vantage point would be from the clubhouse's roof, so I'll set up there. The exchange team should stage at the end of the street. I would put a team between the first and second model homes. Depending on where the Raven stops, they could come up behind him. That leaves one team to cover the south and east sides outside the fence line. They would have to move into place after the Raven arrives to avoid detection."

"I can set up cameras," Kaplan said, "giving me a real-time feed from the street and outside the clubhouse."

"I also want a drone in the air to eliminate surprises," Lexi said. Kaplan concurred. The location and setup were solid, but Lexi was concerned about the timing. "When can we set up?"

"Construction wraps up at six," Kaplan said. "Sunset is around eight. I'll set up the cameras before it gets dark. You should have everyone in place by then. We could schedule the exchange for nine."

"Then I should call the Raven at eight. Not give him time to scout the area. If he balks, we can regroup. That settles the where and the when. Director Keene, Agent Lange, and I have agreed on the how. We're not going to send in Segura. Lange will serve as a decoy."

The murmurs in the room suggested surprise, but everyone's nod said it was on.

Lexi focused on Kaplan again. "We might need to kill the lights at the construction site if they're too bright. We don't want the Raven making Lange before we can move in."

"I'll work on it," Kaplan said.

"Then it's set," Lexi said. "We'll have four vehicles. Keene will be with Lange and me. Noah, you're on your own at the clubhouse. Sinclair and Shaw, you're inside the fence at the model homes. Vasquez and White, you're on the street. I want everyone back here at six with their weapons and vests. I'll have night vision goggles waiting for everyone who needs them." Lexi turned to Kaplan. "I want a broad-spectrum signal jammer with enough range to cover the entire area."

Lexi cared deeply for nearly everyone in this operation. *Take no chances,* she told herself.

Eight p.m.

Lexi rubbed her face with both hands. She was in an impossible situation. They had Robert Segura, but the possibility of him leading Lexi's team to the Raven was secondary to isolating the locust technology. She hated to think it, but having only Nathan's life at risk, not also his son's, made the decision much easier. If his son was involved, Lexi would move heaven and earth to get him back. But that wasn't the case, and Nathan would make the same choice if the situation was reversed. All the players knew their roles. The team was armed, suited up, and in place for tonight's operation. Calling the Raven was the only thing remaining to set everything in motion.

Lexi glanced in the rearview mirror at Willie Lange in the backseat. She wore Robert Segura's clothes, a New York Yankees baseball cap, and dark-rimmed glasses with no magnification lenses. The worry lines had deepened on Lange's face since agreeing to act as a decoy during the prisoner exchange. If her head wasn't in the game, if she lost focus at the critical moment, she, Nathan, and anyone else the Raven had in his crosshairs could be killed.

Lexi turned to Maxwell in the front passenger seat. "Do you mind giving us a moment?"

"Sure." He exited the SUV and stepped away several yards in the dimly lit construction yard.

"Agent Lange, turn off your mic for a moment." Lexi turned hers off and waited for Lange to confirm hers was off too. "If you're not up for this, we can call this off and devise another plan."

Lange looked at Lexi's eyes in the mirror. "I can do this. I have to."

"Why do you have to?"

"I love him."

"I suspected as much after you used your key to his apartment. Does HR know?"

Lange shook her head. "No, and we don't plan to disclose. I'm retiring in June. Once I do, it won't matter."

"Are you sure you can go through with this? Because I need to know you can focus."

"I can do this, Lexi. I would never forgive myself if he died and I failed to do everything possible to save him. Nathan is flawed, but he's a good man and father."

"All right, then. Let's make the call and bring Nathan home." Lexi rolled down the passenger window. "You can come back now, Maxwell."

Once he returned, Lexi and Lange turned their mics on again. Lexi announced. "I'm making the call." The same ominous feeling Lexi had had the night before she was to face off with Tony Belcher in Las Vegas lingered inside the cabin of their SUV. She knew now, just as she knew then, that her nemesis did not intend for her to walk away alive. She would have to stay on her toes to make it back to Nita.

Lexi pulled from her pocket an ATF disposable phone issued for tonight's operation, dialed the number in the Raven's message, and put the call on speaker. It connected. She waited through several silent beats before saying, "Hello, Starshiy."

"Agent Mills, it's about time we spoke directly."

"Yes, it is. Before we get started, I'm curious about something, Raven."

"What has your curiosity piqued?" he asked.

"You left Agent Croft's son behind. Why?"

"This is a business, Agent Mills. My dealings are with you and Agent Croft, not his son. I never involve family like you have. Some things are simply too distasteful."

"Well, that's one thing in your favor." A part of Lexi wanted to believe his line in the sand so she could rest easier about Nita and her father, but Tony Belcher and Noah Black had taught her two important lessons. To never let her guard down with the people she loved, and every line, even those thought forbidden, could be crossed.

"Now for our business," the Raven said. "We both have something the other one wants. Are you prepared to trade?"

"Yes, but I know the capabilities at your fingertips. We meet in one hour at a place of my choosing."

"You're not in any position to dictate terms, Agent Mills. You took a member of my family."

"Oh, I think I am. Don't pretend we crossed the line. You should not have involved family in your work. We have Robert because you sent him. He designs your products. Without him, you'll soon be out of business."

"I see you have an understanding of the playing field," the Raven said.

"You're angry, but I'm just doing my job."

"And so am I," he said. "You either accept my terms, or Croft dies."

"That's unacceptable. It's my way or no way. The exchange is off. Croft accepted the dangers associated with the job the day he put on the badge." Lexi disconnected the call. Her stomach knotted, worried she'd overplayed her hand. Had she sealed Nathan's death?

Maxwell's silence meant he supported Lexi's move.

"What the hell did you do, Mills?" Panic filled Lange's voice.

"He's desperate," Lexi said. "Just wait."

"Trust her, Willie," Maxwell said. "Lexi's gut has never let me down. The

Raven is desperate. We have to control the playing field if we hope to get Croft back and capture the Raven."

"You may have killed Nathan." The anger in her voice could have cut through steel.

One minute passed.

Two. The knot in Lexi's stomach twisted tighter, making her nauseous.

Three. She fought the urge to throw up.

The phone rang. Lexi's shoulders dropped in relief. She answered. "Are you ready to meet, Raven?"

29

The door opened. Light from the corridor flowed inside Nathan's cell, sending a chill up his spine. He braced for more agony when the two men who had dragged him there rushed inside. They grabbed him by both arms, triggering a sharp pain in the left, and hauled him out with urgency. Something was finally happening.

The thugs jostled him down the hallway, clanking the chains around his wrists and ankles and dialing up the pain to a new level. They tugged him violently up a flight of stairs and through a door leading to a bare gravel yard outlined with a chain-link fence. *Wait*, he thought. This wasn't the same door they used to take him downstairs. There must have been two access points to the tunnels.

The sun had set, but the last slivers of light lost their fight against the darkening sky. A black Escalade with tinted windows and its tailgate up was five yards away. The Raven's men steered him toward it. One slipped a cloth hood over his head, sending Nathan into darkness again before both tossed him in the back, aggravating his arm again.

"If you don't want us to knock you out again, don't be a pain in the ass. Be still," one said, shoving Nathan's feet deeper inside until they no longer hung over the opening.

A mechanical sound whirred, and the tailgate latched shut, scrunching Nathan into the rear compartment. Three doors opened and closed. He sensed three people enter the Escalade before it started to move. The woody soap scent in the air told him the Raven was in the car, and the queasiness in his stomach told him this ordeal was about to end for him, but what about his son? The Raven was a ruthless killer and never left loose ends. Everything Nathan had dug up on him pointed to the horrible reality his son was dead. If an opportunity presented itself, even if it meant dying, Nathan would end the Raven for good.

Several minutes, maybe an hour, passed before the vehicle stopped and the doors opened. The doors shut, and they were in motion again. This repeated three more times before the tailgate opened. Nathan had no way of telling where they were, but based on the traffic sounds and road vibrations, he guessed they had left their rural surroundings and were in a city. Something was about to go down.

The cold night air rushed into the cabin. Hands grabbed Nathan's feet and yanked him toward the opening. The back of his head took another beating against the backseat and floor, making him nauseous again. If he survived, which he doubted after his failed escape, his injuries would likely have him out of commission for months.

His feet touched the ground. Standing straight made him dizzy. Multiple head injuries were likely the cause, but he hadn't eaten or drunk anything in a day and a half. Severe dehydration magnified his symptoms. After getting his bearings, he concentrated on his surroundings. The ground was hard, smooth, and flat, like a sidewalk or pavement. No light filtered through his hood, so he couldn't tell whether they were in a well-lit area. The distant noise of vehicle traffic said they were in a populated place. A slight breeze kissed his left side. Winds were out of the west this time of year, so he was likely facing north.

The men tugged on both arms, and the pain in his left roared again, but Nathan remained silent. He didn't want to give them the satisfaction of knowing their beatings had reaped the desired result and that he was on the verge of passing out from pain and dizziness. Nathan needed to grind through whatever this was until Lexi or Willie could find him.

One man removed the cloth hood from his head. Nathan glimpsed the area quickly before they put it back on. Dark street. Lampposts. Construction. Empty lots. Trees. Chain-link fence. No cars. They were in a city, but this place wasn't well-traveled at night.

The Raven appeared from the passenger side of the Escalade, carrying a metal ring resembling a bangle bracelet slightly smaller than a frisbee. His red eyes still gave Nathan the creeps. He flipped up a latch and lifted one section at a hinge before placing it around Nathan's neck.

"What the hell is that?" Nathan asked, but he suspected what it was. His breathing increased rapidly at the realization the Raven had placed an explosive device around his neck.

"It's my insurance policy against your partner. If she tries to trick me, you'll die before her eyes. It contains enough PETN to send your brain matter fifteen feet. It's quite sensitive, so I suggest no sudden moves."

Nathan wasn't familiar with PETN but was sure Lexi knew everything about it down to its chemical composition and could calculate a kill zone for this thing on the fly.

The Raven snapped the device in place and fiddled with it at the back. He stayed there for several moments before returning to face Nathan. "And do be careful with the tether. We wouldn't want you tripping and setting this off too early."

"Tether? What? With Robert gone, you couldn't figure out something more sophisticated than a string and some tin bracelet?"

"Come now, Agent Croft. I expected more from you. Throwing insults is very pedestrian. I know Agent Mills will employ defenses against the locusts, so this is an old-fashioned detonation cord, and I hold the trigger." He held up his left hand. A device attached to the other end of the tether was taped inside his palm with his thumb on the trigger. "Her jamming device will be useless. If she doesn't give me Robert, my associate will shoot, and you will fall and die in the explosion. As a failsafe, I added a timer. If the lock isn't opened within ten minutes, it will go off."

Shit, Nathan thought. Lexi would have her hands full, but he couldn't let the Raven see his worry. "You're a worn-out record, Raven. You've underestimated Lexi so many times you should have it tattooed on your ass."

The Raven harrumphed. "Colorful. I can see why Agent Mills has a soft spot for you. But don't underestimate my determination. Robert is family, and I will stop at nothing to get him back."

"Even though he's helping us."

"I'll know right away if he is and will deal with him if that be the case," the Raven said.

"What are you? Clairvoyant?"

"It will be in his eyes. If he can't look at me, I will know." The Raven gave Nathan the impression he believed Robert had likely betrayed him. That he was there to exact revenge, not rescue a captured brother. "Shall we, Agent Croft?"

The Raven gestured toward the smaller of the two men. He circled the Escalade and got into the driver's seat. The larger man gripped Nathan by the upper arm. This could be his only chance to take out the goon and the bastard who likely killed his son while preserving the life of the only man who could tell them where the locust technology was hidden. If Nathan lunged at him and they fell, the explosion would kill them all. Two years of hunting the Raven would be over, his son's murder would be avenged, and the country would be safe from the most dangerous weapon developed in decades.

Nathan pivoted on his heel, assuming the optimum angle to catch the Raven off balance. An image of how his son might have died at the Raven's hands sprang into his head. A bullet to the gut or a pistol-whipping to the head like Nathan had endured. What kind of man was Nathan if he didn't kill the man who killed his son when given a chance? One sudden move and he would join his son.

Nathan's breathing shallowed. The end was seconds away.

The Raven studied Nathan's eyes. "If you hope to see your son again, do exactly as I instruct."

"He's dead."

"Are you sure, Agent Croft?"

Logic told Nathan the Raven was lying. He would say anything, do anything to get Robert back. But his heart told him if his son was alive, he owed it to Wes to do whatever it took to get out of this. The thought of Wes losing his father too young, like he had, broke his heart. He had to fight to stay alive to avoid foisting immeasurable pain on his son.

"All right, Raven. We'll do this your way." Nathan clenched his fists and stepped backward. He'd have to signal Lexi to protect Segura at all costs.

The large guard yanked Nathan toward the front of the SUV. "Easy there, King Kong, unless the Raven has changed his mind and wants you to blow up with me." Nathan had a hard enough time maintaining his balance without this brute making him a human teeter-totter.

30

Ten minutes earlier

The lights at the end of the model home street went dark, signaling the ten-minute mark before the meeting time and putting Lexi's vehicle in the shadows. The two lights in front of the nearly finished clubhouse, one at the model home with the builder's office, and those on the main access road into the community remained on to better see the Raven when he approached and stopped at the exchange location.

"Thank you, Eagle Eye." Lexi let her vision slowly adjust to the darker conditions before pressing an index finger against her ear mic, securing it more tightly. "All right, people, stay alert. Eagle Eye, anything from the hawk?"

"Nothing," Kaplan replied. She'd had the drone up for the last fifteen minutes, scanning the area from fifty feet above the clubhouse. The early warning would give them a minute to make adjustments, depending on the force the Raven brought and where he deployed them.

Lexi adjusted the rearview mirror to better see Willie Lange in the back-seat. She was chewing her fingernails. "You're still nervous," Lexi said. "There's still time to call this off."

"Being nervous doesn't mean I'm having second thoughts. I'm worried the Raven will figure out it's a double-cross before Nathan is safe."

"I am too, but everyone here tonight is well trained. We've given ourselves every possible advantage. Trust in the plan and the people."

Lange grinned. "You're a natural leader, Lexi." She shifted her stare to the front passenger seat. "Director Keene, you made a wise choice putting her in charge of Task Force Zero Impact."

"From the day we met, I knew Lexi had good instincts. She knows how to work a problem and leverage everyone and everything around her to get the job done."

"I see it too." Lange shifted her attention back to Lexi. "Have you considered putting your name in the hat for my SRT command slot when I retire this summer?"

Lexi had considered the possibility, but commanding a Special Response Team meant more time behind a desk than in the field. She was an explosives expert and wasn't sure if she was ready to put her passion behind her. *Unless*, she thought. Lexi could redefine the role and make the commander an integral part of the team in the field, and not only during specific taskings.

"Maybe."

"Well, I think you'd be a great fit if you do. The ATF could use more commanders like you."

"Team One, this is Eagle Eye," Kaplan said over the radio. "I've got movement. One dark Escalade is approaching from the east."

"This could be it, people," Lexi said. Only one vehicle meant the Raven didn't bring a strong force. Maybe he didn't have an extensive network of people like Tony Belcher did and relied on his tools and cunning. "Stay on your toes. Sound off."

One by one, her team reported in—Coby Vasquez and Daniel White from a block away, Noah Black on the clubhouse roof, and Lathan Sinclair with Kaplan Shaw sitting in a car between two model homes. They had every direction covered, including the high ground. She'd instructed the Raven to meet on the street in front of the clubhouse. The position would give Noah an unobstructed view of the exchange.

"Noah," Lexi said, "when you see the red of his eyes, you have a green light to take the kill shot if you think it's safe."

"Copy, Lexi," he said. "I won't let you down."

"Eagle Eye," Lexi said, "give us a play-by-play when they turn onto Hyde Street."

"Copy, Lexi," Kaplan said.

Lexi handed Lange her cuffs over her shoulder. "Make sure they're loose enough to slip off." One ratchet sound, then a second. Lange acknowledged with a silent, nervous nod.

"Target turned onto Hyde," Kaplan said. "They're going through the open gate. Noah, you should have a visual."

"Got him," Noah said. "They stopped short of the light."

The Escalade was in the shadows between the clubhouse and model homes. Its headlights were still on, making it impossible for Lexi to discern who was inside. She grabbed her night vision binoculars and focused on the windshield, but the direct light from the headlamps produced too much glare.

"Front doors opening," Kaplan said. "They resemble the men from the apartment security cameras at Croft's place. They're opening the tailgate. A third man in a hood. It's off. I can't make him out from this angle."

"It's Croft," Noah said. "Identity confirmed. It's Croft."

"Team Four," Lexi said, "move into place."

"Copy. Moving in," Coby said.

"Another door is opening. It looks like the Raven," Kaplan said.

"Do you have a shot?" Lexi asked.

"Negative," Noah said. "He's behind the SUV."

"Raven is putting something around Croft's neck," Kaplan said. "One man went back to the car. He's in the driver's seat. The others are on the move with Croft, going toward the front of the car. There's something between Croft and Raven. A rope."

"Zooming in," Noah said. A pause. "Lexi, the Raven has a dead man switch in his hand. It looks like it's connected to a detonation cord, leading to a collar bomb around Croft's neck."

"Copy." Lexi ran a hand through her hair, considering the dangers at play. "Do not take the shot. Repeat. Do not take the shot."

The Raven's devices had one thing in common—redundant triggers. An explosive collar trigger should have a wire, timer, remote control, or pressure plate. The wired trigger meant the Raven expected her to employ a signal jammer against the locust, eliminating the likelihood of a remote trigger. Lexi's gut told her the Raven pulled out all the stops and added every trigger possible, making the device much more difficult to disarm.

"Can you take out the tether? We need to sever the Raven's control."

"You mean, can I shoot a fly between the eyes while it does a somersault?" The doubt in Noah's voice said his confidence was low.

"Remember David Lindsey at the trailer in Bowie?" Lexi recalled when Noah shot Lindsey in the temple from the hood of an SUV fifty yards away through a dirty window with broken blinds. She didn't wait for a response. "You threaded the needle then. I know you, Noah Black. You can do it again."

"I'll do my best, but I'll need Croft to be still. No somersaults."

"Wait for my mark." Lexi's heart raced faster. The Raven would be within striking distance in moments, but she couldn't get to him while Nathan's life was still in danger. She inhaled the encouraging words she'd given Willie Lange and put her faith in the precision of the people she trusted most in the world to execute the plan. "What are they doing, Eagle Eye?"

"They're waiting at the bumper," Kaplan said.

The Raven was slick. Lexi needed to draw him out more by showing her hand first. "That's our cue." Lexi turned on her headlights to camouflage them from the Raven's line of sight before opening the driver's door. Maxwell followed out the passenger side.

Lexi opened the rear door and pulled Lange from the backseat. Her boss' hands were loosely cuffed at her belly. Lexi patted her on the shoulder with her left hand, feeling the lightweight ballistic vest under Segura's clothes. It wasn't the highest quality protection, but it was the thickest model they had that wouldn't give away its presence.

"Ready, Agent Lange?"

"I think it's time you called me Willie."

"Ready, Willie?"

"Yes."

Lexi said to her team, "Everyone gets to go home tonight. No heroics. Eagle Eye, be sure to get this on tape."

Before Lexi stepped away from their SUV, Lange said, "Wait. If you have to choose between saving Nathan or me, you choose him."

Lexi squinted, reading determination in Lange's eyes. She clearly loved him. "I said everyone goes home tonight."

Lange's grip grew tighter, nearly desperate. "That's an order, Mills. Save Nathan. He goes home to his son."

Lexi acknowledged with a firm nod, hoping desperation would not morph into disaster. She held Lange by the upper arm and guided her toward the Raven's car. While Lange kept her head down and baseball cap low, Lexi fixed her stare at the shadowy figures between the headlights.

"Show yourself, Raven," Lexi shouted. She couldn't see him but felt his presence. Every inch of her skin tingled at being this close. "Let me see Croft."

"I'm sure you've already confirmed it's him and gotten a good look at the device around his neck."

"A tether means you've left your favorite toy at home, which makes the playing field even." Lexi was careful not to mention the locusts by name since Kaplan recorded everything.

"It's safe to say we both anticipated the other's first move. We each have something the other wants. We better get to it. Agent Croft has only ten minutes from when I put on the collar before this trade is moot." The Raven's threat meant Lexi's suspicion was correct. The device also had a timer. "Send Robert."

Lexi spoke softly to Lange and into her mic, "Noah, advise when you have a shot at the tether. Lange, when he fires, I need you to turn and steer Nathan to the model home. Kaplan and Lathan will be your cover."

"Got it." Lange moved forward, taking steady steps while keeping her head down and hands clasped at her belly to prevent the cuffs from falling to the pavement.

Lexi focused on the headlights. Someone moved toward her position. "Eagle Eye, report."

"Croft is moving toward you. Tether is still attached. He's cuffed. Ankle shackles."

Nathan came into focus the closer he came. He limped. No. He wobbled. "Stay upright, Nathan," Lexi whispered. "Lange, make sure he doesn't fall. The collar might be unstable."

"Got it," Lange said softly.

They were ten feet apart.

Five feet.

Two.

Lange raised her head.

No, no, no, Lexi thought. *He could see you.* She didn't trust the Raven's word about not bringing the locusts with him. He might have one up with a camera to identify Segura.

"Brother," the Raven called out.

Lange kept her gaze on Nathan when they came even. Nathan took one more step and stopped before looking over his shoulder.

"I have a shot," Noah said.

The Raven called out, but this time with a questioning tone. "Brother?"

"Take it!" Lexi said. "Take it." *Please*, she whispered.

A shot rang out.

Nathan flinched and wobbled.

"Gun. Gun. Gun." Kaplan alerted.

A hail of gunfire erupted.

"Nooo!" Lange lunged toward him and fell to the ground.

"All teams converge. Noah, fire at will."

One shot after another pierced the night air. Lexi and Maxwell dashed toward the Escalade with their guns out and firing. Kaplan emerged from between the model homes, firing too. A team SUV appeared from Kaplan's position as the headlights of the Raven's car wobbled and moved backward before turning off. He was escaping.

"Raven on the move!" Lexi shouted.

Nathan wobbled again, more than the first time. He was about to topple over.

Another set of headlights appeared. They must have belonged to Team Four. The Raven continued to move backward before disappearing behind the clubhouse. Gunfire continued.

Lexi reached Nathan. He fell into her arms, dropping her to her knees. "I got you."

Nathan's muscles simultaneously relaxed in palpable relief. "Thank God. I thought I was going to kill you." He turned his focus to Agent Lange on the ground. She wasn't moving. "Willie!" Panic coated his voice. He jerked toward her, but Lexi held him firmly.

"Stop," she shouted. "You could trigger an explosion. I'll check."

Maxwell arrived and held Nathan upright.

Lexi crawled to Lange. It was too dark to ascertain her injuries effectively, but the expanding dark pool of liquid around her head wasn't a good sign. Lexi rolled her over. "Willie?" She pressed a hand against her chest but felt no movement of breathing. Two fingers against the side of her neck discovered no pulse. "Call an ambulance. Officer down!"

Lexi started chest compressions. Thinking of how much time was left on the explosive timer jumbled the count in her head. She was the only one capable of disarming the device, but with Maxwell's injured arm, she was also the only one who could keep Willie Lange's heart pumping. She remembered her boss' last order: *Save Nathan.* The blood coming from Lange's head looked devastating. Even if she kept her heart pumping, Lange was likely brain dead. She needed to keep her promise.

Lexi stopped. Her prosthetic slowed her effort to rise from her knees. "I need to disarm the bomb."

"No! Help Willie," Nathan cried out.

Lexi recognized the pain in his voice. It held the same anguish Lexi felt when she discovered her parents lying in blood on their kitchen floor. The same agony when she realized Tony Belcher had abducted Nita. It was a pain that, once experienced, no one was ever the same again.

31

Kaplan ran toward Lexi. Her breathing was labored. "I have the drone circling on autopilot and called 911. Help is coming."

"I need you to take over CPR while I disarm the explosive."

Kaplan started chest compressions on Willie Lange, alternating with breaths at a ratio of thirty to two.

Nathan looked on with horror.

Lexi's heart went out to him, but she had to deal with an equally pressing issue—the explosive around his neck. "I need to get you to a safe distance," she said, estimating thirty feet would be enough for Lange and Kaplan to avoid injury. She and Maxwell tugged him toward their car. "I'll need you on your knees, Nathan." He knelt, facing Kaplan as she continued pumping Willie Lange's heart to keep blood flowing to her organs.

A third team vehicle sped away in the distance. It must have been Noah.

"Maxwell, I'll need light to disarm this thing," Lexi said, moving behind Nathan to inspect the lock and tether. Three feet of cord remained, testifying to Noah's marksmanship.

Maxwell aimed his cell phone flashlight at the device. "Is this enough?"

"It will have to do," Lexi said. "Nathan, did the Raven say anything about the explosive?"

"He said it has enough PETN to send brain parts fifteen feet. The lock activated a ten-minute timer. It will go off if I fall."

Lexi did the math in her head. To send brain matter that distance and considering the diameter of the collar, she calculated the Raven used military grade PETN with ninety to one hundred grains of explosive material. That much PETN would kill anyone within two feet, damage lungs within three, and create ear damage within six.

"Maxwell, I'll need you to stand six feet away."

Maxwell backed up. "That won't give you enough light. How close can I really get?"

"Three feet but no closer." Lexi continued her inspection of the collar. "Give me your phone, so I can see the entire device." She circled Nathan, noting the collar was one inch in diameter with a smooth aluminum casing. It was loose-fitting enough for Lexi to see two wires running the collar's circumference on the inner side. They were likely connected to the timer power source. Cutting it would likely detonate the device, leaving the lock at the back as her only approach.

Lexi returned the phone to Maxwell. "Move back. I need to cut the power first."

The timer wasn't visible, but there was a small metal box, two inches wide by one inch tall, attached to the collar near the latch. The lid was secured by four tiny screws. Lexi suspected it contained the timer and battery. Without knowing how much time was left, she had to hurry.

Lexi dug a set of small screwdrivers from her cargo pocket and retrieved the appropriate flathead to do the job. She spun the screws loose one by one, letting them fall to the pavement. Once the fourth was off, she carefully pried the lid off, exposing a circuit board with a digital timer and a button cell battery with one screw holding it in. The timer had twenty-two seconds. The cell phone light was at the wrong angle and cast shadows on the screw holding the battery in place, but she didn't have time to reposition Maxwell and remove the battery. Lexi had to do her best, given the circumstances.

"Don't move, Nathan." Lexi positioned the screwdriver head over the screw slot, hoping she would hit it dead center, but she missed. With no time to waste, she felt for the screw with her left index finger and positioned it as a guide.

Fourteen seconds.

Sweat dripping from her forehead, Lexi tried again, sliding the tool head down her fingernail until it seated in the slot.

Twelve seconds.

She withdrew her left hand and twisted the screwdriver madly with her right. Time was running out. She had to work quickly. Sweat trickled into her mouth, the salty taste reminding her that precision was critical. If Lexi had followed Lange's order and hadn't stopped to perform CPR on her, she would have had another minute left on the timer and would not have been rushed. The mistake might cost both their lives.

Seven seconds.

The securing arm shifted, signaling it was loose enough to move out of the way.

Five seconds.

Lexi slid the tool between the battery and the metal holder.

Three seconds.

She applied force and popped the battery clear. The timer went dark. Lexi lowered her head and released a long breath. That was too close for comfort, but they weren't out of danger yet. The lock appeared simple, but nothing about a Raven device was ever straightforward. Time was the only thing going for her without the ticking clock. Now she could locate the hidden switch.

"Timer's cut," Lexi said. "You can breathe now."

"How close was it?" Maxwell asked.

"You don't want to know."

Nathan silently shuddered, keeping his stare on Kaplan and Lange. Kaplan hadn't stopped CPR, but Lexi knew her effort was futile. She could do little to help Lange but could do everything possible to reunite Nathan with his son tonight.

Minutes earlier

"All teams converge," Lexi ordered. "Noah, fire at will."

That was Coby Vasquez's cue to block the Raven's avenue of escape. "We're up," he said to Daniel White in the front passenger seat. He lowered his night vision goggles over his eyes, slammed the gear shifter into drive, and pressed the gas pedal to the floor, screeching the tires against the pavement. If he approached in the dark, he could surprise the Raven as he retraced his path to the open exit.

"Raven on the move!" Lexi shouted over the radio.

Coby turned onto the community access road and roared past the gate. The Escalade appeared from the corner with no headlights, going in reverse. It wobbled while turning but gained speed and moved away from Coby's SUV.

Coby gave it more gas, closing the distance between the two cars. They were nearly bumper to bumper. The Raven's car drifted left and suddenly dropped speed. The two vehicles collided, sending Coby's SUV into a fishtail. Daniel braced himself with a straight arm against the dashboard. The force was too great to correct, propelling them into a spinout. They turned around once, twice. Coby couldn't be sure, but he thought the Raven's Escalade executed a J-turn, flipping around and continuing its route forward.

Another team SUV took up the chase. "Team Two in pursuit," Lathan Sinclair said over the radio. Coby rested a little easier, knowing his partner was behind the wheel.

"Call an ambulance. Officer down!" Lexi said over the air.

When Coby straightened the SUV, his heart skipped a beat. He'd prevented a rollover but was more concerned about Lexi's message. Keene, Lange, or Croft was hit and in grave enough condition to require an emergency medical response, but he couldn't stop. His job was to pursue the Raven at all costs.

Coby gripped the steering wheel so tight a stitch in the leather strap snapped. Throwing off his night goggles, he turned on the headlights and pressed the gas. He followed the cloud of dust and picked up the pursuit within seconds.

"Holy shit," Daniel said. "Where'd you learn to do that?"

"Lexi Mills had us take the tactical driving course. It comes in handy."

"I'd say so."

The Escalade crashed through the temporary fence, sending two panels askew like rag dolls. Lathan was seconds behind but kept pace with the Raven.

Coby sped up, staying on their tail. "Team Four, back in pursuit." He sped through the opening in the fence and bounced over the curb onto a street. The jolt reverberated through his jaw. He followed Lathan's taillights along the south end of the neighboring housing community. At the first stop sign, the Raven braked hard and turned left. Lathan followed.

An explosion at the intersection sent Lathan's SUV wobbling, turning it on its side. It slid toward the sidewalk, slamming broadside into a light pole. The turn had reduced most of the force, making the impact survivable, so Coby continued the chase while radioing it in.

"Team Two crashed. Intersection of Hyde and Clairmont. Help needed. Team Four in pursuit."

"Team Three en route," Noah radioed back.

The ticking timer was no longer an issue, and Lexi had reached the point where she should don her bomb suit, but while Willie Lange's life hung in the balance, she doubted Nathan would sit still for it. However, her helmet would provide her with some protection and additional lighting to complete her examination.

"Nathan, I need to get my helmet for the extra lighting. I have the circuit board exposed, so I need you to remain still. Can you do that for me?"

"She's dead, isn't she?" He sounded numb from the harsh reality unfolding before his eyes.

Lexi needed Nathan to focus, so she spoke about facts, not her suspicions. "I'm not sure, but you should know we found your son at your apartment. He's unhurt and is in protective custody at the FBI building."

Nathan slumped slightly. "Thank God."

"I'll be right back. Maxwell, I need you to stay six feet back." Lexi darted to the rear of her SUV, popped the tailgate, and unzipped her gear bag. She pulled out her helmet and paused to text Nita in case something went wrong. It simply read, *Love you.*

Re-pocketing her phone, she dashed back to Nathan, slipped on her helmet, and flipped on the external lights. She focused on the collar's fastener. It was a simple draw latch, utilizing tension to pull two metal pieces, a lever and a keeper, securely together in the same plane. Its presence was a giant warning flag. The design was the primary choice by engineers to reduce vibration or rattling and provide constant compression. Using it meant the Raven wanted to guard against accidental opening or loosening of the latch, which meant any change in pressure would detonate the explosive. The Raven had intended this latch to be for single use. Opening it would be the last thing Lexi did in this world.

Lexi had to find a way around it by thinking it through logically. If securing the latch shut initiated the timer, the mechanism must have had an electronic component requiring a power source. She'd already removed the timer battery, which could have also powered the latch switch, but every Raven device she'd encountered had redundancies. She bet her life—and Nathan's—the latch had an independent power supply. The problem was finding it without disturbing the triggers.

Lexi ran a fingertip across the circumference of the collar, feeling for any difference in composition. The only variation was the timer box. The second battery had to be there, so she used the flathead screwdriver to pry up each circuit board corner from the clips securing it to the bottom of the metal casing.

At least one wire connected the timer to the latch, so Lexi carefully raised one long edge of the board, being careful not to rip it, stopping at a forty-five-degree angle. As suspected, she discovered the second battery to the latch but also found the Raven's surprise—a second wire. The additional wire suggested the design contained a redundant circuit to activate the latch trigger. The device might have triggered if she had inadvertently ripped the wire from the second power source while removing the circuit board.

Lexi had a choice—cut both wires simultaneously or remove the power supply. The availability of space would determine which method was the most viable. Closer inspection revealed a small screw holding in place a securing arm over the battery. To remove it, Lexi would need to flip the board upright at a ninety-degree angle. However, the tension between the circuit board and the primary wire leading to the latch told her the wire was already stretched to its maximum limit. Raising the board to such an angle would break the wire and detonate the device.

Lexi was left with only one complicated option. She needed to prop up the board to free up both hands to cut the wires. She could use a toothpick from her toolkit if the device was stationary. However, the explosive was attached to a man who could do nothing to help while his friend and lover slowly died several feet away. If he flinched at the precise moment Lexi was about to cut the wires, it could mean disaster for them both. To be safe, she would need a third hand.

"I need to take a step back, Nathan. I'll be a minute. Please be as still as possible."

Lexi backed up six feet to Maxwell and spoke softly to explain the two wires and the dangers involved. "Without a third hand to steady the board—"

"Say no more," Maxwell said. "Tell me what to do."

Lexi hated putting her friend in danger, but if she shielded him with her body, he might only lose one arm. Lexi would only lose both with her helmet on, but Nathan would lose his life. "Are you sure?" She searched his eyes for any glimmer of doubt but found none.

"I trust you. Let's do this."

An explosion in the distance boomed, making Lexi flinch. A bright flash in the direction of the car chase caught her eye, taking her breath away. Either her team had ended the pursuit in a fiery crash, or the Raven had laid his escape route with explosives. But who was involved? The overwhelming instinct to jump in her car and help rattled her until the radio chirped.

"Team Two crashed. Intersection of Hyde and Clairmont. Team Four in pursuit."

Lexi gasped. Lathan was in the vehicle that crashed. She brought both hands to the sides of her helmet, thinking how much he had already given to the Boyko case. He'd already taken a beating to maintain Agent Kent's cover. How much more did he have to give?

"Team Three en route," Noah radioed back.

Thank God, she thought. Noah would save him. Lathan would be in good hands.

Lexi released a loud breath, refocused on the danger facing her partner, and fished out two wire snips before returning to her partner. "We have a plan, Nathan, but I need you to remain absolutely still while I cut two wires attached to the collar latch. Can you do that for me?"

"Yes." His response became machine-like as he watched Kaplan exhaust herself, performing lifesaving measures.

"Okay," Lexi said. "Don't move." She raised the circuit board to a forty-five-degree angle and instructed Maxwell to hold it in place with his right hand while kneeling behind her for maximum cover.

Sirens sounded in the distance. Help for Willie Lange was seconds away. And, if Lexi had chosen wrong, the first responders could help her and Maxwell, too.

Lexi gripped a pair of snips in each hand and positioned them over each wire. She silently whispered, "I love you, Nita," before saying, "I'll cut on one."

She took three steadying breaths, rechecked her hand positions, and counted down.

"Three, two—"

An explosion.

32

All hell had broken loose. Nathan Croft had a bomb around his neck. Willie Lange had been shot. Lathan Sinclair had crashed in a high-speed pursuit. And the Raven was getting away. Noah had severed the tether connecting the explosive trigger, but by the time he'd reset to aim at the Raven, his target had already taken cover inside the Escalade. He'd fired several times at the frame and windows to take out the driver or disable the vehicle, but the bullets did little damage. The car was likely reinforced.

Noah sped through the fresh gap in the fence and turned toward the bright flash. Smoke rose through the cone of light cast by the streetlamps at the intersection a hundred yards away and disappeared into the night sky. Suspecting the worst, Noah muted his radio mic to avoid saying something that might distract Lexi. He counted down the distance with each passing yard, hoping the crash wasn't devastating or the car wasn't engulfed in flames.

He braked hard at the corner, preparing to make a left, but he had too much speed and downshifted to compensate like Lexi had taught him. Entering the turn, he saw the crash site at the light pole. Smoke billowed from the hood, but the fire wasn't visible. It was close, too close to stop short of it. He kept constant pressure on the brakes until he straightened out before slamming on them to come to a skidding halt.

Slamming the transmission into park, Noah flew from his car and darted toward the wreckage. The driver's door opened, and Lathan stumbled out, falling to his knees in the gutter.

"Whoa, buddy." Noah rushed over. "Are you okay?"

"I'm fine, just a little shell-shocked." Lathan shook his head hard as if clearing out the cobwebs. "Let's get that son of a bitch."

"Can you walk?" Noah gripped Lathan by the elbow when he rose to his feet. "Yeah, I'm good." Stepping toward Noah's vehicle, he was slower than usual, taking narrower strides, but at least they were straight.

Noah jogged over, slid into the driver's seat, and waited for Lathan to buckle in before continuing the chase. He activated his mic again to pass along the good news. "This is Three. Lathan is okay. He's with me. Back on the hunt." He glanced at Lathan. "Track Team Four's position on your phone."

"I'm on it."

Noah sped down the street, hoping Lathan would pick up Coby's signal.

"I got him," Lathan said. "A mile east. Go straight."

When Noah pressed the gas more, a second explosion sounded. "Lexi!" He slammed on the brakes, fearing the worst. His car skidded to a stop. "Lexi! Respond."

One second passed.

Two. His breathing shallowed.

Three. His heart nearly stopped.

Four.

"Noah? Is that you?"

Recognizing the pained, rushed voice, Noah released a giant breath. "Yes. Are you safe?"

"I'm fine," Lexi said. "The explosive is disarmed. The ambulance is pulling in."

"Then the explosion must have involved the Raven or Team Four. We had a bead on them. I'm headed there now."

Lathan relayed the GPS instructions from his phone and appeared more alert with each passing second.

Noah made the final turn onto a rural road, discovering a team SUV had flipped over and was on the shoulder. Flames lapped from the engine compartment and tracked to the gravel, following a trail of engine fluids. Gasoline leaked from the tank and spread toward the fire. A body was strapped into the front seat but wasn't moving. The Raven was nowhere in sight, but saving Noah's teammates had become more critical.

Noah stopped the car. Lathan jumped out and took the passenger side. It was the closest. Noah circled the upturned SUV and rushed to the driver's door. Coby was strapped in upside down, unconscious. The windshield was shattered, but the side windows were intact. Noah tried the door, but it was locked. He suspected the same was true for the passenger side.

Gas was still pouring from the tank. Weeds along the roadside caught fire. Time was running out. They needed to get their teammates out now.

"Break the glass with your gun!" Noah pulled his pistol, gripping it by the frame, and struck the window with all his might. It shattered. He heard the other window crack. Reaching inside, he unlocked the door and pried it open with a loud creak. Lathan had done the same. He pressed the seatbelt release button, but the mechanism was jammed. Coby was stuck, but Daniel fell to the roof in a thump, and Lathan pulled him out by the arms.

The fire grew hotter and brighter, washing the interior compartment in an orange glow. The smell of burning chemicals grew stronger. Flames poked through the floorboard near the pedals. They were out of time.

Noah holstered his weapon, retrieved his pocketknife from its sheath attached to his belt, and began slicing through the sturdy strap. Coby thrashed and cried in agony as the flames inched up his leg. Noah ignored his screams and cut at a feverish pace until the belt broke, sending Coby to the roof.

Noah clutched Coby's wrists and dragged him clear of the wreckage. Coby's right shoe was scorched, and the rubber sole was melted, but no flames were visible. Noah didn't stop until they were safely behind his SUV.

A bright flash. Loud explosion. A wave of heat rushed through like a whirlwind. Noah lay on top of Coby, shielding him from flying chunks of metal that crashed to the ground in rapid succession. It sounded like a hailstorm. When the barrage stopped, Noah popped his head up and looked Coby in the eye.

Coby's breathing was labored, but he smiled and said, "Thank you, friend, but I usually like to be wined and dined first."

The second Lexi placed the collar bomb in a bucket for safekeeping and removed his shackles, Nathan darted toward Willie Lange and fell to his knees near her head. Kaplan didn't stop performing chest compressions despite appearing fatigued.

Maxwell stepped beside Lexi, shoulder to shoulder. Both looked at the sad scene several yards away. "Nathan was right," he said. "She's dead."

A heaviness weighed on Lexi, like wading through a stream that kept getting deeper and deeper, but Maxwell deserved an answer. "Yes, she is."

She considered relieving Kaplan, but the distinctive red glow of approaching emergency vehicles came into view. The ambulance rig and a police cruiser rolled onto the street, stopping near the clubhouse. Paramedics jumped out, opened the back, and retrieved a gurney loaded with multiple boxes of equipment.

Lexi and Maxwell stepped closer. Their friends would need them.

One medic urged Nathan back while another rested a hand on Kaplan's shoulder. "You did well. We'll take it from here."

Maxwell guided Kaplan back to a safe distance. Her shoulders sagged, and her arms hung limply like windblown laundry on a clothesline.

Lexi gently pulled Nathan to his feet. "They need room to work, Nathan. Let's step back a few feet."

Nathan backpedaled with Lexi. "She hasn't moved an inch since being shot."

"I know," Lexi whispered and clutched his hand.

He gripped it tighter. "I should call her sister."

"Let's wait until we know something for sure."

The medics worked at lightning speed, assessing vitals and attaching leads. One resumed CPR while another prepared the defibrillator. The machine hissed a high-pitched sound until one announced, "Clear." He pressed the paddles against Lange's chest and torso, arching her back violently. She twitched once but showed no other signs of life.

"Still a flatline," the other said.

They charged and zapped Lange again and a third and fourth time before the older medic made the call. "It's time." He glanced at Lexi and others, shaking his head. The news wasn't good. Willie Lange was dead.

33

Six hours ago, paramedics said Willie Lange had died. Lexi hadn't left Nathan Croft's side since, not at the scene and not at the hospital to get his injuries tended to. Numb was the word he could find to describe himself. He and Willie had an on-and-off thing since his divorce five years ago. It was more off than on at times, but they always gravitated back to each other when things got rough or were flat-out lonely. Love was there, but not the "can't live without you" type in the movies. Losing her still hurt.

Boarding the elevator in the FBI building, Nathan tried putting the horrible image of the medics giving up their lifesaving measures out of his head to stay in the now. Lexi stood to his left, and Maxwell Keene was at his right. But his mind kept drifting back. Keene had taken charge of the scene. He'd called in an FBI forensics team and had their two wrecked vehicles towed to the FBI compound for examination. Noah Black boarded the elevator next. He'd kept close to Kaplan Shaw since explaining the events at the crash site. He and Lathan Sinclair were damn heroes for rescuing Daniel White and Coby Vasquez before the SUV exploded.

All eight crammed inside the elevator, and a gloomy silence hung over them while they rode to the fourth floor. According to the Emergency Room doctors, White, Vasquez, and Sinclair should have been resting at home for several days, but they were here, sticking together like a family should after the traumatic loss they'd been dealt. The only positive notes tonight were Lexi disarming the bomb and what was about to transpire.

The elevator door opened. Weary and beaten, the ragtag team exited two by two with Nathan and Lexi in the lead. The entrance to Maxwell's office near the end of the hallway opened, making Nathan's breath hitch. Wesley had stepped into the corridor. His slow, sad smile told of exhaustion from hours of worry about his father. The feeling was mutual.

Nathan increased his speed, pulling away from the group. Coming face to face with Wesley, he pulled him into a long, emotional embrace, quaking in relief. He'd spent most of his captivity convinced his son was dead, and it nearly broke him.

Wesley released his hold and took inventory of his father. "Lexi said you were hurt."

"Nothing is broken, but I'm bruised as hell. The ER doc popped every-thing back into place and gave me some pain meds." Nathan gripped his son's upper arms and inspected him from head to toe. He tried hiding the worry in his eyes. "But you. Did they hurt you?"

"No. They knocked me out with some drug. The next thing I know, Lexi and Willie were waking me up." Wesley looked over his father's shoulder, studying the faces in the hallway. "Where *is* Willie?"

Nathan felt the blood rush from his face. He opened his mouth to explain but could utter only one word, "I..." before his voice fell off.

Lexi stepped forward and rested a hand on the small of Nathan's back. "Let's take this inside." She ushered them into Keene's office. The agent Maxwell had assigned to guard Wes stood from his chair. "Thanks for watching Wes," Lexi said. "Can we have the room?"

"Of course."

Once the agent left, Lexi sat on the guest chair. Nathan was glad she stayed. He invited Wes to sit on the couch. His son's questioning expression said he already suspected the news wasn't good. "Was she hurt?"

"Wes," Nathan started, but he couldn't find the words. He lowered his head, thinking of Willie's lifeless body on the street.

"She's dead," Wes said slowly. Sadly.

"Yes, she is. She died rescuing me. Now I need to work with Lexi and the team to find the man who killed her."

"It was the Raven, wasn't it?"

"Yes." Nathan formed his hands into fists, feeling the heat rise in his belly, the same fire he felt when he'd thought Wes was dead. "And when we find him, I guarantee he won't take another breath. Until then, I've arranged for you to stay at Director Keene's house. He has a security team around his place."

"Then get the son of a bitch."

If it was the last thing Nathan did, he would do precisely that.

The team gathered in the control room next to the high security holding cell where they'd kept Robert Segura since his capture. Their goal was to get Segura to give up the Raven. And based on what Kaplan cobbled together, Lexi was convinced it wouldn't be as difficult as the others suspected. She'd seen the doubt in Robert's eyes the last time she questioned him, and now she had the ammunition to push him over the edge.

Lexi glanced at Nathan. His face was still pale, and he moved more slowly than his usual sure pace, but he had a fire in his eyes. She grew concerned, pulled him into a corner to speak privately, and whispered, "Are you sure you're okay? I need to know your head is straight. This might be our last chance to smoke out the Raven."

"If you're asking if I'm as good as ever, the answer is no. If you want to know if I'm well enough to find the bastard who killed Willie, the answer is hell, yes. Remember when you jumped out of a speeding car seconds before it blew up and went right back to work? You were beat up then, but I never questioned your ability."

"I had a few cuts and bruises," Lexi said. "You have a concussion and had a partially dislocated shoulder."

"But I'm still standing. Don't take this away from me, Lexi."

Nathan was still in charge of the case, but Lexi could invoke ATF protocols following injuries like his and sideline him. However, she was sure he would go around her if she did. Having him working with her would be safer than chasing after him.

"All right, but I call the shots. You follow my orders."

Nathan offered a sharp salute. "Yes, ma'am."

They placed their weapons and electronics on the plastic tray, and Lexi nodded to Kaplan, queuing her to unlock the door. Once Lexi and Nathan entered the cage area, communication would be available over the landline phone on the wall or by giving hand signals through the six cameras to Kaplan.

Lexi pushed the door open at the buzz and flipped on the bank of wall switches, bathing the room in bright fluorescent lights. After pressing the button to slide open the plexiglass covering the bars at the cell door, she and Nathan grabbed two hard plastic chairs and slid them across the linoleum floor. The screech was loud enough to wake the dead.

Segura popped up from his bunk. "What the hell?"

"Rise and shine," Lexi said.

Segura threw the blanket off and swung his feet to the floor, rubbing his eyes. "What time is it?"

"Almost three-thirty."

"Morning or afternoon?" Segura asked.

"Does it matter?"

"I guess not. What do you want?"

"We have something you might like to see." Lexi twirled an index finger over her shoulder, Kaplan's cue to bring up the sizeable flatscreen monitor on the wall behind Lexi. The thirty-second video would play on a loop while she talked.

"What is this?" Segura asked.

"A prisoner exchange. My partner," Lexi wagged her thumb toward Nathan, "for you." The video showed the aerial view of the doomed exchange from the drone Kaplan had hovering over a model home. It stopped before showing the Raven getting away and Lexi rushing to Lange to check for signs of life. She wanted him to think his mentor was weaker than he believed and was in federal custody. If Robert knew they were still desperate to find the Raven, he might not cooperate without a deal. "As you can see, it didn't go as the Raven had planned."

A grin formed on Segura's lips when Lange fell to the ground. "Your decoy must not have been convincing."

"Don't be so sure. The video clip was enhanced to eliminate shadows and magnify the low lighting." Lexi twirled her finger again, the cue to bring up the unaltered version of the video. "These were the actual conditions last night."

Robert squinted, focusing on the screen.

"It was too dark for the Raven to make out the decoy's identity before he shot. I've asked myself a dozen times tonight, why did your so-called brother fire, and why did he only fire at you before trying to flee. Then I wondered how long it would be before the Raven leveraged the technology you designed to finish the job. As you know, he has a long reach, even from behind bars."

Segura stepped up to the bars and studied both versions of the video, watching them repeatedly. He kept his eyes on the screen and asked, "What do you want?"

Lexi had him, and the Raven being on the loose was still her ace in the hole.

"We want his toys. The more we can take away from him, the less he can use against you. After seeing the video, do you want him to have the locusts at his disposal?"

Segura stared at the screen for several beats before saying, "I should have taken Starshiy's advice long ago and called my grandmother's place home. I'm no longer a brother to him, so his ranch house will never be my home again."

34

Lexi glanced at Noah in the driver's seat of their SUV. With Nathan still questionable with a concussion, having Noah by her side made her more confident of a successful outcome. If she lost sight of Nathan during the breach, Noah would have her back when the dust settled. She shifted to glimpse Nathan in the back seat behind Noah at the wheel. He was wide awake, which was a good sign, and he had a determined look, an even better sign the concussion wasn't affecting him. At least not much.

Kaplan was seated next to Nathan on her laptop, digging up ownership and tax records of the property at the address Robert Segura provided. Having only a brief look at the outside before the Raven's men had slipped a hood over his head, Nathan thought the property in the satellite photos resembled the place where the Raven had held him hostage. His recollection was enough for Lexi to be confident Segura's information was authentic and to get a search warrant.

"Find anything we can use?" Lexi asked Kaplan.

"The property comes back to a shell corporation. I'm looking for other properties the company or its two officers listed might own. It could give us other locations if this doesn't pan out."

"Keep at it," Lexi said. "If we don't find him quickly, I sense we never will."

"I'm on it, Lexi."

Noah followed the directions on the car's navigation system and pulled over at the GPS coordinates for the rally point. The rest of her team in the second SUV followed them to an empty field one mile from the Raven's lair. They were the first to arrive. With less than an hour before sunrise, they would quickly lose the advantage of breaching under the cover of darkness if the FBI Special Weapons and Tactics Team didn't arrive soon.

The team exited their vehicles while Kaplan remained inside to dig deeper into the Raven's footprint. Lexi walked up to Daniel, Lathan, and Coby, assessing their visible cuts and black eyes. "You three look like you went a few rounds against Rocky."

"It feels like I did," Coby said, gently pressing two fingers against the shiner under his left eye. "But I'm ready for another round."

Each looked ready and eager to go the distance.

Four sets of headlights approached from the east and veered into the empty lot. The specific models were hard to determine in the dark, but Lexi recognized two silhouettes as mine-resistant heavy armored vehicles. The other two were an oversized SUV and a pickup truck. Each crunched the gravel on the ground while maintaining their position and spacing until coming to a stop.

Every door opened, and nineteen tactical operators stepped out, armed to the teeth with military-style automatic rifles, sniper rifles, SIG Sauer pistols, and a complement of stun grenades. Each operator was equipped with tactical green uniforms, helmets, and ballistic vests. They were prepared for whatever the Raven threw at them, including a small war.

The team commander approached Maxwell Keene and Lexi, carrying a tablet. He removed his helmet and cradled it under an arm against his torso. "Director, any last instructions?"

"If we don't find his weapons cache, it's imperative to take the Raven alive," Maxwell said. He was right. Securing the locust technology was critical to ending the Raven's terror. "The suspect is a master at building bombs and traps, so every member of your team will have to be on their toes."

"If you run into a trap, radio me," Lexi said. "I can walk you through disabling it. If for any reason we lose comms, back out and get me."

The commander showed Lexi and Maxwell the tablet screen with an aerial view of the Raven's compound. "We sent a drone ahead. It has shown no activity in the compound in the last three minutes. We'll set up snipers at these points for containment," he said, pointing to two scalable trees along the south and eastern perimeter and two ground-level positions behind a short garden wall on the west side and a rock pile on the north.

"The high ground isn't optimal, but it will have to do," he continued. "Once they're in place, Teams One and Two will roll in through the access road. Their vehicles are designed to withstand small IED explosions, so hold back until they've cleared. Team One will take the main building, while Team Two will focus on the garage with the second access point to the tunnels. We'll first use a tactical through-the-wall imaging system to assess for targets and will breach using flash-bang grenades if necessary. We'll clear the buildings, working in squads of two. Your guys can fall in behind either breaching team. Stay behind us. We're like a freight train. Once we start moving, we're hard to stop until we pull into the station."

Maxwell turned to Lexi. "How do you want to deploy your team?"

"Nathan thinks he was held in the main house basement complex, so I want him and Lathan with me, trailing Team One. Noah, Coby, and Daniel will trail Team Two. Director Keene, I'd like you to stay with Kaplan as overwatch. She can be ready with the jammer."

"A jammer? There's no need." the commander said. "Each of my teams is equipped with a low-level jammer to disrupt most wireless security systems. If they detect sensors, the jammers can easily bypass them."

Between his team and Lexi's, they had twenty-seven people to take down one man, but knowing the Raven, Lexi didn't like the odds. The locusts were a force multiplier and were more lethal than a battalion-sized force. She and Maxwell had left out that tidbit during the initial brief, but now it was go time. She couldn't let this team go in blind.

"I'm afraid it won't be enough for what the Raven might employ," Lexi said. "He has acquired top-secret military technology known as the locust. They are micro-drones the size of a horsefly and can be equipped with video cameras, electromagnetic charges, poison, electric charges to spark a fire, and enough explosive material to kill if they get close enough to your head. I can personally vouch for the fire ones. Those hurt like the dickens."

"Jesus. Who is this guy? James Bond gone rogue?"

"More like Dr. No. He's evil to the core and won't hesitate to kill. The only defense against the locusts is to deploy a broad-spectrum signal jammer, which will knock out your comms. We have a choice. We can proactively activate the jammer, but you won't be able to talk to your teams. Or we can hold off. If your teams spot anything suspicious, we can turn it on."

The commander blew out a sputtering breath while running a hand through his hair. "My teams are trained to operate in radio silence, but I'd like to hold off as long as possible since we have two buildings to clear and two access points to breach."

"My thought exactly," Lexi said.

"All right," Maxwell said. "Warn your agents, but they need to know this information is top-secret. They share it with no one."

"Got it. We leave in two minutes." The commander turned on his heel and returned to his team. "Listen up..."

Lexi's team returned to their SUVs, shuffling vehicles based on Lexi's assignments. Before Noah hopped into the second car, she pulled him aside and popped up the tailgate where she'd stowed her gear. "I have a feeling the breaching teams will run into traps. Since I can't be in two places at once."—she handed him a screwdriver set, a pair of wire snips, a roll of electrical tape, and a mirror before clasping his hands with hers—"you're the only one I trust to follow my directions to disarm traps. I need you on the other team." Lexi left out a morbid point. If something went wrong on her end, she wanted Noah nowhere in the vicinity.

"But what if you have to deploy the jammer, or we lose comms?" he asked.

"Back out. I suspect the Raven wouldn't leave himself with only one way out. We'll flush him out from our end."

The Raven leaned back in his chair, resigned that once Lexi Mills had captured Robert, it was only a matter of time before he gave up his location. He'd hoped their decades of friendship outweighed self-preservation, but their falling out had spooked him. The speed at which the ATF and FBI had located his home and were approaching it proved his suspicion. He and Robert would never work together again.

He brought up the live feeds from the security cameras around his compound. The wireless ones were still broadcasting, a sign Mills had yet to deploy a signal jammer to counter the locusts. But when she did, it might be her last mistake. The teams on the ground would be out of communication, and if they didn't work in unison, one wrong step by either team would kill them all.

The outermost feeds showed the tactical team deploying their snipers for a three-hundred-sixty-degree containment coverage. With their night vision goggles, escape was impossible. Once they were in place, two heavy armored response vehicles crashed through the gate. One skidded to a stop at the main house, while the other stopped near the detached garage. Two SUVs fell in line, one following each of the armored vehicles.

Agents jumped from each automobile and fell into line like a trail of ants. They moved slowly in unison, crouched low for protection. Each line leader held a ballistic shield to counter small arms fire. The agent behind each leader carried a battering ram to break through the door. A third man had a metal case. The rest held rifles or handguns.

The leaders issued hand signals. The third man in each line darted toward the building, unfolded the case, and attached it to the exterior wall. If the Raven's memory served him correctly, the devices were high-tech sensors to retrieve thermal and energy readings from inside the entry rooms. After ten seconds, the men recovered their sensors and darted back into position. The leaders counted down with hand signals.

Three. Two. One.

Both lines moved forward, with the shield paving a safe path. Having met no resistance, the second men jumped from the line and swung the battering rams with strong arcs, splintering the entry frames and sending both doors turning on their hinges. The Raven expected a quick entry since every room in the single-story house was unoccupied. However, he didn't expect the agents to find the hidden entrances to the basement so quickly and be one door away from his workplace. It was time to rethink his timeline and collect what he was owed.

35

Lexi descended the barely lit stairwell to the basement directly behind the last member of Team One. Nathan was on her heels and said, "This is the place. I was down here."

"This is Alpha One. Can confirm correct location."

"Fox One, copy," Maxwell radioed back.

"Sierra One, copy," the tactical commander replied.

Team One leader ditched the ballistic shield and stopped his progress at the reinforced metal door. He tried the handle. It was unlocked, but he didn't open the door. Instead, he raised three fingers and gestured toward the door. The third man darted forward and attached the sensor to the door.

"Team One and Team Two, no human targets visible," a SWAT tech radioed. "I'm picking up other heat signatures on the upper right corner of both door frames."

Both team leaders acknowledged the presence of sensors and advised they would deploy under-door cameras. After the third agent retrieved his detector and retreated, another agent stepped forward and slid the camera under the gap at the floor. The team leader manipulated the focus direction until he saw the device mounted to the door frame.

"Agent Mills," he said, "you're up."

Lexi moved forward and studied the leader's mini tablet screen. Three bricks of C4 butted against the frame four feet off the ground. A blasting cap stuck out of each brick with a wire running to a control box next to a magnetic door sensor at the door's upper corner.

"Alpha One to Alpha Two, what are you seeing?" Lexi radioed Noah. He responded with a description of the identical setup at his location. Lexi replied, "Copy. We need to disable the magnetic sensor. It looks like a commercially available wireless sensor."

The Team Two Leader broke in. "We can block the signal with our handheld jammers."

Team One Leader retrieved a jammer from his utility belt and tuned it to the appropriate range.

Lexi considered the basic configuration and the simplicity of defeating it. Yes, Lexi had captured his engineer, but from what she'd gleaned from Robert before leaving his cell, the Raven was also technically inclined. This was too easy. She recalled what he'd said at the prisoner exchange when she noted he'd used a wired device instead of deploying the locusts. *"It's safe to say we both anticipated the other's first move."* The Raven wanted her to use the signal jammer, but why? He always used redundant—

"Stop!" Lexi shouted. "Don't cut the signal. Repeat. Do not cut the signal." Her heart raced, hoping the other leader had heard her command in time. "Noah, come in. Noah, come in."

One second of silence.

"Lexi, this is Noah. Standing by for your order."

"The Raven wants us to use the jammer. That's him anticipating my first move. A signal loss might activate a secondary trigger."

"If we can't use the jammer, how can we disable the sensor?"

"Magnets, but if my instinct is right, we'll have to do this at the same time. The Raven's devices are all about redundancy. He likely added multiple triggers on each door and daisy chained the explosives together."

"Like the proximity devices at the grocery store in Gladding."

"Exactly. One will trigger both, and we'll be trapped if it detonates when we're inside."

"Just like Gladding," Noah said. "Where can I find a magnet?"

"Cell phone cases. Check everyone's phone. You'll need at least three layers to provide enough pull through the frame. They need to be touching, so you'll have to break off the edges to make them flat." Lexi had a magnetic case, so she pulled out her phone. She turned to the SWAT members waiting in the hallway. "Who has a magnet on their phone case?"

Three agents raised their hands, ripped the case from their phones, and broke them down until the magnet section was flat. When she placed them back-to-back, they stuck together. "We're set here, Noah. How about you?"

"Almost there," Noah said. "We're breaking up the pieces now."

"Good. They'll stick together naturally. You'll need to tape the stack against the frame at the precise location of the stationary sensor. Use their imaging system to determine the location. Be at least forty feet back, then use a line to pull the door open."

"Got it, Lexi," Noah said. "We'll radio when we're ready."

"Once we get the door open, we'll be halfway home. We'll need to disable the explosive's power and remove the blasting caps." Lexi had brought only one blast suit. She knew the steps to disarm the device by heart and could perform them blindfolded, but Noah wasn't as experienced. "Noah, I want you in my blast suit when you work on the power supply."

"But what about you?" Worry cut through Noah's voice.

"I'll be fine. Remember, I've done this a hundred times."

"I wouldn't know how to maneuver in that thing. Just step me through what to do." Noah could be as stubborn as Lexi, and she doubted she could talk him into using it.

"All right, Noah. Let me know when you're ready to open the door." Lexi ushered the rest of the breaching team upstairs and out of danger while she and the team leader remained in the stairwell with the rope tethered to the door handle. If her or Noah's placement of the magnets was more than an inch off, both would blow.

A minute later, Noah replied, "We're all set. Everyone is topside but me and the FBI leader. He'll operate the rope."

"Same here. Pull on the count of one."

"Copy. On one."

Lexi took three calming breaths and counted. She braced herself for multiple explosions. The stairwell would protect them from the destructive part of the blast waves, but the concussion would still knock them off her feet.

"Three. Two. One."

The leader tugged. The rope pulled straight.

A bang.

The door hit the wall.

Glorious silence.

Lexi laughed. "We're good here, Noah."

"Same here." Noah laughed too.

"We're at the fifty-yard line. Let's get to work. Don't step inside because the hallway might have infrared or proximity triggers. Use your mirror to eyeball the wires."

Lexi extended her hand past the door frame and angled the mirror to view the wires from the blasting caps. They were gathered together two inches below the power supply box. The box was covered by a metal lid with four screws. Usually, she would disconnect the power before cutting the wires, but she doubted she could correctly angle the screwdriver to remove the fasteners. Cutting the cables first wasn't the safest method, but it was the only one at her disposal.

Lexi explained the dilemma to Noah. "So, we're going to cut all three wires simultaneously an inch below where they're gathered."

"It should be easy enough," he agreed.

"The trick is making sure the exposed wires don't touch each other once cut. We'll need to make a second cut."

"Just above the gathering strap to create a gap." Noah finished her sentence.

"Right. Ready with your snips?" Following his affirmative response, Lexi said, "On the count of one, make the first cut, then move on to the second." She counted down, made the cuts, and listened for an explosion.

Nothing.

"Lexi, I made the cuts. We're still kicking."

Lexi released a long breath of relief. "We're almost home. Remove each blasting cap from the C4 and place them where they won't get knocked around."

Once they finished, Lexi said, "Let's clip the Raven's wings."

Both team leaders radioed a green light to begin searching the underground tunnels. Lexi, Nathan, and Lathan stayed close at the end of the line. Her heart thumped harder with each passing second. She was inside the Raven's lair, in the very spot where he and Segura had built hundreds of weapons and bombs that had taken dozens of lives. She was hot on his tail and tasted blood.

The maze of tunnels and rooms was more extensive than Lexi expected. Nathan pointed out the cell where he was held and the one where the Raven made him think they were holding Wesley. Based on Segura's description, one room the agents cleared looked like his lab, but there was no sign of the Raven or his weapons. He had to be hiding.

She held out hope as long as both teams hadn't met in the middle and run out of areas to search. However, at the next corner, her hope was blown to bits. The Team Two leader stared her in the eye. He said, "All clear. No Raven or weapons, but we found something you should see." He guided Lexi to an office.

While the rest of the rooms were industrial or bare like the one Nathan was in, this one was plush. The bookshelves, leather couch and chairs, and ornate wood desk made Lexi think this was a study, the Raven's personal office.

The team leader directed Lexi to a framed oil canvas painting on the wall. It was of the Raven dressed in black with his long, stringy black hair, pale skin, and blood-red eyes. The man defined menacing. A piece of paper with a handwritten note was tacked to the bottom of the frame.

Lexi stepped closer and read the message. "*First things first. You're next in line, Agent Mills.*"

The Raven slid deeper into his seat and slipped his tablet into the pouch attached to its side. Lexi Mills had proved more resourceful than he'd given her credit for. He glanced out the jet's window and looked down at the passing clouds, thinking he had much to do. He had hundreds of weapons and explosives to collect at two more facilities before he cleaned up his final two loose ends. With time running out, he would have to be judicious in what he gathered, and Mills would have to wait until he had collected in person from Anton Boyko what he was owed—his life.

He dialed Anton's number. The call connected. "It's time to pay the balance of your bill, Mr. Boyko. You owe me a million dollars."

"You failed to provide my son," Anton said. "I owe you nothing."

"That was not the deal. The price was one million in advance and one million when the job was done. If your men failed, it is irrelevant to our agreement."

"Well, I'm not paying."

"Then I will collect."

"I dare you to try," Anton said, laughing.

"I will do more than try. I will succeed."

36

Thomas waved at the gate guard as he drove into the Boyko compound. He wasn't expected for another hour to prepare for the trip to Dallas with Viktor to shoot Sasha before he testified, but arriving any earlier might have looked suspicious. He had orders from his handler—hop on a plane to Dallas this afternoon, with or without Anton's ledgers, to testify at the grand jury tomorrow morning. However, he still had Anton's trust and couldn't leave without trying again. The ledgers would make a conviction a slam dunk and open up a vast pool of potential witnesses against him. He was sure they were in Anton's office, and his best bet of getting them rested in the cooperation of his battered wife.

Thomas pulled deep into the compound, noting Anton's car was gone and the workshop door was open. He backed into his traditional spot on the east side of the workshop, hidden from the main house, where he'd discovered a gap in Anton's security web. Cameras were there, but thick trees and brush provided several pockets of blind spots. The parking location had the added benefit of having a direct line to the gate if he had to leave quickly.

Anton's muscle wasn't in the courtyard, so Thomas stepped inside the workshop. Mrs. Boyko was at her wheel, straddling the bench and forming a stubby pot to sell at the weekend flea market. She didn't need the money, but she thrived on the satisfaction when someone bought a piece of art she'd created. Pottery was also her escape. When she needed to get away from the harsh reality of her life, she came here.

Thomas stood quietly near the entrance, waiting for her to notice him. She angled her hands against the spinning wet clay, caressing it like a lover until it took a longer shape. When the wheel slowed, she flipped her right leg over the bench and grabbed the hand towel from the table to her left. "You like watching me, Thomas." Her voice was void of flirtation as if she no longer felt worthy of a man's attention.

"Your work is intriguing, Mrs. Boyko."

"I think we're beyond formality. Call me Darya."

Thomas walked closer and inspected the bruises on the side of her face. "He shouldn't treat you like this."

"And what is this?"

It was now or never. It was time to take a leap. Anton allowed no one to put a hand on his wife, not even Viktor. He stepped within a foot of her to get her attention, tuned her head by the chin, and gave her an intense stare laced with the message that she mattered. "Like he owns you."

Darya slapped his hand away and darted her eyes toward the camera mounted in the corner near the ceiling. She was terrified. "Are you crazy?"

Thomas took one step back. "You don't have to live this way. There is a way out."

"How? With you?"

"Yes. You deserve better." Thomas looked over his shoulder to ensure the courtyard was clear and turned so the camera would not catch his lips when he spoke. "He's going to have Sasha killed at the courthouse when he testifies at the grand jury. I'm supposed to fly out there today and shoot him tomorrow."

Her face went pale. Her lips trembled, but she needed one more push.

"I know people who can keep you and Sasha safe."

"Don't fool yourself, Thomas. You know how dangerous my husband is."

The screen door at the main house's back entrance squeaked on its hinges. Someone was coming. He handed her a bucket of rocks and pebbles from sifting through the dirt collected in the yard for her clay. "I can protect you. Meet me behind your workshop in five minutes."

Walking outside, Thomas saw two of Anton's men emerging from the house. He grabbed a shovel and wheelbarrow by the door and went deeper into the compound to make it appear Darya had sent him on another run for dirt. When he was clear of the men, he dropped the tools and veered toward the far side of the workshop, cutting through the brush to avoid being seen. He stopped near his car at a camera blind spot and waited.

Five minutes passed. Six. At seven, doubt seeped in. Thomas hadn't gotten through to her. At eight, his doubt was proven wrong when Darya appeared carrying the bucket of pebbles. When she scanned the area, he waved her over to the brush.

She approached cautiously, inspecting Thomas as if seeing the real him for the first time. "Who are you, Thomas Falco?"

"I'm not who you think I am, but I can help you and Sasha."

"Sasha? Do you know where my son is?" Darya furrowed her brow with suspicious eyes.

"Yes. He's safe, but unless we put Anton behind bars, he'll continue to come after your son. I need your help to do that."

"My help?"

"Anton keeps ledgers for his business. It has names, dates, amounts, and bank account numbers. If we get those, I can guarantee he'll never hit you again, and you and Sasha can live where he'll never find you."

"Are you a cop?" she narrowed her eyes.

Thomas was at a crossroads. Once he broke his cover, there would be no going back. And if Darya betrayed him, he would have to fight his way out. But he had to be on a plane within hours and owed it to Sasha to not leave empty-handed.

"FBI." Thomas waited to read her facial expression before continuing. She appeared hopeful. "I need help getting into his office. When Anton isn't there, he has a man standing guard."

"That's because he trusts no one. You'll never get to the ledgers. He keeps them in a wall safe behind a portrait next to the fireplace."

"Do you know the combination?"

"No, but he doesn't believe in storing important things on a computer.

He says it can be hacked, so he keeps his important names and numbers in a little black book in the top drawer of his desk. The combination should be in there."

"Anton's car isn't here, so we only need to get past the guard at his office door. Will you help me?"

She nodded rapidly with a palpable sense of relief.

"Do you have a key?"

"Anton keeps one in his cuff link box. Give me a few minutes to get it and come back to the kitchen."

"Then we need to go now. I'm supposed to meet with Anton and Viktor in forty minutes. We'll need to distract the guard."

"Okay." Darya nodded again. "I'll get him to come upstairs."

"I'll need three or four minutes in the office. Once I get the ledgers, I'll wait in my car for you. Grab nothing. Otherwise, you might draw attention. Leave your phone because he can track it. Slip into the back seat and stay low until we're off the compound. I'll take you to the Federal Building in Manhattan."

"Okay," Darya said with determination in her eyes. "I'll go first. Join me in the kitchen in three minutes. We can go from there." She clutched his hand, squinting her appreciation. "Promise you'll protect my son."

"I will."

She gave his hand a firm squeeze and disappeared around the workshop. Thomas waited to hear the screen door squeak to start the timer on his phone. After two minutes, he emerged from the brush, circled the back of the workshop, retrieved the wheelbarrow, and returned it to its usual spot. The two guards he saw earlier were sitting post in the porch chairs.

Thomas approached the house and acknowledged the men with a brief "Morning." They eyed him with mild curiosity but made no move to stop him. When he pulled open the screen door, one called out. "Wait."

Thomas stopped, his pulse popping faster at the possibility of getting caught. He craned his neck toward them. "Yeah?"

"Mind taking in our coffee cups?" The bigger one downed the last of its contents and handed his to Thomas. The other one did the same. "Thanks."

"Sure." Thomas opened the door again, entered the mud room, and continued to the kitchen. Darya was sitting at the granite island. She'd washed up and was sucking down a glass of wine. Second thoughts were plastered on her face as she stared at the key inches from her hand. He stepped closer to whisper. "You need to calm yourself. Otherwise, the guard will know something is up."

"What if this doesn't work? What if he won't go upstairs?"

"Then I'll knock him out, and we'll leave together." Thomas squeezed her hand. "You can do this."

Darya swallowed the rest of her wine, slid the key to Thomas, and led the way from the kitchen to the hallway toward Anton's office. Thomas remained out of sight along the wall in the great room and listened.

"Good morning, Leo," Darya said. "I need help getting something off the top shelf in my closet. Would you mind helping me?"

"I'm not supposed to leave this spot until Mr. Boyko returns," the guard said.

"Mr. Boyko is the one who said he needed to renew his passport and couldn't find his birth certificate. He'll be on a rampage again if he doesn't have it when he gets back. Do you really want that? Fine. If you hear a big crash upstairs, that's me breaking my neck."

"Wait. Make it quick."

Thomas peeked around the corner, discovering Darya and the guard retreating down the hallway. The moment they disappeared into the stairwell, he walked softly on the balls of his feet to the office door. He unlocked the door, keeping the key in the lock so he wouldn't have it on him if he was caught. *Plausible deniability*, he thought. He slipped inside and closed the door behind him. Thomas never liked coming into this room. Viktor was behind him every time he did, and he never knew when Anton's righthand man would put a bullet in his head.

Thomas went to the desk and pulled on the top drawer, which was locked. *It's never easy*, he thought. He grabbed a letter opener atop the desk and jimmied the lock until it opened. The drawer was well organized with pens, paperclips, various papers, and the little black book in the back. He snatched it and sifted through the pages until he discovered the one containing three numbers. *It must be the safe's combination.*

Thomas jotted the numbers on his palm, returned the book to its spot in the drawer, and dashed to the wall safe. He discovered the portrait was attached to the wall by hinges and propped it open to the left, exposing the safe. The door had an electronic lock with a push-button keypad. After reviewing the combination, he entered seventeen, forty-three—

The office door opened.

Thomas froze. Unless Darya stepped inside, he was a dead man. He reached inside his jacket and got his fingers around the handgrip of his pistol when he heard, "I wouldn't do that if I were you." Anton's voice was unmistakable and very readable. He was furious.

Thomas considered making a break for the French doors leading to the back patio, but they were four steps away. He'd never make it, so he rubbed his left hand against his pant leg to smudge the safe combination. He then raised both hands and slowly turned his head. Viktor had his Smith & Wesson pointed at his chest with a hungry look on his face. This was the moment Thomas had feared since the day he'd accepted this assignment. He'd be dead before anyone realized he was missing.

37

Lexi Mills boarded the elevator in the Dallas FBI building with Noah Black, Kaplan Shaw, and Nathan Croft in silence. Each had long, solemn expressions. In twelve hours, they'd been dealt three crushing blows. Willie Lange was dead, and the Raven had escaped them twice. The weight of her failures had her residual limb throbbing inside her prosthetic and the ATF badge dangling around her neck feeling like a lead weight. She had years of training and over a decade of experience, yet she couldn't protect her boss nor capture a wanted criminal twenty yards from her grasp. It had taken her months to overcome the debilitating guilt of failing her wife and parents at the hands of Tony Belcher, and she feared this would require equal effort to defeat.

When the elevator door swooshed open to the basement floor, Coby Vasquez, Lathan Sinclair, and Daniel White were waiting. They looked as tired as she felt, but the Raven was still at large. They couldn't rest. The window to leverage Robert Segura's knowledge of his operations was closing quickly. If they didn't identify all the Raven's known operating locations now, they might never find him.

"Where's Director Keene?" Lexi asked.

"On the phone with the Attorney General. He'll be down as soon as he can," Coby said.

"All right, until then, Agent Croft and I will squeeze every bit of knowledge from Segura," Lexi said. "Kaplan, I need you to keep digging for properties. The rest of you, get some food and sleep while you can but stand by for a quick response."

Noah stayed with Kaplan, offering to help research names and locations on the fly that Lexi might unearth during Segura's interrogation.

"Thanks, Noah," Lexi said. She and Croft had just stepped toward the door to the secure area and stowed their electronics when the elevator door opened. Harlen Landry, Special Agent in Charge of the ATF Dallas Field Office, stepped out. His flared nostrils and clenched fists meant he was mad and had someone in his crosshairs. Lexi whispered, "What the hell is he doing here?"

"I don't know," Nathan said, "but Willie put me in charge, so whatever this is, I'll take the spear." When Lexi opened her mouth to argue, he added, "End of story."

Landry stopped at Lexi's feet. "This was the last straw, Mills. You've embarrassed the agency enough for a lifetime. It's not enough to go off half-cocked and make a mockery of the ATF on the national stage. You got one of our best agents killed."

The truth was a spear through the heart.

Nathan stepped forward, standing toe to toe with Landry. "That was uncalled for. You weren't there. If anyone is to blame, it's me for getting captured."

The elevator door dinged.

"This was her rescue operation." Landry turned his ire on Lexi with fire in his eyes. "I questioned Lange's judgment for putting you in charge, and now she's dead because of your incompetence. You're suspended effective immediately."

"You might want to rethink that order." Maxwell Keene approached from behind as the elevator door closed. He held a secure satellite phone and offered it to Landry. "You'll want to take this call."

"You don't run the ATF, Keene," Landry spat. "This is an internal agency matter."

Maxwell brought the phone to his cheek. "I'm putting you on speaker, ma'am." He held the phone out again, returning his attention to Landry. "It is an ATF matter, but we all answer to the same boss. Madam President, I have Agent Landry, the Dallas ATF SAC, in the room, and he needs convincing."

Landry's eyes widened.

"Special Agent Landry, this is Meghan Brindle. Lexi Mills is on a special assignment for me. Completion of her mission is vital to national security. She will report to Director Keene until further notice."

"I think you're making a big mistake, Madam President," Landry said, stiffening his spine.

"This is way above your pay grade, Agent Landry. You will not interfere with Lexi and her team. You will provide her with every resource she needs to get the job done. Have I made myself clear?"

Landry's expression changed on a dime from furious to defeated. A moment ago, he was ready to feed Lexi to the wolves, but now she was the leader of the pack. He stared at her like he'd been punched silly in a heavy-weight bout. Lexi shrugged and could not hold back a smug smile.

"Yes, Madam President. Agent Mills has the full support of the agency."

"Good. Lexi, are you there?"

"Yes, Madam President," Lexi said. "I'm here."

"Give your wife and father a big hug for me."

"Will do, Madam President. Agent Croft and I haven't given up hope. We'll get him, ma'am."

"I trust you will."

The call disconnected, and Landry stormed off. Lathan Sinclair piped up when the elevator door closed, and her supervisor was gone. "Dang, Mills. That was awesome."

The team looked at her with shock and surprise, some with their mouths hanging open. Noah had a prideful half-cocked smile.

"Yeah, well, let's get to work." Lexi turned to Maxwell, filling her face with gratitude. "You have great timing."

"When the guard warned me he was at the gate, I knew he was coming for you. So, I had the guard stall him until I could put the call through."

Lexi kissed him on the cheek. "Thank you." She turned to Nathan. "Let's talk to Segura."

She and Nathan entered the secured area. Segura was at the bolted-down desk writing with a pencil on loose sheets of paper. He looked up when they approached.

Lexi opened the plexiglass door. "Good morning, Robert. Did you get any sleep?" She brought a chair closer and sat. Nathan did too.

"I should ask you the same. You look tired. So does Agent Croft."

Lexi needed to hold back information about the Raven's escape unless she couldn't get what she needed from Segura. "We went to the compound. Unfortunately, nothing was there. It had been cleaned out, including everything at your lab. Where would the Raven have taken the locusts?"

"We have two storage facilities, but—" Robert stopped, angling his head as if ciphering a puzzle. Then, his eyes twitched open wider. "You don't have him. He wouldn't have had time to clear out the compound, store things in the desert, and return in time for the prisoner exchange." Robert paced his cell like a trapped animal. "He will get to me."

"Not if we put our heads together. He left me a message tacked to the portrait in his office. It said, 'First things first. You're next in line.' Who would be ahead of me in line? You?"

Segura stopped and shook his head. "No. Starshiy is obsessed with Anton Boyko."

"Why?"

"He used to work for Anton, but Anton double-crossed him and tried to kill him."

"But why would Anton work with him again? We know he hired the Raven to retake his son. That's how we captured you."

Segura shook his head harder and approached the bars to look Lexi in the eye. "He doesn't know Starshiy is the Raven."

"So Starshiy took this as an opportunity to even the score while bilking him of tons of money. We might be too late."

"Before you captured me, Anton still owed a million dollars. Starshiy wouldn't leave that much money on the table. But, since we didn't retrieve his son, I doubt Anton paid up."

Lexi rose from her chair, stepping up to the bars and standing nearly toe to toe with Segura. "Then we need to go to Brooklyn. Write down anywhere else Starshiy might have taken the locusts so we can get them back."

38

Brooklyn was a long way from Texas. Lexi had thought Dallas was a traffic nightmare, but this New York borough took the prize for rude drivers and nowhere to park. The parking issue complicated the night surveillance of the Boyko compound, making it less than optimal. On the bright side, two Boyko guards were at the gate, so they weren't too late. The Raven had yet to strike.

Lexi had seven people in three vehicles for the operation. However, only one SUV and three people were on the same street as their target. The others were at least forty seconds away by foot. Their only tactical advantage was Kaplan's drone which required frequent battery changes to maintain an eye in the sky. The drone feed confirmed activity in the compound. Lights were on in the main house, but the garage and workshop were dark. Two men stood watch at two corners of the porch, giving them a three-hundred-sixty-degree view of the house.

The property configuration was better than the parking problem. The only vehicle access was through a gated paved road off a residential street. The back of the compound was composed of a solid nine-foot-tall cinder block wall. The front and two sides were protected by a seven-foot-tall iron non-scalable fence, with the ends of the pales sharpened to a deadly point. No one was getting over it. Old-growth trees and shrubs along the fence line provided privacy. The compound was the only house on the block. Its only neighbor was behind the solid wall in the rear.

The three hours of sleep on the plane had done everyone good but Nathan. He remained quiet in the back seat, lost in his thoughts. The few moments he'd gotten with his son before agents whisked Wesley off to Maxwell's house for safekeeping clearly weren't enough to comfort each other. If they captured the Raven tonight, it would not surprise Lexi if Nathan retired after his trial. If it got to one.

Lexi glanced at Noah in the driver's seat. He hadn't said anything about the president since the phone call, but she could tell he was dying for details. She shifted in her seat to look at him straight on. "Are you going to ask?"

"I figured you would explain why you're suddenly tight with the president when you were ready," Noah said. "But based on the conversation, I guess it has something to do with the locusts."

"It does. When Nathan and I were in Napa chasing down leads on the Raven, we came across the locusts. They are a game-changer, Noah. Those little things ripped the presidential motorcade to shreds, and we barely escaped with our lives."

"But you figured out how to defeat them with the wide spectrum signal jammer."

"Yes, it's the only defense, but employing it is a tradeoff. You're either safe against the locusts or—"

"Or you're in a full communications blackout and vulnerable to a myriad of other attacks. It would be like being back in World War I without radar."

"Which is why we need to recover the technology before someone else gets their hands on it."

Noah leaned back in his seat, absorbing what Lexi had said. "Since we found only firearms and traditional explosives at the two storage facilities Segura told us about, the locusts are still out there. We have to take the Raven alive so he can lead us to them."

"If we don't, warfare as we know it may change." Lexi's phone buzzed with an incoming call and a recognizable ringtone. She answered it. "Hi, Maxwell. Still nothing."

"Lexi, Agent Thomas Kent missed his flight and hasn't checked in for twelve hours. I sent agents from the Manhattan field office to check his apartment, but he's not there. All his stuff is gone like he intended never to return, but no one can locate him. Even his burner phone is offline. His last message said he was heading to the Boyko compound to look for the ledgers one last time."

"You think his cover was blown, and Anton Boyko has him, or he's dead."

"I'm afraid so."

"I understand." Lexi completed the call with a heavy heart and explained the situation to her team members over the radio. "So, when we go in, we need to search every inch of the place until we find Thomas."

Each team acknowledged with a single word, "Copy."

Minutes later, Kaplan radioed, "Eagle eye at ten percent. Bringing it down in one minute."

"Copy, Kaplan," Lexi replied. "Coby. Lathan. You're up."

The pause in aerial surveillance meant her team was blind. During each battery change, Lexi moved her people on foot to watch the side fence lines while Lexi, Nathan, and Noah watched the front of the compound. She kept the foot patrol to a minimum to avoid detection by Boyko's web of security cameras while one person remained in each vehicle at all times.

"Copy," Coby said.

"Copy. Getting in my steps," Lathan said.

Lexi chuckled. She could always count on Lathan to provide the levity.

The live drone feed on her tablet went dead, signifying Kaplan had landed it and was changing the battery. The fifty seconds it took to replace the battery and reposition the drone was their most vulnerable window of missing the Raven's approach.

Lexi picked up their night vision goggles to watch the guards at the entrance. One was street side, and the other was inside the gate. Both had radios and were armed with handguns and sawed-off shotguns inside their jackets. Since coming on shift an hour ago, these two had spent more time jawing with each other than watching their surroundings.

The one outside the fence jerked oddly and wobbled. Then the second one. Both fell to the ground. The gate opened, and a shadowy figure slipped inside.

"Gate guards down," Lexi radioed. "Subject going inside. This is it. Eagle Eye up. Kaplan and Daniel, containment at the gate. Coby and Lathan, take the garage. We'll take the house."

Lexi, Noah, and Nathan flew from their government SUV. Her heart sped. Within minutes, Lexi would have the Raven in her grasp.

A fist the size of a grapefruit collided with Thomas' gut for the seventh, no, eighth time this session. The force was enough to rock him in the chair Viktor had tied him to. The pain would be more manageable than the brute's kidney punches if not for the cracked ribs on his left side. It was infinitely better than the strikes to his jaw and eye. Thomas already suspected several broken bones on the left side of his face and could hardly open his mouth beyond the amount required to groan in agony.

"Who are you working for?" Viktor demanded for the hundredth time since he and Anton had caught him at the safe. Anton remained in the chair behind his desk, unmoved by Thomas' misery. He was looking for answers about the safe and his son and would not stop until he got them. Thomas' only solace was Anton not catching onto Darya helping him. Or so he hoped.

If the pattern for the last ten hours held, Thomas could rest for an hour if he withstood the next five minutes of pounding. He'd been through hostage training and had learned settling into a predictable pattern was the worst thing Viktor could have done. It had given Thomas a finish line to imagine and to last through.

Viktor wound up and let another punch fly to his left flank. Again, a painful kidney shot radiated through his entire core. "What were you looking for?"

Thomas coughed and would have spit, but he was too dehydrated to generate enough moisture in his mouth. "Nothing." He gritted, pushing past the pain to work his jaw more. "Leo wasn't here. I found the picture open over the safe."

Viktor picked up the burner phone he'd found hidden in Thomas' crotch and shoved it in Thomas' face. "What about this? Two phones."

"My dealer. I use coke sometimes." The Boyko's dealt in drugs and prostitution and thrived on addiction. Anton had a rule about not tasting the product, so reluctantly admitting to drug use was plausible. "Not a lot. Only when I don't get enough sleep for a pick-me-up."

"Bullshit." Viktor prepared for another blow but stopped in mid-rewind when the sound of breaking glass came from the front of the house.

Anton knitted his brow in curiosity before jutting his chin toward the door. "Check it out." When Viktor exited the office, Anton circled his desk, approached Thomas, and lifted his head by the chin with a firm grip. The pressure antagonized the cracked jawbone, shooting sharp pain pounding through Thomas' skull. "I have more important things to deal with tonight, Mr. Falco."

Thomas tasted the coppery flavor of blood in his mouth when he nodded. "The Raven."

Anton narrowed his eyes and gripped Thomas' chin harder. "What do you know?"

"He's dangerous." Thomas tugged on his wrist bindings to determine if the beatings had loosened them, but they hadn't. "Those bombs he built and little drones he used. They're nasty stuff. Word on the street is that he leaves no loose ends. You'd be crazy to cross him."

"I'm dangerous as well. No man would have enough bravado to take me on." Anton threw off his grip, pain punctuating his forceful release. "Rummaging through my office and trying to break into my safe borders on stupidity. Are you working for the Raven or the feds? Tell me what you were looking for, and we can end your suffering."

Thomas knew he was a dead man if he admitted the truth. The only thing keeping him alive was his ability to hold out. Surely Lathan had figured out by now he had never made a flight to Dallas and hadn't checked in during the designated window. The FBI had to be looking for him. He simply had to hold out a little longer. "I work for you, Mr. Boyko. Haven't I done everything you've asked of me?"

"Those who don't stay in their lane have an agenda. What is yours, Mr. Falco?

A popping noise in the hallway caught Thomas' attention. He turned his focus to the doorway. Anton followed his stare. Viktor had appeared, but he remained still at the opening. His expression was blank, as if he were staring off into space.

"What was it, Viktor?" Anton asked. "What was the noise?"

Viktor took a step in. Blood trickled down the side of his head when he turned. His ear was missing, and the same side of his face was mangled and charred. When he collapsed to the floor with a loud thud, a swarm of large flies a dozen strong flew in behind him and made a straight line for Anton. They were the same flies Thomas had seen at the safe house when the Raven helped break out Sasha.

"The Raven is here," Thomas yelled.

Anton backpedaled with panic in his eyes until his butt hit the edge of his desk. He raised his hands to protect his face. The great Anton Boyko was terrified.

39

Guns were drawn. Radio earpieces were in. The drone was in the air.

Lexi, Noah, and Nathan dashed across the street to the gate of the Boyko compound. Her residual limb slipped lower into the prosthetic socket, flesh squeezing tighter against the polymer shell, but Lexi ignored the discomfort. She'd worn it for thirty-six hours straight, removing it for only a few minutes to change the liner around her leg and the layers of cotton socks for added padding. She was long overdue for skin care with a prosthetic salve and should have performed it on the plane, but sleep had taken precedence. Thankfully, Lexi had her most flexible, high-tech ankle on and was ready for the chase of her lifetime. More than catching the bad guy was at stake. The president counted on her to recover the locust technology before it got into enemy hands, no matter the cost.

Within minutes, after months of searching and a trail of bodies from Texas to California, Lexi would be within striking distance of the Raven in New York City of all places. He'd escaped every time before, but tonight was different. He wasn't primarily focused on her. The Raven was at the Boyko compound to exact his pound of flesh from Anton for an attempt on his life years ago. His emotion would be her advantage.

Noah was in the lead. Lexi was steps behind, and Nathan limped along, bringing up the rear. Noah reached the gate and rolled the downed guard with his right foot. The man flopped over but showed no signs of voluntary movement.

"He's dead," Noah said.

Lexi continued through the partially open gate without breaking stride and rolled the second guard over as Noah had. The lights at the entrance cast a sufficient amber glow for her to make out a traumatic injury to the head. It was the same damage found on Senator Jackson's aide, later determined to be from a locust attack.

"Locust strike confirmed," Lexi said over the radio to the team. "I'll hold on deploying the signal jammer so we won't lose comms. Coby. Lathan. Do not split up." Surviving a locust attack was possible if they stuck together. "Clear the garage. Disable all vehicles." If every car had flat tires, anyone alive on the compound could only flee by foot. "We'll check out the workshop. Meet at the house."

"Copy."

Noah and Nathan slipped inside the gate. Noah took point, and Nathan stayed at Lexi's side. The three held their weapons at the ready position. The illumination from the landscape lighting was insufficient to scan the overgrown trees and shrubs effectively on both sides for threats.

"Eagle Eye, we need you to be our eyes for our approach," Lexi radioed.

They started a fast walk up the paved driveway after Kaplan's confirmation. "No movement on either side. I'm picking up six bodies on the ground. Two near the workshop and four near the house."

"What about the garage?" Lexi whispered.

"Nothing visible."

Lexi's group glided up the driveway. The brush ended where the asphalt widened, exposing the three structures on the property. The four-car garage was on the left. The workshop sat a little farther up on the right. The main house was back on the left, and a paved courtyard connected the three buildings. Lights were on in the house, but the other two were dark.

Footsteps down the driveway announced Coby and Lathan were inside the fence line. Lexi issued hand signals for them to go left. Meanwhile, she veered her group right. She and Noah checked the two men lying on the ground. Both were dead.

The workshop door was open. Noah entered first, turning left. Lexi went next, going right. Nathan followed, heading straight. Glow from the courtyard light spilled into the space, highlighting a pottery workbench, shelves with dozens of clay pots, and a kiln large enough to stuff a man inside.

Nathan disappeared into the seven-foot-tall labyrinth of shelves. "Jesus," he said.

Lexi followed his voice, turning the corner and finding a horrible scene. A woman in her fifties had been beaten to a pulp. She sat limply on the ground with her arms spread above her head and anchored at the wrists to the posts of a pottery shelf.

Nathan knelt in front of her and checked for a pulse. "She's alive."

Lexi moved in for a better look. Despite the swollen, bloodied, and bruised face, she recognized the woman from Delanie Scott's pictures regarding the Boyko case. "She's Anton's wife."

Noah approached from the other end of the shelf. "The Raven couldn't have done this."

"This is Anton's handiwork," Lexi said, "which means Thomas Kent is in trouble."

Noah retrieved his pocketknife and cut both ropes restraining the woman. Her arms flopped to her lap. "She needs medical attention."

Lexi already had a thin team, but saving and preserving life came first. Considering Nathan's injuries, Noah was the strongest and fastest. "Noah, take her to Kaplan and Daniel at the gate. Then return."

Noah lifted the woman. Barely conscious, she wobbled to her feet and hung her head low. He slung her left arm across his shoulder and guided her through the maze of shelves with his right arm pressed against her torso. "I'll be back in two minutes."

Two minutes might be too late, Lexi thought. "We're heading to the house." Noah locked eyes with Lexi. His sad, piercing stare said he worried about her hunting the Raven without him. She caressed his cheek. The world needed more brave, loyal, and kind men like Noah Black. "Nathan and I have this. Save the woman." He acknowledged with a firm, silent nod before slipping through the workshop door and turning left.

Lexi and Nathan followed but continued straight toward the main house. She glanced toward the garage, noting the side door was open. Coby and Lathan must have still been inside. "Kaplan, Noah is heading your way with an injured woman."

"Copy," Kaplan replied. "Be careful, Lexi."

The team had the Raven trapped. The fence was unscalable, and the wall had no foot holdings. Coby and Lathan were disabling the vehicles. The only obvious way out was through the gate, which Kaplan and Daniel had blocked with their SUV and were guarding. The only other way out was up. Lexi had the Raven precisely where she wanted him—cornered.

She ascended the two steps to the wraparound porch. The exterior lights were on, bathing the entire underbelly of the roof eaves in a warm amber glow. Chairs were positioned at the corners as guard posts, not for lounging. Two corners were visible from Lexi's perspective, and one man lay lifeless at each. The main entrance was farther away, so Lexi headed toward the secondary door facing the courtyard. The wood slats creaked beneath her feet, tossing the element of surprise out the window.

She tested the knob. It turned. Easing the door open, Lexi clenched her gun tighter, feeling her pulse vibrate in a rapid rhythm against the hard-shell grip. The first notable thing was the distinctive sound of a baseball game on television. She entered the mudroom. It contained jackets hanging from wall hooks, boots in cubby holes beneath a stained wooden bench, and white shelves with storage baskets.

The room was dark, but the adjoining kitchen fifteen feet away was lit like a baseball stadium. Lexi stepped toward it quickly, pausing at the door-frame to peek around the corner and expose as little of herself as possible. Holding her service weapon flat against her cheek, she leaned toward the light, discovering a blood bath. Two men were prone on the floor, blood pooling around their dead bodies. Another man was slumped over the granite island. Chunks of tissue or brain matter littered the countertop, and blood dripped to the tile, forming a gruesome puddle.

Lexi stretched to step over the first body, leading with her natural foot for added balance. Falling on a bloody corpse was not a pleasant thought. Once past the island, she reached the great room, expecting more carnage, but the space was surprisingly vacant. Several lights were on, beer cans and half-eaten plates of food were scattered on the coffee table, and a seventy-inch flatscreen was tuned into a Mets home game. A sliding glass patio door was open. It was too dark outside to see beyond a small, covered patio with a barbeque grill, table, and chairs.

Lexi heard muffled voices when she reached the hallway leading deeper into the house. They were difficult to discern, but she distinctly heard the name Raven. He was here, and she was only a few yards away. Her breathing shallowed, thinking of the many people who died because of the devices he created. Many of his victims were bad in some way, but some were good, like Sheriff Sam Jessup from Harrington, Texas. He was merely a public servant elected to clean up a corrupt town and died because a greedy man hired the Raven to build a bomb to get him out of the way. Still, others were collateral damage, like Willie Lange. She made the ultimate sacrifice twenty-four hours ago, doing what was necessary to protect her people. The Raven needed to die, but not before they learned where he kept the rest of the locusts and the blueprints to the dangerous technology.

Thomas split his attention between Anton trembling at his desk, the open doorway leading to the corridor, and the French patio doors. The Raven must have been close and was coming for them, possibly through either entrance. His man at the safe house had told him the locusts could carry poison, an explosive charge, or a fire spark, each capable of injuring or killing him. Thomas wasn't likely on the Raven's hit list, but, tied up, he could easily become collateral damage.

Then.

A shadow darkened the interior doorway. A tall, thin man wearing a black suit, shirt, and tie stepped inside. When he turned, revealing his piercing red eyes, an ominous chill overtook the room. The man's long, stringy black hair contrasted with his pale skin, making Thomas wonder if he was there to blow them up or drink their blood.

"I'm here to collect, Anton." The Raven had an electronic device larger than a smartwatch strapped to his wrist. He slid a finger on the screen and moved the locusts closer.

Anton's eyes widened in fear. He shimmied across the desk's edge and backstepped to a corner of the room. "I'll get you the damn money, Raven."

"I'm not here for money, Anton Boyko. I'm here to collect on an older debt." The Raven stepped forward. Slowly. As if savoring each inch closer.

Anton stopped his trembling long enough to flinch his head back. "What older debt?"

"You don't remember me?" The Raven paused while Anton examined his face.

"Who are you?" Anton asked, still squinting with curiosity.

"I was a little heavier and my hair was a lot shorter then, but it has been twenty years."

Anton cocked his head left and right, digging deep for a stubborn memory. He relaxed some, forming a slight grin on his lips. "Savva. Savva Morozov. That little dog who used to follow you around. What did he call you?" Anton snapped his fingers. "That's it. Starshiy."

"That little dog, as you call him, turned out to be an engineering genius. He's designed many weapons, including this one that has you quaking in your shoes."

"What do you want, Savva?"

"My pound of flesh for trying to kill me."

"It was business, Savva. The weapons you sourced were promised to another family. I had to offer a sacrifice to keep the peace among the New York families."

"And I was your lamb." The Raven stepped closer. "This is your day of reckoning, Anton Boyko. Your lamb is now a raven, and I will pick at your bones when you are dead."

This is not good, Thomas thought. He wasn't caught in the middle of an arms deal gone wrong but a sworn oath of revenge between two ruthless killers. Tonight would not end well for anyone in this room.

40

Tingles went up Lexi's spine. Within moments this entire ordeal would be over. The trail of bodies she and Nathan came across getting to this point made her wish she'd issued Kevlar helmets to everyone in addition to ballistic vests. Her heart sank a little at the thought. If her people had helmets at the exchange last night, Willie Lange's cover might have been blown, but she would still be alive.

This was not the time for regret. Lexi took a deep breath to purge the distracting, negative thoughts. Another. And another until a sense of calm overtook her. Her mind drifted to Nita and the life they'd built. It wasn't perfect, but it was perfect to Lexi, and she wanted many more decades with her to work on those rough edges. She whispered, "I love you, Nita."

Nathan put a hand on her shoulder. Lexi would have taken it as an attempt to provide calming reassurance if it were soft and gentle. However, the level of force he used and the tug on her vest strap signaled impatience. He was hungry for the confrontation. She glanced over her shoulder. His narrowed eyes and the seething anger she saw in them confirmed it.

Lexi continued down the hallway. Light from the living room and an open door lit her path. Voices became louder with each step closer. She recognized one as the Raven's and heard the name Savva. Could it have been the Raven's real name? After all this time, she only knew him by his alias and Robert Segura's nickname for him.

Before reaching the room, she assumed a two-handed grip on her pistol, noted the door opened to the left and decided to line up against it. She continued to the opening and pressed against the door, making herself a tiny target.

Lexi took a second to assess the room. It was an office with a desk, fireplace, and seating area with a couch and chair. A man lay dead on the floor three feet past the door with similar injuries as the other victims in the house. Agent Thomas Kent was beaten as badly as Anton's wife and was tied to a chair in the center of the room. Anton Boyko was backed into the corner behind his desk with his hands raised head high, protecting himself against a small swarm of locusts buzzing around him. The Raven had his back to the door and was closing in on Anton.

She trained her gun on Willie Lange's killer. Finally, the roles were reversed. He was in her crosshairs. "This is the end of the road, Raven."

The Raven stopped in his tracks. His back stiffened. Ten feet separated them, close enough to smell the woody scent of his cologne. It had an undertone of citrus. *Cedarwood*, she thought.

"Raise your hands slowly, put them behind your head, and lace your fingers." Lexi sidestepped the body inside to enter the room. She gestured her chin toward Nathan after he slid in behind her. "Check on Thomas."

Nathan tended to Agent Kent, cutting his restraints with a pocketknife.

Anton's expression changed from nervous to furious. "I knew you were a damn fed." He threatened to move forward, but the locusts buzzed faster and closer to his head.

"Uh-uh," the Raven said.

Lexi adjusted her focus to Anton in the corner. The swarm of a dozen locusts was still hovering inches from him. "I know you're here for revenge, Raven, but I need you to kill the locusts. Now."

"You have horrible timing, Agent Mills." Anger dripped from the Raven's voice.

Lexi refocused on the Raven. He hadn't complied with her order. "I'll say this only one time. If you don't put your hands up, I will shoot you where you stand." Every synapse fired at a haunting realization. Months of hunting the Raven culminated in this flashpoint. Comply or die.

Several tense, silent moments passed before he turned at an agonizingly slow pace, revealing a self-satisfied grin. Lexi Mills and the Raven were finally face to face. He wasn't nearly as scary as she'd built him up to be in her head. Though, the red eyes were a nice touch. He was merely a sick, demented man with a slanted view of the world. That making a profit from killing was an acceptable way of life.

The Raven inched his hands up and put them behind his head. Lexi thought she saw something on his left wrist, but he'd positioned it behind his head too quickly to get a clear glimpse. "Your persistence has become tiresome, requiring a change in the natural order of things." He moved his right arm up and down an inch behind his head.

The order of things, Lexi thought. The message the Raven had left for her at his hideout gave the impression he intended to take out Anton before her. Switching things up now meant—

Lexi reached for the signal jammer clipped to her waistband, but several locusts were already heading toward her.

Nathan called out, "Lexi!" He dove, tackling her to the floor with half his body pinning her down.

Gunfire erupted. The rapid barrage made it impossible to determine who was firing and from which direction, but Lexi was sure she heard it coming from multiple directions. Her right hand was free. She searched for the jammer blindly on the floor, first touching the lifeless hand of the dead man. At the same time, she sensed Thomas had dived to the floor with them.

A crash. The sound of breaking glass.

An explosion.

Lexi's fingertips located the device. She powered it on.

Nathan rolled off Lexi, allowing her to see the chaotic scene unfolding.

The locusts lay still on the wood floor.

The Raven was gone. The French doors were broken and wide open. Anton was firing in their direction.

Thomas located a pistol on the dead man and fired at Anton, hitting him in the shoulder.

Silence.

Lexi scrambled to her feet. "Thomas, are you okay?"

"Yeah." He mumbled his answer without moving his jaw and kept his gun trained on Anton. His tormentor had slid to the floor on his butt against the wall.

"Help is coming." Lexi lunged toward the mangled French doors. She would have barked commands to position her team, but she needed the signal jammer to prevent the Raven from activating the locusts again. Her team must have heard the commotion and gunfire before she cut the comms and would be right on her heels.

Nathan followed her to the patio. A trail of blood started at the broken door and disappeared at the edge of the concrete and the available lighting. "The Raven is hurt," he said.

Lexi heard rustling in the brush beyond the patio. With her team still sitting tight at their posts and the locusts no longer a threat, they had the Raven cornered on the property. His only way out was to scale the back wall, which was impossible without a ladder or another form of lift.

Lexi pulled her mini flashlight from her belt on the fly. Holding it in her left hand and her weapon in her right, she darted through the brush, following the noise. After several yards, she lost the trail and froze. Nathan stopped too. Rustling started again from her right, moving toward the work-shop, but the fence along that side was not scalable. Lexi's gut told her the Raven would double back to find a weakness along the back wall. She and Nathan had to box him in.

Lexi signaled for Nathan to go right and force the Raven left. They would narrow his escape circle until they met in the middle. He took off. She went straight, deeper toward the back of the property. If her internal compass worked correctly, she should end up ten yards left of the property line with an unscalable fence.

Lexi directed the beam of her flashlight low to illuminate the ground between the trees and shrubs. The footing was uneven, slowing her pace. The rustling noise continued, telling her the Raven was still on the move. She broke through at the wall. The left corner was clear, so Lexi turned right.

Nathan shouted, "Raven, stop! Lexi! Up!"

Lexi continued her approach and shifted her focus from the ground to the trees.

A gunshot whizzed past her head and plinked off the masonry wall. Lexi ducked and aimed her gun and flashlight up into the trees. A shadowy figure was high in the network of branches. She considered firing, but they needed the Raven alive to locate the remaining locusts. He shimmied across a thick branch extending across the top of the back wall. The offshoot appeared sturdy enough to hold his weight for several feet but not the entire length to safety.

"Stop, Raven!" Lexi ordered. "You're cornered. There's no way out."

"That's what you think, Agent Mills." The Raven was halfway to the wall. The branch cracked, but he continued to hurry.

"You're not escaping, Raven." Nathan appeared from the darkness near the wall on the other side of the tree. He opened fire. The Raven's body jerked three times. He wobbled, lost his balance, and fell to the ground with a loud clunk.

Lexi raced toward him as Nathan closed in. The Raven rolled in pain, but Nathan fired again, putting three more bullets into him.

"Nooo!" Lexi yelled. She dropped her flashlight and holstered her weapon before rushing to the Raven's side. Turning him onto his back, she revealed his gun on the dirt before grabbing him by the jacket collar with both hands. "Where are the rest of the locusts?"

The Raven coughed, spitting up blood.

Lexi tightened her grip, raising his head off the ground. "Where did you hide them?"

The Raven gurgled and choked out, "They're home." His body went limp.

Lexi checked for a pulse, but the Raven was dead. Nathan stood over his body, still holding his service weapon. His chest heaved with satisfaction. Lexi locked eyes with him. "We needed him alive, but you killed him."

Nathan sneered. "Good."

"Was he reaching for his gun?"

"Does it matter?" Nathan spat on the Raven's lifeless body. "Rot in hell, you son of a bitch."

41

Multiple FDNY ambulances, NYPD cruisers, and NYC medical examiner vans lined the Boyko driveway and the street in front of the compound. The number of flashing lights and first responders was reserved for spectacles of the highest magnitude. Three injured and eleven dead qualified as sensational headlines and had also attracted a media circus at the end of the block.

Lexi gathered her team in the courtyard while medics worked on Thomas Kent, preparing him for transport to the hospital. Lathan Sinclair remained close, gathering what information Thomas could pass along in his state. Before the medics wheeled his gurney into the waiting ambulance, every team member patted his leg, telling him he was a damn hero.

Once the rig drove off, Lathan walked up to Lexi, holding the ledgers documenting Anton Boyko's drug and human trafficking operation in a sealed evidence bag. "If we can get these to Delanie Scott by morning, she'll have what she needs for the grand jury."

"Take one of our vehicles and the FBI jet back to Dallas. The rest of us will search for the Raven's weapons." Lexi would not go home empty-handed. She wasn't prepared to explain to the president why the Raven was dead, but they failed to recover the locust technology.

Coby tossed him a key fob. "Tell Delanie good luck."

After Lathan departed on his mission to put Anton Boyko behind bars, Kaplan pulled Lexi out of earshot of the group. "I went through Boyko's security footage. A camera caught everything on video at the back wall with the Raven." She handed Lexi a USB stick. "This is the only copy. You decide what is done with it."

"Thank you." Lexi stuffed the storage device into her pocket. Any assistant U.S. attorney would consider shooting the Raven out of the tree as justified after he'd fired at Lexi. However, putting three more bullets into him while he lay on the ground was questionable. While she discovered his weapon under his body, she could not tell from her position whether he still posed a threat when Nathan pulled the trigger. She had a decision to make that could taint both their careers. "What about the other footage and the locusts?"

Kaplan held up two evidence bags, one containing the locusts, the other a hard drive. "It shows the locust attack, so I pulled everything for national security concerns."

"Good call," Lexi said. "We'll see how the Attorney General wants to handle it." They returned to the rest of the team. It was time to get to work. "Coby and Daniel. Since Boyko is an FBI case, I'll need you to accompany him to the hospital. Babysit him until you can transfer him to a federal holding facility while we look for the weapons."

Coby and Daniel acknowledged and boarded the waiting ambulance with Anton inside. Lexi regrouped with the remainder of her team— Kaplan, Noah, and Nathan. "Before the Raven died, I asked him where he took the rest of the locusts. He said, 'They're home.' We need to figure out what he meant." She turned to Kaplan. "Any luck on more properties the Raven may have used?"

"We know the two storage facilities in the Arizona desert didn't have the locusts," Kaplan said. "Unfortunately, other than the Raven's lab, I can't locate any other properties owned by the shell corporation. The only other place we know about is the apartment Segura inherited from his grandmother."

"Could that be what the Raven meant when he said the locusts were home? The locusts are at Robert's home?"

"It's the only thing we have to go on," Kaplan said.

Lexi glanced at Nathan. His jaw muscles rippled after Kaplan's reply. He'd killed the man who kidnapped his son and killed his lover, leaving the team with nothing else to go on, and clearly regretted the byproduct, not the act.

"Then let's get a warrant," Lexi said.

Lexi and her small team were at Robert Segura's apartment building four hours later. Unsure what they might find, they evacuated the building. Lexi donned her bomb suit and went inside with a key provided by the homeowner's association manager while the rest of her team remained across the street. She stepped off the elevator and shuffled down the hallway, the bulky legs of her Kevlar suit creating a rhythmic swoosh. The mechanical whir of the demister fan in her helmet kept her company during the long silent walk to Segura's door.

"I'm at the door," Lexi announced over the radio in her helmet. "Deploying the through-the-wall imaging sensor." She unfolded the device in her hand and attached it to the door before stepping back to get feedback from Kaplan with the live stream. "What are you seeing?"

"No heat signatures in the first room, not even a door sensor," Kaplan replied.

The absence of proximity devices using infrared motion or battery-operated magnetic sensors at the door was a good sign. However, considering the Raven's haste, the possibility of low-tech mechanical tripwires or pressure plates remained high.

"I'm going in." Lexi detached the imaging sensor, gripped it in her left hand, and flipped on the bright lights mounted on either side of her helmet.

"Steady hands, Lexi," Noah replied in her ear.

Lexi inserted the key, turned the knob, and opened the door. The helmet lights shined into the dark, sparsely decorated living room. As she turned and focused on each item, the beams highlighted a couch, two chairs, one bookshelf, and a television stand. With no signs of storage containers, she focused on the next room.

A thin carpet runner covered the wood floor along the path to the next room. Leary of pressure triggers, Lexi laid down the imaging sensor and flipped back the rug several feet at a time until she reached the end. After retrieving the detector, she continued deeper into the apartment. The kitchen came into view. The only items visible were a square dining table with chairs and countertop appliances.

Lexi turned down the hallway toward the bathroom and two bedrooms. Two doors were open. One was closed. She peeked into the bathroom and searched the open bedroom but found no hidden treasure. However, she located a wireless base station for a driveway alert sensor, which made her suspicious of a trap in the final room. She unplugged it.

Lexi attached the imaging sensor to the closed bedroom door. "Anything on the imaging sensor?

"Yes," Kaplan said. "There's a faint heat signature at your upper right-hand corner of the doorframe."

"I saw a wireless receiver in the other bedroom and disconnected it. I'm deploying the signal jammer to be on the safe side. Will reestablish contact after I've cleared the room."

"Understood." The silent pause before replying was loud and clear. Kaplan was worried. "Catch you on the other side."

Lexi turned on the broad-spectrum signal jammer in her front pouch, cutting her off from Kaplan, Noah, and Nathan. She took three calming breaths, twisted the knob, and crept the door ajar.

Then.

Nothing.

Lexi pushed the door open slowly, discovering a cache of boxes and storage containers. Her heart raced faster, realizing this was it. This had to be the Raven's most prized designs. She reached up, tore the door sensor from the frame, and removed the rechargeable battery.

Lexi took a step closer but froze before taking a second. "Redundant triggers," she whispered. Something one foot off the floor shimmered in the light cast by her helmet. She bent lower to get a better view, and a stretch of fishing line came into view. It stretched the width of the room. One end was attached to the wall through an eye bolt. The other connected to a military M68 hand grenade taped to the wall.

Lexi sidestepped to the explosive, retrieved her snips, and cut the trip-wire. She then carefully removed the grenade from the wall and taped down the safety lever to prevent it from exploding.

A laptop was atop a stack of boxes. It must have contained the Raven's designs.

Lexi removed the lid from a neighboring container, revealing a metal case inside. She opened it, revealing hundreds of deactivated locusts. If the remaining boxes contained the same number of devices, she'd discovered at least ten thousand.

Turning off the signal jammer, Lexi said, "All clear. We've got them. The hunt is over."

42

Three hours later

The blades of the VH-60N helicopter twirled at a slow pace while it idled on the soccer field at Betsy Head Park in the heart of Brooklyn. The loud engine hum cut through the dark sky as the first streaks of light to the east signaled the coming dawn. Lexi and Nathan dashed across the trimmed grass toward a Marine pilot dressed in a flight suit and helmet waiting at the base of the boarding stairs.

Reaching the craft, she flashed her badge and spoke loudly over the revving engine, now bringing the blades up to speed. "ATF Agents Mills and Croft."

"Welcome aboard, Agent Mills." He gestured for them to go inside.

Lexi climbed the stairs and entered the plush interior of the executive military helicopter, sat in a leather seat against the back wall, and buckled in. Nathan did the same beside her. They each grabbed a headset to enable communication during the flight.

Once the pilot raised the stairs, closed the hatch, and joined his partner on the flight deck, Lexi pressed her mic button and asked, "Gentlemen, how long is the ride?"

"Ninety minutes, ma'am."

"Thank you." Lexi would have an hour and a half to catch a nap and decide what to do with the USB stick in her pocket showing what really happened at the back wall of the Boyko compound. Nathan had yet to give her a straight answer whether the Raven had reached for his gun before he put another three bullets into him. With the engine's roar drowning out their voices, this might be her only opportunity to ask.

Lexi tapped Nathan on the leg and gestured for him to remove his headset. She did too. The engine noise was deafening, so she leaned closer and spoke into his ear. "I have the only recording of the back wall. I need to know what happened before I decide what to do with it."

Nathan cocked his head to look her straight on. He didn't have to say it. The bloodthirsty look in his eyes said emotion had dictated him shooting the Raven on the ground, not justification. But who was to say the original three bullets hadn't already fatally wounded him?

Nathan leaned toward her and spoke into her ear. "I did what I had to and would do it again. I can't ask you to cover for me. Turn over the recording."

Lexi pulled back silently, squeezed his hand, and closed her eyes for the remainder of the trip. She must have drifted off because she startled awake when they landed with a gentle thud. After stretching and shaking off the fog of sleep, she looked out the small portal window. The White House was less than fifty yards away. They must have landed on the south lawn.

The engines wound down, and everyone unbuckled. The Marine pilot opened the passenger hatch, lowered the stairs, and waved Lexi and Nathan forward. "Good luck, ma'am."

Lexi thanked him before stepping onto the grass. She and Nathan jogged toward the building. Martin Torres, the president's chief of staff, waited at the end of the covered walkway leading to the White House entrance. He waved them over, greeting them with firm handshakes. "The president is waiting for you in the oval." He led them into the White House and through the West Wing corridors, stopping at the president's outer office. Three assistants occupied their desks. Torres approached the one farthest into the room. "Is she ready for us?"

"Yes, Mr. Torres," she replied. "Go right in."

Torres knocked three times on the door before opening it and stepping inside. Lexi and Nathan followed. The Oval Office was much like the depictions in Hollywood movies but seemed a bit smaller than Lexi had expected.

President Brindle rose from her chair and circled the Resolute Desk. She hugged Lexi and shook Nathan's hand. "I'm so glad you two are safe." She turned to Nathan. "And your son. How are you two doing?"

"We'll be fine," he said. "Thank you for asking, Madam President."

She gestured for everyone to sit on the twin couches at the center of the room. "I understand you have good news."

"Yes, we do," Lexi said. "The Raven is dead. We secured all video evidence of the locusts and will turn it over to whomever you instruct." She reached into her pocket and slid a USB stick across the table. "This is the only copy showing the Raven's death. I take full responsibility for what is on the tape and accept whatever punishment you deem appropriate."

The president rose from the couch, tossed the stick on the floor, and stomped on it, crushing it into an unusable mess. "My orders were to recover the locusts and neutralize the Raven by any means necessary. Whatever was on the recording is proof of a job well done and nothing more. A picture of the body is all the proof I need."

Lexi had expected President Brindle to order the Director of National Intelligence to review the shooting but was happy with her decision. What was done was done. The threat to national security was over.

"Understood," Lexi said. "It took some doing, but we recovered what we believe is his entire stock of locusts and a laptop with the design schematics. I have a team of FBI agents securing everything for transport to the storage facility in Pantex. They should be in the air within the hour."

"Storing them alongside the nation's nuclear stockpile was a stroke of genius, Agent Mills," the president said. "No one will access it. Thank you for suggesting it."

Lexi acknowledged with a nod. "We also have his engineer in custody. As far as we know, he's the only person with the knowledge to make the locusts functional. He's ready to make a deal. We'll await orders from the Attorney General."

President Brindle smiled and shook her head. "I knew you were the right people for the job. The country and world are safer because of the gallantry you two possess. You've earned any job you desire. Name it."

Nathan shifted uncomfortably on the couch, grimacing in pain. "These old bones have had enough, ma'am. I'm ready to retire."

"Then I'll make sure it's at full salary." The president turned her attention to Lexi. "How about you, Agent Mills?"

"I'm an explosives expert, Madam President. I'm not ready to give it up, but I'm sure my wife would like me to spend more time behind a desk."

"Do you have something in mind?"

"Yes, I do."

EPILOGUE

Two weeks later

Sunday at the Ponder house meant one thing—a cookout. Lexi's father had been in his element all afternoon. He'd overseen the grill, cooking steaks and chicken for sixteen people while the others had brought a side dish or dessert. Lexi's guest list was long, but after the last two weeks, everyone involved in the Boyko and Raven cases needed to celebrate their closure and unwind. Lexi had expected them to divide among case lines, but they surprised her. Everyone mingled, bonding over food, beer, music, and cornhole.

Kenny Chesney played in the background, and Coby's wife lined up, tossing her beanbag perfectly into the board's hole. The guests cheered, raising their beer bottles in appreciation. Kaplan was next on the opposing team and made an equally fantastic shot to another round of cheers.

Nita and her father had started clean-up duty, bringing food and dishes into the kitchen. Lexi picked up a bowl with the last bits of pasta salad and the empty breadbasket. Maxwell and Amanda snatched up other serving bowls but paused to take in the jubilee in Lexi's backyard.

"This was a great idea, Lexi, and the weather was perfect today," Maxwell said.

"This was a good day. I'm glad everyone made it and has gotten along with each other so well."

Amanda placed an arm around Lexi's shoulder. "You did this, Lexi. Everyone here loves and respects you. I was a believer the day you saved my life. So, take pride. You created this family."

Lexi took stock of everyone present—Noah Black, Kaplan Shaw, Maxwell and Amanda Keene, Nathan Croft and his son, Delanie Scott, Coby Vasquez and his wife, Lathan Sinclair and his wife, Daniel White, and Thomas Kent. She pressed her lips into a straight line, pushing back emotion welling in her eyes with tears. "Yeah, I guess I did."

"More dishes, please," Nita shouted through the open porch door.

"We better get these inside." Lexi headed toward the house.

More guests joined in, clearing the serving tables of dishes and plates. Lexi held the door open, allowing everyone to file inside. The kitchen became crowded, but it was a good type of crowded. Everyone laughed and pitched in to store the leftovers and wash and dry everything by hand.

Delanie sidled next to Lexi at the kitchen table. "I thought you would like to know Anton Boyko took a deal on Friday."

"Please tell me it's good news."

"You taught me murderers never walk. I took the death penalty off the table, and he accepted a life sentence."

"That is good news. What about his son and wife?"

"Sasha and Darya went into witness protection yesterday. They should have a good life together."

"That's wonderful," Lexi said. "With Robert Segura serving twenty-five years, the country will be safe for a long time. How are things with your parents? Are they still furious about you faking your death?"

"They're coming around. I'm taking a week off in San Antonio to make it up to them." Delanie focused on Noah and Kaplan at the granite island, wrapping leftovers. "But this is more interesting. What's up with those two? How long have they been a thing?"

"Officially? A few weeks. In reality? Since the first day they met. Noah gave his ninety-day notice at the Nogales Police Department. He's moving to Dallas in the summer and will be on Sarah Briscoe's Texas Ranger tactical response team."

"That's wonderful. I bet his moving back makes you happy."

Lexi gazed at Noah. From day one, they'd had a special connection. They'd put their lives in each other's hands countless times and would do it again without hesitation. She couldn't be happier seeing him in love. "Yes, it does."

The guests had gone home, each dish and fork was back in its proper place, and the front door was locked. Securing the back door and turning on the alarm was the final nightly task. Lexi headed to the kitchen but found the door open and the porch light on.

Odd, she thought. Her father had said he would lock up before going to bed. Perhaps his memory issues still lingered after the doctor adjusted his medication. She went to close the door but stopped when she saw the lights on in the garage. Of course, he would be out there tinkering.

Lexi grabbed her light jacket hanging near the entryway before crossing the yard. The bay doors were closed, but the entry door was ajar, spilling light onto the gravel driveway. She went inside. Country music played softly from the radio on the back workbench. The hood on Deputy Thomas Perez's Camaro was up, and her father was bent over the front fender with his head in the engine compartment.

"Hey, Dad. Isn't it a little late to be working?"

Her father poked his head up. "Says the woman who takes off for days at a time for a case."

"Things will change starting tomorrow. You'll see."

"I'll believe it when I see it." He harrumphed.

Lexi stepped closer to the car. "What are you working on?"

"I noticed a small coolant leak after we moved it last week. It was only a few drops, but I wanted to put in a new hose."

"You are a perfectionist."

"The apple doesn't fall far from the tree," her father chuckled.

"Yeah, yeah, yeah. Let's get you to bed. I have an early day tomorrow."

After Lexi got her father inside and locked up the house, she went upstairs. Nita had changed into her night clothes and was sitting on the bed, applying lotion to her legs. Lexi paused in the doorway to take in her beautiful, perfectly imperfect wife. She didn't believe in destined soulmates but did believe two people could complement each other emotionally and intellectually so profoundly, in heart and mind, that imperfections were invisible. And the life they shared was the only one they could imagine. Her mother and father had such a relationship, and Lexi had concluded she and Nita had the same enduring, unbreakable bond.

Lexi inhaled her happiness and stepped inside. "Now, this is an irresistible sight."

Nita snickered and patted a section of the mattress next to her. "Come to bed. Let's do your limb care."

Lexi changed into her night clothes, brushed her teeth, and removed her prosthesis bedside, resting it between the headboard and the nightstand. She scooted to the center of the mattress and angled her residual limb toward her wife's side of the bed.

Nita inspected the flesh around the nub and gave an encouraging nod. "It looks good."

"The new socket fits like a glove with two layers of socks. I don't feel it until I'm home and ready to take it off."

This was Lexi's favorite part of her day. No matter how challenging the day was or how dangerous the situations she'd found herself in, she could count on this moment of intimacy with her wife. Sometimes her nightly limb care evolved into making love, but if she had to choose between one or the other, it would be this. The way Nita looked at Lexi with love in her eyes when she was most vulnerable was a testament to enduring trust. The way Nita caressed her partial leg made her feel whole.

"We'll have to send your prosthetist a bottle of wine for this one." Nita poured an ample amount of salve into her hand and rubbed it onto the parts of Lexi's skin covered by the prosthetic socket.

"That's a great idea."

When Nita finished, they curled beneath the covers, and Lexi took her into her arms.

"Ready for tomorrow?" Nita asked.

"I hope so." Tomorrow would mark the start of a new chapter for Lexi. She hoped she was up for it. "I have some pretty big shoes to fill."

"You'll see. Like your prosthetic, the new job will fit you like a glove."

———

Lexi stepped off the elevator at the Dallas ATF building, feeling the weight of doubt creep in. Was she ready for this? She'd taken the lead on many cases, including Tony Belcher and the Raven, and she was damn good at herding a small, agile unit. What she was about to take on wasn't too different. However, as far as the men and women of the ATF knew, she was still the screw-up who'd embarrassed the agency on a national stage. Would they now accept her? Respect her?

Lexi took three calming breaths like she did before putting herself into any dangerous situation and walked through the cubicle maze to the space she and Nathan had shared for six months. She'd come a half hour before her traditional arrival time intentionally. She wanted to gather the few things from her workspace and be relocated before the other agents rolled in.

The only thing on her desk not related to work was a box of tissues for the dreaded allergy season, which was about to come into full bloom. A black feather, the calling card the Raven had dropped at the scene after killing ATF Agent Kris Faust, was at the corner of her desk. A picture of Kris was tacked to the wall above the feather. It was a daily reminder of why she'd first chased the Raven. She removed the tack, pulled the picture from its six-month home, and studied it. Kris was a competent explosives expert and died much too young. Lexi did not doubt she would have evolved into one of the agency's best experts.

Lexi thought of her promise to Kris' mother at her funeral to get the man who had killed her daughter. "I got him, Kris. The Raven is dead. He'll never kill again."

She tucked Kris' picture and the feather into the folder she'd assembled on the Raven and placed the folder atop the one on the Gatekeepers and Red Spades. She slung her backpack over her shoulder, gathered the files, tissues, and government laptop into her arms, and stepped out.

"Good morning, Lexi," Ronald said. "I mean Agent Mills. Now that you're the boss on the floor, I gotta get used to calling you by your rank."

Ronald had been her co-worker and office neighbor since her first day at the Dallas office when she was confined to desk duty after losing her leg. He was the best damn logistics clerk she'd had the pleasure of working with and was likely the best in the field office.

"Good morning, Ronald. Lexi is fine when it's just us. We've been through too much to change things up now."

"Lexi it is," Ronald said with a mischievous grin. "Let me know if you need anything for your new office. I'll put a rush on it."

"I appreciate that. Catch you later." Lexi navigated the maze again, stopping at what was Willie Lange's office door until two weeks ago. The label on the wall beside the doorframe read, Deputy ASAC, SRT Commander. She juggled her things into her left arm before running the fingertips of her right hand across the lettering. "Mighty big shoes, Willie. I hope to do you proud."

"You will, Lexi." Nathan's voice sounded over her shoulder.

"Thanks, Nathan. It means a lot coming from you."

"I'd offer to help you move in with your things, but you take minimalist at the office to a new level."

Lexi gestured with her chin for him to join her inside. The office had been emptied of Willie's personal items, leaving only government-provided furniture. She placed the tissues and laptop on the desk and stowed the files in the bottom drawer before sitting in the chair. Lexi ran both hands across the desktop, feeling odd about being on this side of the desk. She'd been in this office a hundred times, but this was her first time in this chair.

"You'll do fine at this job, Lexi. Listen to your gut. It's never failed you," Nathan said.

"I feel old sitting in this chair."

"It comes with the territory. Own it," he laughed.

"Have you put in your retirement papers yet?" Lexi asked.

"Signed, sealed, and delivered. I leave at the end of the pay period."

Lexi did the quick math. "That means we have two weeks together." Her desk phone rang. She picked it up. "This is Agent Mills."

"Agent Mills, this is Operations. We have an active bank robbery with a bomb. Your Special Response Team is in the batter's box."

Lexi jotted down some notes before hanging up. She smiled at Nathan. "Time to get to work."

MURDER BOARD
A BOSTON CRIME THRILLER NOVEL
by Brian Shea

On the tough streets of Boston, justice requires a detective who isn't afraid to break the rules.

The crime sent shockwaves through the entire city.

But for Boston homicide detective Michael Kelly, the case hits particularly close to home.

Kelly was born and raised only a few blocks from where the girl's body was found. He still has friends living in the old neighborhood.

Some are cops.

Others run the Irish mob.

And when Kelly's investigation uncovers a shocking conspiracy, he realizes that he'll need to use all of his unique connections to solve the case.

Because Kelly is determined to bring the killer to justice.
Whatever the cost...

ABOUT BRIAN SHEA

Brian Shea has spent most of his adult life in service to his country and local community. He honorably served as an officer in the U.S. Navy. In his civilian life, he reached the rank of Detective and accrued over eleven years of law enforcement experience between Texas and Connecticut. Somewhere in the mix he spent five years as a fifth-grade school teacher. Brian's myriad of life experience is woven into the tapestry of each character's design. He resides in New England and is blessed with an amazing wife and three beautiful daughters.

Sign up for the reader list at
severnriverbooks.com

ABOUT STACY LYNN MILLER

A late bloomer, award-winning author Stacy Lynn Miller took up writing after retiring from the Air Force. Her twenty years of toting a gun and police badge, tinkering with computers, and sleuthing for clues as an investigator form the foundation of her Lexi Mills thriller series, as well as her Manhattan Sloane novels. She is visually impaired, a proud stroke survivor, mother of two, tech nerd, chocolate lover, and terrible golfer with a hole-in-one. When you can't find her writing, she'll be golfing or drinking wine (sometimes both) with friends and family in Northern California.

Sign up for the reader list at
severnriverbooks.com

Printed in the United States
by Baker & Taylor Publisher Services